It's Murder,
Dontcha Know?

It's **Murder,**

Dontcha Know?

Book One in the *It's Murder* series.

A quirky murder mystery with recipes.

By Jeanne Cooney

NORTH STAR PRESS OF ST. CLOUD
WWW.NORTHSTARPRESS.COM

ISBN: 978-1-68201-133-1

North Star Press of St. Cloud Inc.
www.northstarpress.com

First Edition

Cover and interior design by Liz Dwyer of North Star Press.

Other Books by Jeanne Cooney
Hot Dish Heaven: A Murder Mystery with Recipes
A Second Helping of Murder and Recipes
A Potluck of Murder and Recipes

Dedication

To the memory of Mom, Rosemary Cooney.
And to Natalie. The circle of life continues.

Disclaimer

This is a work of fiction. Characters and incidents are the products of the author's imagination or are used fictitiously. Any resemblance to actual people, living or dead, is entirely coincidental. Many of the towns, roads, establishments, and landmarks, however, are real, and the author encourages you to visit them. They help make the Red River Valley the unique place that it is.

Acknowledgements

Lots of people helped me pull together this book. Thanks to Jodee Sugden for sharing her knowledge of medication protocol, Jill Swanson for teaching me a bit about banking, and Kittson County Sheriff Mark Wilwant for explaining a few local law enforcement procedures. Any mistakes in the book in those areas are mine, or I may have made changes for the sake of the story. Thanks to Mary Cooney, who continues to serve as my first reader and sounding board. To the women of Camp Candace, my writing sisters, for their expertise, support, and encouragement. Thanks to my agent Krista Soukup and Blue Cottage Agency, simply the best in representation and marketing; and to development editor Charlie Johnson. Thanks also to Corey Kretsinger and MidState Design for developing and maintaining my website. And, finally, thanks to my publisher, North Star Press, along with Curtis Weinrich and Liz Dwyer, as well as final editor Anne Nerison of Inkstand Editorial.

Chapter 1

The evening breeze caressed my cheeks and propelled shivers down my arms. It was the closest I'd come to a sexual experience in more than a year. Physical intimacy had been missing from my relationship with my husband, Bill Connor, during the last three months of his life.

I became Mrs. Doris Connor four decades ago and a widow when Bill died of a massive heart attack while harvesting soybeans last fall. I'd stopped sharing a bed with him last summer after learning of his affair with Destiny Delovely, the oversexed overnight waitress at the truck stop out on I-29.

With a name like Destiny Delovely, "trampdom" was inevitable. And because the Red River Valley of northwestern Minnesota, where we lived on Bill's family farm, was sparsely populated, it was only a matter of time before she got around to hitting on him. But as I explained after happening upon her leopard-print thong in the lunchbox Bill had forgotten in the tractor, he didn't need to accommodate her.

Of course, he may not have understood me as words and sobs spewed from my mouth like vomit. And once rage replaced shock and I threw my coffee in his face, he surely stopped listening altogether. Still, I wasn't done demonstrating the depths of my anger. Hence, the no-sex thing. Then before I settled on my next move, he died.

"How come you're so quiet?" Grace, my Barbie doll–like sister, asked from the wooden porch rocker next to mine.

"No particular reason." Rather than allowing her to catch the lie in my eyes, I tucked my platinum-gray hair behind my ears and stared into the darkness as leaves stole across the front lawn, the earthy smell of autumn chasing after them.

Grace and I had often debated the worth of my marriage, even before Bill's "date with Destiny." But those arguments were no longer relevant. I was a widow and planned to maintain that status for the remainder of my life.

"We certainly put in a hell of a few days." An assortment of moans and groans accompanied Grace's words. She reached for the wine bottle on the wicker table in front of us. Because she was a short Barbie doll, it was quite a stretch.

"Sounds like you're about to keel over, Grace. You're two years younger than me, for Pete's sake."

With a huff, she plunked the bottle down after shaking it to confirm that it was empty. "Most of the time I think of myself as twenty-nine, but tonight I feel every one of my fifty-nine years." A short, aging Barbie doll.

I slipped my arms into my jean jacket, and a spasm near my tailbone made me flinch.

"You feel it, too," she added into the wind, "whether you own up to it or not."

Instead of responding, I bit into a cookie I'd claimed from the tin on the table and mentally calculated its calories. When I passed "way too many," I quit calculating.

"Can you believe it?" she went on to say. "We literally moved your house all the way from the farm into town."

I mumbled around the oatmeal and M&Ms. "It's not like we carried it on our backs or anything." Even though it felt that way.

"Quite a feat just the same." Grace set her chair in motion, the light from the battery-operated lanterns on the porch playing off the paint splatters in her tousled, dyed-blonde updo. "While I've seen houses relocated before, watching your place make its way down the highway on that flatbed trailer was still pretty darn amazing."

I inhaled a calming breath. When it failed to do its job, I drew in another. Grace may have been amazed by the process, but I'd been worried sick about it. I'd never before been in charge of anything more complicated than a school fundraiser or a church bazaar. True, houses were routinely moved away from the Red River after falling victim to repeated floods. But because mine hadn't suffered the ravages of a flood, transplanting it was unnecessary, as more than a few people had pointed out.

The house had been in my deceased husband's family for over one hundred and twenty-five years, and while my children showed no interest in it, I wanted to retain it on the off chance that someday they might change their minds. If left vacant on the farm, it would fall into disrepair in short order. Besides, I loved the place—cracked plaster, creaky floors, and all. I couldn't imagine living anywhere else.

Three days ago, a crew that specialized in house relocation had hoisted the old Victorian via hydraulic jacks, set it on a trailer equipped with specially designed dollies, and towed it to the edge of town, not far from the sign that read, "Hallock, Population 988." There, the clapboard three-story was lowered onto a freshly dug crawl space.

My new yard featured scrub oaks, a gravel drive, and the meandering Two River out back. As for neighbors, the closest was a hundred yards away, on the other side of a thick stand of pine trees, just like I had wanted.

Sitting there on the porch, I wondered what the old house thought. In 1893, Bill's grandparents had ordered it through the Sears, Roebuck and Co. catalog, and it was shipped to Hallock in pieces by way of the train. Bill's grandfather and neighboring farmers assembled it. And afterward, it stood among the grain fields like an overseer for more than a century. Not anymore.

"What are you going to do now?" Grace inquired over the rhythmic creaking of her rocker.

"Give me a break."

"I don't want you depressed again."

I flexed my long legs in an attempt to relieve my achy joints. "I'll be fine."

"We had a deal, Doris. You promised to get on with your life once we got settled. Well?" Grace waved her hand like a church choir director, probably an ill-chosen simile considering my sister hadn't stepped inside a house of worship since eleventh grade, when she got caught playing sink the sub in the choir loft at Red River Lutheran with bad-boy Donny Hanson. "The house has been moved, and the workers are gone."

"They only left two hours ago. And they'll be back on and off over the next several weeks." I pointed to the lantern. "We don't even have all of our electricity yet."

"I don't care. I won't let you get down in the dumps again. You're not going back to sitting around in your bathrobe all day, doing mindless needlework, and eating nothing but Hostess Ding Dongs."

"That 'mindless needlework' resulted in the afghan that's keeping you warm as we speak."

4

Grace rewrapped the crocheted blanket around her shoulders. "Along with four or five others scattered about the house."

"So?" Not much of a retort, leading me to take another route. "You're really pushy, you know that?"

Finishing her own cookie, Grace sucked the tips of her index finger and thumb, ending with a kissy sound. "With good reason."

She may have been right. Following Bill's death, I had remained cooped up on the farm for three months, doing pretty much what she'd just accused me of doing. I steered clear of everyone, going so far as to have my groceries delivered and left on the porch so I wouldn't have to face a soul, not even the sixteen-year-old, acne-pocked delivery boy. Not that he would have noticed me. Middle-aged women were invisible to young people.

My kids had attributed my desire for seclusion to grief. My sister, on the other hand, speculated that I merely felt lost because my children were grown and on their own, and my husband was... well... dead. Grace said it was a tough spot for me, someone who'd spent her entire adult life playing wife and mother, à la Ma Walton.

She'd shared her theory after driving out to the farm one day, where she'd found me in my pajamas at three in the afternoon, cupcake crumbs stuck to my cheeks and Hostess wrappers littering the floor. That's when she presented me with an ultimatum: Either I get some counseling or she'd convince my children, Will and Erin, to intercede. Because I hated the idea of anyone dictating the terms of my existence, despite it being as bleak as a three-day blizzard, I polished off my last chocolate Ding Dong—no sense in letting it go to waste—showered, and began my search for a counselor.

My first therapy session almost didn't happen, but not because I was a stoic Scandinavian who avoided sharing my troubles. No, the reason was, the northern Red River Valley was thick with Scandinavians who avoided sharing their troubles, choosing instead to shove them deep down inside, which more than likely explained their ruddy complexions: they were on the brink of exploding from suppressed emotions. Anyhow, since there were few requests for therapists in the area, weeks passed before I found one. The proverbial needle in a haystack.

The wind tinkled the chimes I'd hung from the porch earlier in the day, yanking me back to the here and now. "I'll admit I was stuck for a while, Grace, but I've done a lot in the last nine months."

"Such as?"

"Well, for one, I managed Bill's affairs—"

My sister guffawed at my poor choice of words, then coughed so hard I thought she might choke, which would have served her right.

"You know what I mean." I washed my cookie down with the last of my beer. The mishmash of tastes made me wince. "I signed the farm over to the kids and turned the day-to-day operations over to Will. I bought this lot and arranged to move the house. And because you insisted, I did a stint in counseling."

"You make it sound like a prison sentence."

"Well?" Although I wasn't about to admit it, especially to Grace, counseling had been good for me. Among a myriad of revelations, I had realized that I needed to move on. And not just figuratively. I couldn't keep farming or remain in the country. There were too many memories—some of them nearly debilitating. Did I mention finding Destiny's underwear in Bill's lunchbox? Still, the prospect of leaving my home of forty years proved so unnerving that I took it with me.

Following the move, Grace and I had spent two days spackling the fissures in the walls caused by lifting the house off of its original foundation. We also painted. And unpacked boxes. That's when I found the porch chimes—in a box marked "Christmas Dishes."

At the same time, the moving specialists leveled floors. The plumbers connected pipes previously laid in the crawl space. And the electricians began the arduous task of rewiring the entire house. As of a few hours ago, we all needed a break. The tradespeople went home, with plans to return tomorrow afternoon, while Grace and I sought refuge on the porch.

No doubt about it, relocating my house was the craziest thing I'd ever done or, perhaps, the second craziest. Number one may have been convincing Grace to move in with me. Then again, I probably needed Grace for the same reason I felt compelled to remain in my home: starting over was scary. Nevertheless, as I rocked on the porch, I couldn't help but wonder if I'd been too hasty in proposing that my sister become my roommate. She'd only spent two nights under my roof and already was driving me crazy.

"Why don't you work with me down at the café full time?" she posed for the umpteenth time, the lantern illuminating her dirt-smudged cheek.

"I don't want to get more involved in the café than I am. Owning it was your dream, not mine."

"But you have no dreams."

My back grew rigid. "I'm not you, Grace. I didn't long for a college education or big-city life when I was younger, and I don't need to take the world by storm now."

7

"Waitressing wouldn't exactly constitute 'taking the world by storm.'"

"You know what I mean."

"I'm worried about you, Doris. That's all. Like your therapist said, you're less likely to lapse into another depression if you do something constructive with your days."

I blew air from my puffed-up cheeks. "Grace, from this point forward, all I want is a peaceful, solitary life. No men. No demands. And no more therapy."

"I get the 'no man' thing, given that you were married to Bill. But no therapy? You'll get depressed again."

"No, I—"

"What's more, if you really wanted a solitary life, you wouldn't have moved to town or begged me to live with you."

I raised one finger. "I moved to town because I had to get away from the farm." Then another finger. "As for asking you to live with me, believe me, I'm having second thoughts."

She raised a finger of her own.

"Besides," I proceeded, pretending not to notice her extended middle digit, "I intend to start my new life tomorrow morning, right after you go to work. First off, I'll put an hour in on the treadmill. I'm determined to drop the fifteen pounds I gained during menopause. It's been twelve years."

"Okay, that's one hour. Then what?"

"Well, I'll unpack more boxes, finish painting the kitchen, and finalize the plans for the new garage."

"What about the day after tomorrow? Or the day after that?"

I visualized my to-do list. "There's more painting. I have to design my new flower beds, so I can till the ground right away next spring. And I want to start the first book on my list of a hundred novels to read before I die."

Grace opened her mouth, most likely to offer another

snarky comment. But before she got the chance, her cell phone rang. Unable to ignore any call—ever—she answered and puckered her face. "Oh, no. Really?" Her eyes drifted from her lap to me and back to her lap. "Are you sure?" She scooted forward in her rocker, the afghan sliding off her shoulders. "We'll be there in a jiffy."

She returned her phone to the table. "That was Erin. She couldn't get through to you."

I set my beer bottle on the porch deck and patted the pockets of my jean jacket. "I must have left my phone inside. What's up?"

"The pharmacy at the medical center just got robbed."

My heart slammed into my tonsils. "Is Erin all right?

"She's fine. She only got there a few minutes ago."

"What about Rose? How's she?"

Ninety-year-old Rose O'Brian was my late mother-in-law's sister and our own deceased mother's best friend. We were the only "family" she had left. She resided in the assisted-living section of the medical center, down the hall from the pharmacy.

"She's okay physically, but she's pretty upset. She witnessed the whole thing. Erin wants us to get over there right away."

Chapter 2

The pharmacy was located in the two-story medical center on the south side of town. The expansive sand-colored brick building also accommodated the hospital, clinic, nursing home, and assisted-living facility.

After I parked my car, nose to the curb, we rushed through cones of light emanating from lampposts bordering a long sidewalk. As was common this time of year, two combines in a nearby field growled like they were complaining about the late hours, while the tangy smell of newly threshed grain filled the air and tweaked my nose.

Once inside both sets of glass doors, Grace and I met shocks of corn, clusters of pumpkins, and Dr. Osgood. The corn and the pumpkins were meant to spruce up the place, but the young doctor did a superb job of that all by himself.

"Be still, my heart," Grace murmured under her alcohol-laced breath. She ogled the handsome man, starting with his chiseled face and moving to the muscular torso his lab coat couldn't disguise. She even licked her lips.

While I, too, appreciated the latest addition to the medical staff, I managed to maintain my composure—and keep my tongue in my mouth—because I'd limited myself to a single beer, whereas Grace had polished off an entire bottle of wine.

"I'm glad you're here." Dr. Osgood spoke in a smooth baritone as he gauged my sister's disheveled appearance. "Rose has been asking for you." He swiped at his clean-shaven jaw, evidently to ensure that unlike Grace's face, his was dirt free. "She's really shaken."

"Can we see her?" Anxiety pricked me like stick pins.

"Uh, yeah, of course." The doctor forced his eyes away from Grace's chest, where, predictably, they had stalled.

Grace was well-endowed, and despite her age or the weather, she wore tight t-shirts with odd sayings. This one was paired with an open, flannel-lined chambray work shirt and read, *Don't believe everything printed on a tight t-shirt. William Shakespeare.*

Embarrassment colored his face—the doctor's, not Shakespeare's—although, if there, I'm sure old Will would have felt heat along the tips of his ears, too.

"She's in my office." Dr. Osgood then ushered us there before muttering something about attending to another matter and racing down the hall.

His office was smaller than I'd expected, and it smelled of cinnamon. But beyond that, I didn't notice much other than Rose perched on the edge of an upholstered armchair in front of a stately wooden desk and my daughter, Erin, rooted alongside her.

Rose appeared diminutive and frail, not at all the fierce woman she'd brought to mind when I was young. Her white fleece robe nearly gobbled her up whole, and the thin, pale line of her lips trembled.

My sister squatted in front of her, clutching Rose's knees in what I suspected was an effort to steady herself as much as to offer comfort. "How are you, Rose?"

"Oh, fair to middlin'. I suppose it could of been worse."

Rose and her family had emigrated from Ireland when she was an adolescent. After living in the Gopher State for three-quarters of a century, she, like most long-time Minnesotans, regularly spoke in negatives and was seldom emphatic about anything. I recognized both traits because I wasn't all that different. In this instance, though, I demanded more definitive answers and turned to my daughter.

Erin looked to be the consummate professional, her strawberry-blonde hair in a tight bun at the nape of her long neck, her khaki uniform neatly pressed, and her gun holstered on her hip. As for her eyes, they belied her job as a deputy sheriff and, instead, expressed the concern of a child for her "Nana," Rose's role in my daughter's life ever since my mother's death.

"She was wandering the halls as usual," Erin volunteered, "only this time she observed a man break the glass on the pharmacy door, rush in, and clear the shelves of pill bottles. He may have gotten away with no one else spotting him."

"Uff-da." Rose uttered the Scandinavian expression with an Irish brogue that normally grew thicker as she became more upset. "It happened so fast. No more than thirty seconds." She clutched the sash of her robe like a lifeline.

"Did you get a look at him?" Grace wanted to know.

"Well, the light in the hallway shined on him some, so, yah, I got a halfway-decent look. Not at his face, though. That was shadowed."

Erin retrieved a notebook from her breast pocket and flipped through the pages. "Average height and weight. Wore a baseball cap, a hooded sweatshirt, cargo shorts, and—"

"Shorts?"

"That's not unusual, Mother." My daughter's voice was ripe with condescension.

"The thought of it makes me shiver," I countered. "It's practically winter."

"It's barely fall."

Erin was clearly ready to contest whatever I said, and while I understood her remarks were nothing more than bids for independence, they still bugged me. I didn't recall ever speaking to my mother in that manner. Then again, Grace may have been disrespectful enough for both of us.

"Anyway," Erin resumed, "he threw the pill bottles into a dark backpack and ran off." She closed the notebook. "Nothing's been recovered from the scene as of yet. And while there doesn't appear to be other witnesses, Dr. Betcher's checking for sure."

"Dr. Betcher?" Grace's inflection was sharp enough to cut stones.

"He is the chief of staff," Erin reminded her.

"He's a pig. And he has no business assisting in a law enforcement investigation."

"Oh, come on," Erin groused. "The residents in assisted living are used to him. They're more apt to open up if he poses the questions."

"But he's 'Betcher the lecher.'"

Erin shook her head. "Really, Grace? Betcher the lecher? How old are you? Thirteen?"

Uncomfortable with their terse back and forth, no doubt fueled by frayed nerves, my sister's alcohol consumption, and my daughter's contempt for excessive drinking, I made an effort to defuse the situation with humor. "Grace, I hate to break it to you, but Dr. Betcher has to pitch in sometimes. Dr.

Osgood can't do everything, in spite of what he's capable of in your dreams."

"Ish!" Erin shuddered. "That's gross. Les Osgood is like thirty years younger than you guys."

Grace opened her mouth, but it was Rose who spoke. "Sorry, Erin. I wish I remembered more."

Erin nuzzled the top of Rose's head, squishing her snow-white lambs' curls. "No need to apologize, Nana."

"Is there any chance he caught sight of you?" That was me.

"I hope not." The wrinkles on Rose's face grew more pronounced. "I hid around the corner. I never imagined he might of seen me."

I mentally cuffed the back of my head. Way to go, Doris. Now you've frightened her even more. "Sorry, I didn't mean to cause you alarm."

Rose shouted, "Beg your pardon?"

"Nothing," I replied almost as loudly. "Nothing at all."

Rose absently wrapped and unwrapped the sash from her robe around one of her skeletal hands. "I suppose you're just gettin' settled over at the house there. And you probably have a real mess with all the boxes and such. Still, I was wonderin'…" She left the sentence dangle.

And Grace picked it up. "What is it, Rose? What's on your mind?"

Rose peeked over the top of her wire-rimmed glasses. "It's just that I don't wanna sleep here tonight. Not if that hooligan saw me."

My sister wasted no time in glancing over her shoulder at me, the message in her unfocused eyes nonetheless clear.

I, in turn, reached out and cupped Rose's cheek while chastising myself for having mixed emotions about inviting her home with us. It wasn't that I disliked her. To the contrary. But I was about to embark on what my therapist had termed "Act III of my life," and it didn't include caring for a ninety-year-old.

Even so, I couldn't refuse Rose. She was a second mother to Grace and me. She was Erin's "Nana." And it was only for one night, right? "Well, Rose, if you'd rather stay with us tonight, you're certainly welcome."

"Really?" The word was filled with hope. "I wouldn't be a bother?"

"No, not at all. Erin can come, too. We'll have an old-fashioned slumber party." And Erin could also pick up any slack caused by me being less than an eager host.

But it wasn't meant to be. "Mom, I have to work. The likelihood of capturing a criminal drastically decreases with every hour."

Rose rested her gnarled fingers on Erin's arm. "I wish…" Her words faded while she gazed beyond me, her rheumy eyes, the color of dishwater, appearing to stare back in time. "Yah, the hood of his sweatshirt was up, over his hat, and the brim was pulled down." She knitted her brow in concentration. "Wait a second." True to her words, she let another moment lapse before she added, "I just thought of something."

"What?" We sounded like a trio of crows.

"A tattoo. The robber had a tattoo."

"What kind of tattoo?" Erin again went for her notebook.

"A snake." Rose scratched the textured arms of her chair, as if clawing for a clearer image. "A snake wrapped around his left calf. I'm not sure why I didn't recall it earlier." She peeked up at my daughter. "Will that help ya, dear?"

Erin's face had gone ashen.

"What's wrong, honey?" I reached out to her.

She stepped back. "Nothing."

16

An obvious lie, leading me to nudge my sister. "Take Rose to her room, so she can dress and pack an overnight bag. Get her something to eat, too. It might settle her nerves."

Color returned to Rose's face. "We had wild rice hot dish for dinner, and it wasn't half bad." She stage-whispered in Grace's direction, "I snuck some back to my room. It's in my fridge. I may even have enough to share."

When Grace neglected to move, I glared at her until she grumbled, "Okay, Rose, let's go." But as they strode past me, she hissed into my ear, "You will fill me in later."

Chapter 3

Once we were alone, I studied my daughter in an effort to get a read on her. When I gave up, I asked her outright, "What's troubling you, Erin?"

"Like I said, nothing."

I employed the I'm-your-mother-so-you-better-tell-me tone of voice. "I'll be the judge of that."

"It's just..." She shuffled from one foot to the other in a nervous dance. "Buck Daniel, the guy I've been dating the last few months—"

"The one who's been working for your brother out on the farm? The one you still haven't brought by for me to meet?" According to my children, I nagged, but I usually injected humor into my remarks, which, in my opinion, made them tolerable, if not downright funny.

My kids didn't always agree, as illustrated by the stubborn line that creased the space between Erin's brows. "He matches the general description of the robber and has a tattoo around his left calf. A snake tattoo." She hesitated for a two-count. "We broke up last week. Afterward, Will fired him."

"Hold on. Will fired someone during harvest?" Naturally I was concerned that my daughter may have dated a criminal, but I was downright flabbergasted that my son had fired a hired hand this time of year. Harvest was payoff for all of the hard work put in during the spring and summer. No farmer willingly became shorthanded then.

"I lied." Erin touched the magenta bruise along her jawline. "I didn't get this from breaking up a fight outside the Eagles." She dropped her voice, and I barely caught her confession. "He hit me, Mom. Buck hit me, and Will found out. Buck had never lifted a hand to me before. But over the past month, he got mean."

"Oh, no. I'm so sorry." I clasped her shoulders but didn't go so far as to embrace her. Remember, I'm Scandinavian. "What did Karl say?"

"I lied to him, too."

I backed an arm's length away. "But he's the sheriff, Erin. Your boss."

"I'm well aware of that. I just didn't want him or anyone else to think I couldn't manage my personal life. I still don't." Her tears fell.

"Erin—"

"I mean it, Mom. You can't say a word." She wiped her wet, freckled cheeks. "I heard that Buck was in the Eagles the night before last—drunk. He called Hallock a hellhole and said the people here were 'ripe for the picking.'"

"That doesn't mean—"

"I've got a strange feeling about this." She visibly shivered. "If I'm right and Buck was the robber, I could lose my job."

"You won't lose your job because you went out with a creep. You broke things off as soon as you discovered what kind of person he really was."

I skimmed her discolored chin with my fingertips. She was the precious gift that had saved me from utter despair twenty-eight years ago. True, we currently were experiencing a rough patch as she flexed her will, doing her best to become her own person, but she remained my little girl, and I'd do anything for her. "I want to strangle him, Erin." My voice had an unfamiliar edge to it. "Truly strangle him."

"We'll find him, Mom, and if he's the robber—"

"I don't care about the robbery. Other than it scared the bejeebers out of Rose. But he has to pay for what he did to you."

"Trust me, Mom, Will gave him what for. Truth is, he beat the crap out of him."

◎ ◎ ◎

There was a knock at Dr. Osgood's office door, and Erin wiped her runny nose with the back of her hand, inhaled deeply, and exhaled a shaky breath before twisting the knob and peering into the hallway. "You're done?"

She eased aside, and another deputy entered the room. "Mom, this is Deputy Ed Monson. The two of us are investigating the robbery until the sheriff gets back to town later tonight. Ed, this is my mother, Doris Connor."

"Nice to meet you, ma'am."

I nodded by way of greeting.

Erin hadn't shared much with me about Ed Monson. But as I'd just learned, she hadn't shared much with me about a lot of things, including her recent breakup or her former boyfriend's abusive behavior.

I did know that Deputy Monson was a couple of years younger than my daughter and had worked in the sheriff's office for about four months, ever since moving to town. Erin had described him as "nice enough but not particularly memorable."

Giving him a quick up-down, I had to agree, at least about his appearance. While not tall, Deputy Monson wasn't short, either. He had a medium build. His hair was drab brown. And his eyes were the color of dry grass.

"Yeah, I'm all finished in the pharmacy." Even his voice was unremarkable. "I came up empty. The security camera wasn't working. Dr. Betcher said it's been on the fritz."

"Did you speak to Old Man Olinski?"

"The pharmacist? Yeah, I woke him. He had nothing to add. He offered to come down, but I told him someone would interview him tomorrow."

"What about the patients and staff?" Erin asked. "Did Dr. Betcher check with all of them?"

"Yep. As we suspected, Rose was the only witness."

Erin chewed on her bottom lip. "She just recalled that the robber had a snake tattoo on his left calf."

"Still not much to go on."

"We've got to try."

"Why?" Ed challenged. "It's a waste of time. Nobody robs a place in the boonies, then sits around and waits to get caught. For all we know, the guy's somewhere in Canada by now."

"The border's not easily crossed undetected."

"Maybe he went in on foot, between ports of entry."

"It's a twenty-mile walk from here, Ed."

"So?"

"Let's continue this discussion back at the car." Erin drew in air long and hard through her nose. "I may have a line on a suspect." And with that, she exhaled and worried her bottom lip again.

◎ ◎ ◎

After Erin and Ed left, I wandered the freshly mopped corridor, the pungent smell of Pine-Sol scratching my nostrils as the evening's events tripped through my mind: Rose O'Brian had witnessed a crime, and my daughter suspected her jerk of an ex-boyfriend—and my son's former hired hand— had committed it.

Preoccupied with those thoughts, I rounded a corner and literally ran into Dr. Betcher. I pressed my hands against his chest to put some distance between us, but he captured my wrists and held me in place. "Are you all right?" he asked.

I couldn't form so much as a single-word response. In spite of being in the hospital where Dr. Betcher served as chief of staff, I was taken aback by his presence, undoubtedly because my last encounter with him had been just down the hall, in the emergency room, when he'd pronounced my husband dead. I gave my head an Etch A Sketch shake to get rid of that image. "Uh-huh." I twisted my hands out of his grasp. "I'm sorry, Dr. Betcher. I didn't see you."

He examined me through thick glasses, the eyes behind his lenses magnified yet beady, like those of a lab rat. "Call me Andrew." He actually twitched his nose. "We've been acquainted far too long to be so formal, right, Doris?"

While I had no wish to contradict him, I didn't share his appraisal of our relationship. I could count on one hand the number of interactions we'd had over the years, and since the most prominent in my mind remained that afternoon in the emergency room, I felt as awkward around him as a cow on ice.

"I'm on my way to Rose O'Brian's room." I wrung my hands, a longtime nervous habit I couldn't seem to break. "I'm bringing her to my place for the night."

"Oh?" With the tip of his left index finger, he shoved his horn-rimmed glasses up his pinched nose. His hand then continued north, over his furrowed brow and through his white, slicked-back hair, leaving behind rows of scalp a shade darker than his face. "Do you think that's wise?"

"It's what she wants. And since my house is now in town, we'll be close by."

"But a shock like Rose experienced this evening can be terribly hard on a person, especially an older person. They start imagining all kinds of things." He absentmindedly adjusted his crotch, and I averted my eyes.

"Grace and I can manage," I assured him, staring at his rodent face.

"Oh, that's right. I heard from one of the nurses that Grace moved in with you. How's that going?"

"She's only been there a couple of nights."

"Yet you want to care for Rose, too?" He rocked back on his heels, offering me a close-up view of his oversized nostrils and a bumper crop of nose hair. While I longed to drop my gaze, I feared he might not be finished with his game of pocket pool, so, instead, I retreated another step. And that's when I banged my head against the concrete wall.

Dr. Betcher appeared oblivious. "Doris, while I'm sure you mean well, I strongly recommend that you leave Rose here, where medical professionals under my tutelage can keep an eye on her. In light of my training and experience, I know what's best."

If my day had gone better, I may have dismissed his superior attitude as a bunch of baloney and accepted his suggestion as the sensible medical advice it probably was. But I was exhausted from working at the house, then worrying about Rose, not to mention my daughter. And now I also had an achy lump on my head. So, yes, through no fault of my own, I was crabby and prone to acting a bit contrary.

I drew myself up to my full height of five foot eight and spoke in a voice that left no room for misunderstanding. "Dr. Betcher, while I appreciate your concern, Grace and I are taking Rose home with us. We have that right. We're her guardians." I yanked on the cuffs of my jean jacket, imitating the strong-willed women in the 1950s' movies I'd watched late at night ever since menopause had rendered me an insomniac. "Now if you'll excuse me, we'll be on our way."

He retrieved a pen and a business card from the breast pocket of his white coat. "If you insist." Holding the card in his right hand, he scribbled on the back of it with his left before handing it to me. "That's my personal cell phone number. When she gets to be too much for you, call me directly. I'll talk you off the ledge."

Careful not to touch his fingers, given where they had been, I accepted the card and slid it into my purse. "I don't foresee any issues."

"Maybe. Maybe not." He appeared to debate the wisdom of saying anything more, but in the end, "more" won out. "Just remember not to give much credence to what she tells you about the robbery." He was quick to add, "Or anything else."

"We only want her to feel safe."

"From whom? The robber? I guarantee he's long gone. So if that's why you're—"

"Stop! She's coming with us."

Sidestepping him, I started down the hall, wondering what the heck had just happened. He was advocating for what I wanted—namely, Rose to stay put. Still, I was about to take her home. No doubt about it, some days felt like a test, and I'd forgotten to study.

Chapter 4

Early the following morning, the rich aroma of fresh coffee stirred me awake. Wrenching my eyes open, I discovered my sister sitting in semi-darkness on the opposite end of the couch, her hands clutching two mugs. Tossing aside the afghan I'd used as my blanket, I sat up, kneaded the crick in my neck, and relieved her of one of the mugs.

"Spending the night on the sofa should be avoided after age sixty," she uttered.

I slurped, too desperate for the nectar of the Folgers gods to be worried about burning the roof of my mouth. *Ouch!* "Why didn't you tell me that last night?"

"It didn't occur to me that you'd sleep out here. When we got home, I was exhausted."

"You were tipsy."

"It's not my fault you hate wine and I was forced to drink it all myself."

I breathed in and out of my mouth to soothe my burn. "They make bottle stoppers, you know. You didn't have to down an entire bottle in one sitting."

Grace scrunched her nose in the dim light of the battery-powered lantern perched on the end table next to her. "Within five minutes of my shower, I was sound asleep. I really like my attic suite." Her eyes twinkled, which was remarkable. After a night of drinking, my eyes resembled fried eggs with broken yolks.

"I'm glad you're comfortable. But where'd you think I'd end up? Rose took my bed, and..." I gestured at the space around us. Moving boxes were stacked high. Framed pictures were slanted against the wall. Clothes were strewn about.

"Speaking of Rose," Grace said as she leaned in, "what are we going to do? She made it clear in the car last night that she doesn't want to go back to assisted living until the robber's caught."

"You mean Erin's no-account ex?" Disdain for Buck Daniel bubbled up inside of me, and undeterred by my burn blister, I downed more coffee to get rid of the foul taste in my mouth.

"We don't know for certain he did it."

"Erin's pretty darn certain." I filled her in on what my daughter had shared with me, ending with, "You can't say a word. Especially about him hitting her. No one knows. She's afraid it might jeopardize her job."

"He's a jackass! I've dealt with him a few times in the café." Grace tapped a scarred finger against her burgundy lips. "I'm surprised he and Erin were an item. Whenever he came in, he flirted with Tweety if she was waitressing, and she flirted right back. Led me to believe that they were dating."

"Tweety comes on to every guy who crosses her path. In that respect, she's nothing more than a younger version of Destiny."

Grace flashed stop-sign hands at me. "Do not mention Destiny Delovely. In fact, don't even think about her—or the truck stop. She's supposed to stay away from the café, and you have to keep clear of her."

"Good grief. Relax. I haven't been out to the truck stop in over a year."

My sister shook her head. "To this day I can't believe you poured rice down the heating vents in her Mustang. You're usually such a goody-two-shoes."

"She should have locked her doors." Indignation seasoned my words. "Besides, she couldn't prove it was me. She only guessed."

"I'm pretty sure the sheriff figured it out. That's why he warned you to keep your distance."

"And I will, even if she's a homewrecker who deserves far worse than getting pelted with rice every time she turns on the heater."

"Doris, it wasn't like she was Bill's first fling or anything."

"I know." I toyed with the tassels on the afghan as I replayed the last years of Bill's life in my mind. "But toward the end, he seemed past all of that. Then I discovered he'd been carrying on with that man-eater right there on the farm. In the machinery, no less. It proved to be too much."

"We're idiots when it comes to guys. You know that, don't you?"

"Wait a second." In assessing my ability to gauge the integrity of members of the opposite sex, I didn't care to be lumped in with Grace. Her history with men was abysmal. "I've only been with one guy."

"But he was a doozy. And Erin seems to be following in our footsteps. Buck Daniel and, before him, that weird doofus. What was his name?"

"Don't start," I warned. "Erin's not here to defend herself. And you've gone out with way more buffoons than either—"

"That's my point! We're all drawn to buffoons."

Having no desire to engage in a debate about the men in my daughter's life, the reprobates who'd hooked up with my sister over the years, or my own asshat of a husband, I returned to the actual subject at hand. "I've never been crazy about Erin carrying a gun, but until they catch that sleazebag, I'm glad she has one." Another thought occurred to me. "And while Ed Monson doesn't impress me, he is a deputy and hopefully can provide her with added protection."

My sister followed my conversational U-turn and dropped all further talk of any man other than Buck Daniel. "You really think he'd hurt her?"

"He already hit her. And now she's hunting him down for questioning in a robbery."

Grace nodded, the light from the lantern catching a long hair sprouting from her chin, and despite the seriousness of our discussion, a snicker bubbled up inside of me.

"What?" My sister squeezed her face in puzzlement.

"You know how you complain that your eyebrows are disappearing as you get older?" I pointed at her jaw. "Maybe they're just relocating."

She grabbed her oversized leather bag and scrounged around inside until she found a vinyl makeup pouch. Unzipping it, she retrieved a tweezers and a small, oval mirror. "How on earth did I miss that? It's long enough to braid." She plucked the offender and checked the rest of her face.

Grace's makeup bordered on excessive, which was fitting since the hair piled on her head was equally outrageous. Streaked pink and swept into a fuzzy knot that tilted to the side, it called to mind a twist of cotton candy.

"When I lived in Minneapolis and Chicago," she explained as she primped, "I must have passed robbers and murderers on the street every day and wasn't fazed in the least. But the idea of a criminal skulking around here gives me the willies." She actually shuddered. "That's why I can't fault Rose for being afraid to return to the scene of the crime."

"Grace, when Karl called last night, he said there really wasn't any reason for us to be concerned."

"Then why'd he assign extra patrols past the house?"

"To make Rose feel better. And it worked. Overnight I heard nothing but her snoring and the buzzing of the space heaters."

"Which begs the question, when will the gas get hooked up?" She peered longingly at the fireplace in the corner, its pilot light unlit. "The space heaters aren't cutting it. I have goosebumps."

"Supposedly today."

She dropped her makeup pouch into her bag and smirked. "Anyway, it's really sweet of the sheriff to show such interest in your family."

I rolled my eyes so far back in my head that I worried I might lose them. "It's his job. Nothing more."

"Yeah, right."

"You're ridiculous." I flung a sofa pillow at her.

And she batted it to the floor. "As for Rose, you have to let her stay here. At least until they catch that nitwit."

"But I can't keep sleeping on this lumpy thing." I slapped the threadbare sofa cushion.

"Then take one of the bedrooms on the second floor."

"And leave Rose down here alone?"

"You just got done saying she wasn't in any real danger."

I sighed. Did I mention that Grace could exhaust me? "What if she needs something? We won't hear her. Besides, the electrical work's not done. Our heat's questionable. And who will watch her during the day, when you're at work?"

Her eyes revealed her answer.

"Oh, no." I shook my head so hard my brain rattled. "I've spent the last forty years watching out for other folks."

"Which means you're perfect for the job."

"No, it means I'm done!"

"Come on, Doris. Don't be selfish."

"Selfish? You're the one who's encouraged me over the past nine months to start living for myself."

"We're talking a couple days at the most. The police will have everything wrapped up by then."

"You don't know that. A couple days could stretch into a couple months."

Grace dismissed my remark with a flick of her wrist. "That won't happen. But even if it did, it wouldn't matter because you don't have any true plans."

I wanted to throw something else at her, but most everything was still packed away. "Yes, I do."

"Doris, wishing for a life devoid of expectations and commitments does not constitute a plan."

"You're mean. You know that?"

"I thought you learned your lesson while holed up on the farm. Isolating yourself isn't the way to go. You need to interact with people. You need a reason to get up in the morning." She dropped her voice but not low enough to keep me from hearing, "More counseling wouldn't hurt, either."

"Mostly I need you to back off and accept that I want to live—"

"Yeah, yeah. 'A quiet, solitary life.'" She splayed her hands in surrender. "Okay. If you're hell-bent on becoming a recluse, go right ahead, as soon as the robber's caught. But until then you have to let Rose stay here. And you have to keep an eye on her during the day. Remember, she's ninety, and she's scared."

While I longed to whack Grace at least one more time,

doing so wouldn't make her any less right. Rose was in the last years of her life and deserved to feel at ease. And even though she had put on a brave front the previous evening, she'd been unable to disguise her anxiety.

After leaving the care center, she'd made a half-dozen comments about how assisted living wouldn't offer "any peace or quiet durin' the next several days because forensic guys will be swarmin' all over, just like on television." I doubted our county, one of the least populated in the state, had much in the way of "forensic guys," but that was neither here nor there.

"All right." I sighed like a martyr, a role I had played far too often over the years because of my nincompoop of a husband. "She can stay with us for three days. But that's it. Then she goes back, whether or not Buck Daniel's been captured."

My sister sniggered, as if she had me pegged.

"I mean it, Grace. Three days. No more." I massaged my arms to tamp down my own goosebumps, knowing full well they had nothing to do with the lack of heat. "I have a terrible feeling about this."

"Oh, you're just put out because you may have to wait a bit longer to become the shut-in you long to be."

"Don't you have to be somewhere?"

Grace checked the time on her cell phone. "Yeah, and I better get going. I don't want to keep Dr. Oh-So-Good—I mean, Dr. Osgood—waiting. He's my first customer every morning. Except on Wednesdays. The garbage-truck guys beat him on Wednesdays. They're usually in the alley, biding their time, when I get there. But they only want their thermoses filled. Dr. Osgood orders a complete breakfast."

"Well, Grace, it's Wednesday."

"Shit!" She jumped to her feet and straightened her t-shirt. It read, *The Wizard of Oz: Proof that a new pair of shoes can change a girl's life.* After that she wiggled into her pull-over chef's smock, yanking on the hem until it covered her hips and the top few inches of her leggings. And, finally, she wrestled into a short corduroy jacket.

Grace wore snug clothes and layering them over her curves required significant effort. More often than not, I couldn't help but laugh at her gyrations.

"Put a sock in it," she barked when I did just that.

"I would but it appears as if you've stuffed them all in your bra."

She stuck out her tongue, and I copied her.

Yes, Grace and I often acted like the children we were fifty years ago: Doris Day Anderson and her younger sister, Grace Kelly Anderson. That's right. Our first-generation, Swedish-American mother had named us after matinee idols because a supermarket tabloid claimed that doing so would shape our personalities and talents, not to mention our physical attributes and our futures.

By the time we'd reached high school, Mom knew better. But by then it was too late to change our names or our "attributes." Despite being blonde and attractive, Grace was short, voluptuous, and totally outrageous, her class voting her "least likely to be mistaken for Princess Grace of Monaco." Not really, but it could have happened. And me? Well, even though a number of people had insisted over the years that I was the spitting image of Doris Day, no one ever suggested I could act. As for singing, Grace often compared my voice to that of a cat in heat.

"You coming to the café later?" With the lantern from the end table in hand, my sister skirted the paint cans and tarps cluttering the foyer, the heels of her knee-high boots clicking against the hardwood floor.

34

"Probably not." I shuffled after her in wool socks and an oversized sweatshirt, my afghan draped across my shoulders.

"Don't pout. In all likelihood, Buck Daniel will be captured by the end of the day, if he hasn't been already." She passed me the lantern.

"Erin would have called if he were in custody."

Grace opened the front door and a blast of cold air burst inside, previewing the winter to come. "Regardless, the café's bound to be a madhouse. Everyone will be out and about, gabbing about the robbery. I'll be desperate for help." She nodded toward the back of the house where Rose slept, her snoring strong and rhythmic. "Who knows? Rose might appreciate an outing. And she'll be safe in the café. Nothing ever happens there."

Chapter 5

Around nine o'clock that morning, Rose and I hobbled along the frost-covered sidewalk, our shoulders hitched above our ears and air escaping our mouths in white, icy puffs. Before leaving the house, I'd checked the thermometer outside the kitchen window. Thirty-two degrees and it wasn't even October. Why on earth did we live here?

We were headed for More Hot Dish, Please, the café my sister owned on Main Street. Since we were relegated to a parking spot a block away, I periodically checked over my shoulder for Buck Daniel. Yes, he probably was long gone. Still, I checked.

Notwithstanding Grace's earlier comments, I'd been surprised when Rose requested that we drop by the café. Over a breakfast of microwaved cereal and toast, courtesy of a small generator, she declared she would even risk meeting up with that "no-account hoodlum" because it had been ages since anyone had taken her anywhere.

Hearing that, my guilt cells had multiplied and divided until I felt too bloated to finish my oatmeal. You see, I hadn't visited Rose much during the preceding year and a half, allowing my own difficulties to take precedent over everything else. As a result, my you're-a-pathetic-friend-and-guardian shame remained long after we got to the café, although my Buck Daniel–related nerves dissipated with the jingle of the bells hanging from the door.

My sister had initially expressed interest in the white stone building that now housed her café while home for our mother's funeral, sixteen years ago. Ten years later she bought the place after Margie Johnson, an old family friend and the owner of the Hot Dish Heaven Café in the nearby town of Kennedy, convinced her to open a restaurant.

Margie's café had burned down, and she insisted she was too old to start over. She gave Grace her recipes and helped to get More Hot Dish, Please up and running. But once it was operational, Margie left the area, choosing to winter with her husband in Arizona and summer at their cabin in central Minnesota.

To justify returning to rural Minnesota to run what amounted to a diner, Grace had professed to being fed up with kowtowing to the temperamental head chef and arrogant patrons at the five-star Chicago restaurant where she'd been employed as sous-chef. She also maintained that while she had enjoyed living in Chicago and in Minneapolis before that, she was weary of city life.

Upon signing the purchase agreement for the two-story building that was formerly a jewelry store, Grace had the top-floor apartment remodeled as a rental unit. On the main floor, a professional kitchen was built in the back, while the original tin ceilings and wood-plank flooring were retained throughout. In what became the dining area, Grace installed a black-and-white Formica countertop and black Naugahyde booths along the white walls. Chrome-trimmed tables and chairs filled the middle of the room, and massive windows stretched across the front of the space, overlooking Main Street.

Because Grace had racked up decades of cooking experience after graduating from the Institute of Culinary Arts in New York and possessed a business degree to boot, I was certain she'd do a bang-up job of managing the restaurant. But I questioned whether her menu might be too highbrow for the farmers in the area, many of whom thought of sushi only as bait.

I had no reason to worry. A half-dozen years later, More Hot Dish, Please was still going strong. Open from 6:00 a.m. to 2:00 p.m. Monday through Saturday, it featured the dishes made legendary by Margie Johnson—everything from hot dish and Jell-O to cake and bars. And while Grace added big-city pizzazz to some of the menu items, customers liked them just the same.

As Rose and I entered the café, the farmers playing dice at the counter craned their necks in our direction, as did practically everyone else in the place, including the five young women seated around one of the large tables. They were stay-at-home moms who met at the café one morning a week. They ate and shared horror stories or bragged, depending on their children's recent behavior. As for the kids, they sat in high chairs or booster seats and played with their Mickey Mouse pancakes and sippy cups when not terrorizing the other diners.

After shoving her gloves into the pockets of her woolen car coat, Rose wiped the condensation from her John Lennon glasses and rehooked the bows around her ears. She then nodded at the quartet of elderly self-important women seated in the window-framed booth in the front corner. It was their favorite spot because it enabled them to watch the doings along Main Street while listening to the gossip offered by the café's other patrons.

In the café, gossip was served with almost every cup of coffee. But along Main Street, there really wasn't much for the ladies to see. Hallock, like farming communities across the country, was struggling to survive. The advent of mammoth equipment and changes to federal farm programs had led to a dramatic increase in the size of farms in the area but a substantial decrease in the number of farmers needed to work the land.

Still, Hallock was luckier than most farm towns. While relatively few in number, the residents managed to support a school, the medical center, a smattering of businesses, and a host of recreational facilities, including a swimming pool, golf course, curling rink, and hockey arena.

Nevertheless, the town wasn't exactly a tourist destination. It wasn't situated on a lake or in a forest or among rolling hills. In fact, the terrain was book-page flat, treeless, and stark. At night you could actually see the lights in the next town down the road, some ten miles away. Kind of cool but not exactly tourist-brochure material.

The land was ideal for farming, however. The thick gumbo was some of the richest soil in the world, making local farmers fairly rich, too. In early fall, when tens of thousands of acres were ripe with wheat, soybeans, sugar beets, canola, corn, and sunflowers, the valley resembled a country patchwork quilt that stretched one hundred-fifty miles from top to bottom.

Winter was another story. The post-harvest stubbled earth couldn't halt the howling wind and blistering snow come November. And while some townspeople boasted surviving temperatures of forty below zero and winds of fifty miles per hour, many did their darndest to escape to warmer climates for extended vacations.

Not the four old ladies in the corner booth, though. No matter the time of year, they held court every morning, the sun shining on them as if to highlight their prominence. And evidently Rose had become something of a celebrity, witnessing the pharmacy robbery and all, because one of them motioned her over to join them.

A few folks greeted me, too, wondering aloud if it was cold enough for me. And while no one invited me to sit down, Ole Svengaard hollered as I threaded my way around the tables, "Hey, Doris, what do you call it when a cow climbs over a barbed-wire fence?" He yanked on the bill of his John Deere cap with his right hand and stirred his coffee with the index finger of his left. "An 'udder' catastrophe."

The men with him at the counter joined in as he yukked it up.

Ole, age eighty-five, was a fixture in the café and good for at least one corny joke a day. But when it came to real information, he and his buddies couldn't keep anything straight. That's why I declined to ask them about the robbery and, rather, followed my nose and growling stomach into the kitchen, where Grace stretched over a sizzling grill full of eggs, hash browns, and an assortment of breakfast meat.

"You're limping," she observed after giving me a quick up-down.

"And you're a master of the obvious."

"Owly, too."

"It's this dang sciatic nerve. It's bothered me ever since I got off the couch this morning."

If I hadn't been cranky, I would have appreciated the savory breakfast smells wafting through the air. As it was, I stole a sausage link from the paper towel on the stainless-steel counter and devoured it without really smelling—or tasting—it.

"I bet you didn't take any ibuprofen last night," my sister accused more than stated. "Even after working on the house all day."

I licked grease from my forefinger and thumb. "I guess I forgot."

"I never forget. Years ago, weed was my drug of choice. Now it's ibuprofen." Her head drooped. "How sad is that?"

I flicked the brim of the tie-dyed baseball cap she wore to keep her hair out of the food. "Anything new on the robbery?" I asked. "Erin never called."

"I haven't heard a thing."

"Got a newspaper back here? They're all gone out front." I pilfered another sausage.

"I had one." She readjusted her hat and surveyed the harshly lit kitchen, my eyes following hers along the stainless-steel counters and past the equally shiny industrial appliances. "Someone must have snatched it up."

"Was there anything in it about last night?"

"No pictures," she replied, "and only a short article that didn't go into much detail."

The lack of depth didn't surprise me. Because our town only published a weekly paper, we had to rely on the *Grand Forks Herald* for our daily news. And since Grand Forks was seventy miles away, local stories were slow to get told.

"So, Grace, you really know nothing more than when you left the house?"

42

The corners of Grace's mouth twitched. "I shouldn't worry about you locking yourself away and getting depressed again because you won't be able to do it. You're too nosy. Most likely, that episode last year was just an aberration caused by Will's wedding and Bill's funeral occurring so close together."

"I am not nosy. I'm simply interested in the community I've called home my entire life."

My sister regarded me as if I were one can of cream soup short of a hot dish. "Oh, pul-eeze."

"Besides, I have a stake in this. The sooner the police catch this guy, the sooner Rose goes back to assisted living and I move on with my new life."

Grace scowled, seemingly disappointed in my attitude.

Yet I wasn't about to let that stop me. I had a number of questions to pose. "So?" That was the first one.

"So the paper called Buck Daniel a 'person of interest.'" She aimed her spatula toward the dining room. "You might learn more out there. Tweety didn't show up today, leaving me stuck back here with no chance for a break."

"That's odd."

"Huh?"

"I don't mean it's odd that Tweety skipped work. She does that on a regular basis. I mean it's odd that no one's kept you updated. It's not as if robberies happen all the time around here."

"Like I said, you might hear more up front."

"Well, I'm only staying for a while."

She redirected her attention to the grill. "Then get busy. Allie's waitressing all by herself." She waited a beat. "Moving around will be good for your leg."

I stole another sausage. "Your concern for my well-being is heartwarming." My reply came with a side of sarcasm and a fist to my sternum, followed by a burp.

"Hey," she called as I shouldered the saloon doors separating the kitchen from the dining area, "did you invite Rose to stay on with us?"

I ambled back her way, the doors screeching as they waffled. "Yeah, I told her three days, and she jumped at the offer. Well, she didn't actually jump, but you get the idea."

"See? She's scared."

"Or bored." The guilt over her comment about not getting out was unrelenting.

"Is that why you're in such a foul mood? You may have to be responsible for Rose for the next few days?"

"Nope. It's my leg. Spending time with her won't be a burden."

Grace eyed me suspiciously.

"Really." It's the least I could do after being such a neglectful, self-absorbed jerk the past couple years. "I'll sleep in one of the second-floor bedrooms, and I'll borrow a baby monitor to listen in on her."

"Did she say any more about last night?"

"Not much. Dr. Betcher implied she'd go on and on, but she didn't."

Grace flipped eggs and hash browns, the grill hissing in response. "Betcher's a cretin."

"He also warned me not to place much stock in anything she did say because she'd be confused due to shock. But this morning, when I got her to open up a little about the whole ordeal, she didn't seem the least bit mixed up."

"Yep, a true cretin."

"You sure have it in for the guy, Grace. One of these days you'll have to fess up as to why."

"It wouldn't be worth the breath."

Chapter 6

Folks chattered and silverware clattered as I ditched my quilted vest behind the counter, tied an apron around my Minnesota Gophers sweatshirt, and grabbed a pot of coffee from the service station. The café featured two types of coffee: dark roast, which offered a rich aroma that routinely permeated the air, and Scandinavian coffee, brewed with two eggs per pot and so weak that it barely registered as brown and possessed no aroma whatsoever. Even so, it remained the more popular choice among the older farmers.

I refilled the dice players' coffee cups, then homed in on the talk at the mothers' table. While most customers rehashed versions of the previous night's criminal activity, the mothers debated whether a member of their group should alter her son's Halloween costume after failing to make it big enough to fit over a snowsuit "just in case." Having dealt with that issue a time or two when my own kids were young, I couldn't help but snicker.

Sheriff Karl Ingebretsen lumbered in around then, the bells on the door announcing his arrival. He started my way only to be brought to a standstill by Gustaf Gustafson, who yelled from a booth, "Hey, Sheriff, I've got some information about the robbery."

With a sigh, Karl requested a dark roast, altered his direction, and eased in across from Gustaf, who was visibly pleased that his announcement had drawn almost everybody's attention.

In that respect, Gustaf, a high school classmate of mine, hadn't changed much over the years. When we were seniors, he'd become class president after buying votes with beer and was named captain of the football team after his father purchased new practice dummies. Yeah, Gustaf and his father, the president of the local bank in those days, had a penchant for remaining front and center.

Now Gustaf was in charge of the bank and deemed himself the star of the show that was the town of Hallock. In reality, he was no leading man. When younger, he was handsome enough, but time had not been kind to him. His hair had disappeared except for a few strands he incorporated into an elaborate comb-over. He had a moon face. A ginormous beer belly. And breasts bigger than mine, a fact Grace claimed made me jealous.

I wasn't. Especially not that morning. Gustaf was a drinker and appeared to have spent the previous night pulling double duty as a doormat. His whisker-stubbled cheeks were mottled, his clothes were wrinkled and stained, and in spite of being all the way across the room, I could tell that the bags under his eyes were big enough to hold groceries for a family of six.

To say I didn't care for Gustaf Gustafson was an understatement. I'd never forgiven him for dropping his pregnant high-school girlfriend to hook up with the shrew who later became his wife. On the flip side, he'd never forgiven me for being part of the group of girls who, in retaliation against him for doing his girlfriend wrong, stole his dingy white underwear from his gym locker, wrote "Gustaf is a Man Whore" on them in red lipstick, and hoisted them up the flagpole during the homecoming football game. Still, because I was desperate for robbery news, I put my feelings for him aside and snaked around the tables and chairs to his booth, a coffee pot in hand.

"It's so cold out there I swear I'm farting snowflakes," Gustaf informed the sheriff with a chuckle.

The sheriff only responded, "What's up?"

"Well," Gustaf said, "I know some stuff about Buck Daniel, the guy who robbed the pharmacy." While Gustaf had ratcheted up his volume to a few decibels beyond obnoxiously loud, he probably found it just about right because it kept most everyone riveted on him.

Karl, conversely, spoke quietly when he said, "We aren't even sure he was the perpetrator."

"Yeah, yeah, innocent until proven guilty and all that." Gustaf gulped the last of his coffee and edged the standard-issue restaurant mug toward me with the back of his hairy hand. "Buck supposedly came to town earlier this year to help his grandma, but I guaran-damn-tee ya he had other plans, like helping himself to her cash." He shook his head, and his chins followed. "After he moved in with her, he became a signee on her bank accounts. And when she went into the nursing home a couple months back, he stayed on in her house and kept right on withdrawing funds to 'cover her expenses.'"

While Gustaf droned on, as he was prone to do, I poured the sheriff some coffee, and he thanked me with a wink. My stomach somersaulted like a young Mary Lou Retton, even though I reminded myself that women my age weren't the recipients of winks, so odds were, it wasn't a wink but just a blink, and I only caught half of it. Or, perhaps, my flip-flopping innards had nothing to do with the sheriff's rapid-eye movement. Perhaps they were caused by my Rose-related guilt. Or the sausages I'd scarfed down disagreed with me, and I was about to throw up.

Whatever the reason, I decided it'd be prudent to take my leave and was just about to do that when Gustaf declared, "Buck Daniel came into the bank late yesterday afternoon and cleaned out his grandmother's accounts. That's right. He withdrew every last dime she had. Wanted it in cash—$100 bills. I ordered the girl to give it to him. I couldn't very well deny him, being his name was on the accounts. So she handed it over, and he stuffed it in a backpack and traipsed on out the door."

Yes, Gustaf was loud and overbearing, and he resembled a carp. Yet he seemed to possess information unknown to most people in the place, myself included. Consequently, I warned my stomach to behave because I wasn't going anywhere. Granted, I could have heard him from across the street, but I wanted to stay put, where I could also read his face.

So I watched him while he spoke. And when I didn't dare stare any longer, I pretended to check the creamer and sugar supplies on the table.

"Yeah," he continued, "Buck claimed he had to liquidate his grandmother's assets 'cause the law office was revamping her estate plan. Of course, that made no sense whatsoever, but being the total withdrawal was less than ten grand, I figured, what the heck?"

In addition to his other deficiencies, Gustaf suffered from chronic nasal congestion. He always sounded as if he had packed his nose with tissues, a few of which he could have used right about then because he was sweating like a sinner in church, as Rose liked to say.

Beads of perspiration trickled down his face. "This morning, when I learned about the robbery and that Buck Daniel was the likely thief, I called the law office. And guess what? No one over there was doing any work for Wilma Daniel."

Although I had promised myself that I'd ignore Karl, I couldn't stop from glimpsing at him to gauge his reaction.

He rested against the booth's seat back and folded his arms over his chest. I was determined to keep my glimpse from stretching into a gawk, but it was difficult since he reminded me of the Marlboro man, and what sixty-something woman hadn't at one time or another fantasized about the Marlboro man?

Karl was tall—six foot four or more—and in pretty good shape for someone approaching Medicare. His hair was black, thick, and streaked with silver, particularly along his temples. His cheekbones were cut glass, and his complexion was caramel-colored, the result of some Ojibwe blood coursing through his veins. He also smelled like a campfire because he lived in a wood-heated cabin on the shore of Lake Bronson, about seventeen miles from Hallock.

After a minute—or six—I ordered myself to lower my gaze. The man was capable of setting me on my heels, especially when he peered into my eyes, and I was determined to keep him from doing that. He was incredibly sure of himself, a trait I found both aggravating and, I'm ashamed to say, somewhat alluring.

"I already got filled in," he advised Gustaf. "A few guys from the law office came by the courthouse earlier."

I stole a peek at Gustaf. He appeared deflated. Given his size, in the figurative sense only. "Well, I bet they didn't tell you that Buck's face was battered, like someone wanted to whoop his ass but got him turned around."

I fumbled the sugar shaker, barely catching it before it fell into Gustaf's oversized lap. Gustaf, in turn, nailed me with a bloodshot glower, his capillaries resembling a map of his favorite watering holes. "I know you don't usually eat during your coffee break," I hurried to say before the sheriff had a chance to respond to Gustaf, "but Grace made some scrumptious cinnamon muffins. Would either of you like one?"

I really didn't care if they ate muffins or not. God knows Gustaf didn't need one. I merely wanted to derail their conversation before Gustaf named the person responsible for pummeling Buck Daniel on the off chance that the sheriff wasn't already privy to that information. Of course, the fight had no bearing on the robbery, but if the sheriff discovered that Will had done the beating, he still might demand details. And if that happened, I'd be obliged to lie or break my promise to Erin about the origin of her bruise. Because I wasn't keen on doing either, I preferred to dodge the subject altogether.

"Yeah, Buck was a real mess," Gustaf said, sending me into a panic, "but to this day, I have no clue who got the best of him." Those last words stopped me just short of creating a diversion by dumping what remained in my coffee pot over the guy's head.

As my pulse dropped back to its customary rate, I sighed, and that sigh must have caught the sheriff's attention, leading him to remark, "No, Doris, we're fine." I glanced at him, as he arched a quizzical eyebrow and added, "But how about you? Did you find out all you wanted to know?"

Gobsmacked, I cleared my throat, resolving to respond with an equally scathing retort, but I couldn't come up with one, which left me with only one recourse: to shoot dagger eyes at him, while my cheeks burned hot enough to fry bacon.

As for the sheriff, he tipped his head back and guffawed, the sound shaking the walls, or so it felt. And I, in turn, scurried away, running the gauntlet of toddlers at the mommy table and getting smeared with pancake syrup.

◎ ◎ ◎

I made excuses to remain in the kitchen until the sheriff was gone, leaving Allie to do all the waitressing. I didn't care. Allie was an actual waitress who made great tips, whereas I was mediocre unpaid help who usually went home with empty pockets.

I had just started the dishwasher when my son wandered through the back door. "Hi, Grace," he called to his aunt, who stood along the opposite wall, hunched over the grill, offering up empty threats about kicking Tweety to the curb.

Will pivoted in my direction. "Got a second?"

He showed signs of worry. Then again, he always showed signs of worry. He was a serious guy. Not yet forty, he had permanent frown lines etched across his forehead and gray hair sprinkled throughout his beard and the curly rust-colored mop that stuck out from beneath his Minnesota Twins baseball cap.

"Is Sophie all right?" Using the sleeve of my sweatshirt, I wiped steam from my face before slouching against the conveyor dishwasher, the dishes inside clinking against one another.

"Yeah, she hardly ever gets morning sickness anymore. She hasn't requested a sub at school all week."

"That's good."

He stuffed his thick hands into the pockets of his worn jeans and slumped his shoulders. "I just visited with Erin out back,

51

in the alley," he halfway whispered, even though the rattling dishes and the hissing grill made it impossible for Grace to decipher our conversation. Besides, he had to realize I'd share with her whatever he said, anyhow.

"What's she doing in the alley?"

"I don't know. But she said she told you I slugged Buck Daniel." Like his sister, he had nervous feet and scuffed his thick-soled work boots against the hardwood floor.

"That's right. And while I don't blame you for defending her, I wish you would have worked it out some other way. Flying off the handle doesn't accomplish anything."

"Yeah, yeah."

"It only causes a bigger predicament." Actually, if given the opportunity, I'd have punched Buck Daniel, too. But I couldn't say that. Will was a known hothead, and it was my job to discourage his reckless behavior. At least it had been until last year, when he married Sophie.

"I know. I'm too much like Dad."

True, he was a lot like his late father, from his Irish complexion and compact stature to his quick temper. But while Bill had enjoyed hearing himself talk, Will was reserved. Will also valued family, which had led to the altercation with Buck Daniel in the first place. Ironic, considering that Bill, too, had been eager to use his fists to settle scores but never regarded his family as worth the fight.

"I wasn't comparing you to your father." At least not out loud. "I don't want you to wind up in a jam. That's all. And I would have preferred finding out about the fight right away."

"Erin and I are adults, Mom. We can solve our own problems. We don't need to depend on you."

Okay, that hurt almost as much as if he had punched me. Yes, he was a grown man, but I was still his mother.

"Order up!" Grace hollered.

Will straightened. "Do you have to—"

"No." I attempted to shake off the emotional blow he had landed. "Allie will get it."

I then snared the sleeve of his oil-stained Carhartt jacket. "You'll soon discover you never quit worrying about your children. You never stop being a parent."

"Mom, you had enough on your mind."

"I'm not fragile. I may have been down for a while, but I've been better for some time."

Allie retrieved the plates from the ledge of the pass-through window, delivering them and the aroma of grilled-beef patties smothered in fried onions to a group of early lunch customers.

Once she was out of earshot, Will picked up from where he'd left off. "You had your hands full with the move."

"I'm able to do more than one thing at a time." I had progressed from hurt to peeved.

"All right, Mom. All right. But that's not what I wanted to talk to you about."

Lowering his head, he examined the worn floor before refocusing on me. "Promise you won't tell anyone that I hit Buck Daniel."

I creased my brow and momentarily wondered if my forehead was as wrinkled as his. "Excuse me?"

"I already have a full plate: Sophie's pregnancy. Finishing our new house. And being in charge of harvest for the first time. I don't want to deal with any other crap."

Because my brain didn't move as fast as his mouth, I couldn't make heads or tails of what he had said. "Is this about Erin? Are you worried she'll lose her job if word gets out?"

"No. Not really. It's just…"

When my brain finally caught up and I grasped what was going on, it hit me so hard I almost got a headache. "Oh, I get it. Sophie has no clue about the fight. And if she hears about it, she'll be furious with you, right?"

"After the brawl last year, I swore I wouldn't get into another one, no matter what." He stroked his closely cropped beard. "So, yeah, she'd get worked up. Might even get sick again. And I can't risk that."

No doubt about it, Will loved his wife. It was evident in his eyes, an expression I'd never seen in his father's eyes, and somehow that felt unfair. Why didn't I get a husband who really loved me? Someone who really cared? I discreetly covered my mouth, as if that would silence my brain. It didn't. *Are you jealous of your son, Doris? Sure, he made it clear you're obsolete now that he's married, but that's no reason to begrudge him the love he feels for his wife.*

Ashamed of myself and eager to make amends, I agreed to his request. "Okay, I won't say anything, but someone else might." Although if Gustaf couldn't identify the person guilty of beating Buck Daniel, no one else probably could, either.

"Erin and I didn't tell anyone, Mom. And the sheriff would have said something by now if he knew."

"I hope you're right, Will. I hope you're right."

Chapter 7

After Rose and I left the café, we dropped by the Farmers Store, the only grocery store in town, to pick up a few things for Grace and a couple items to take home with us. Rose was too worn out to go inside but assured me that she'd keep the car locked while I was gone.

As I selected a chicken from the rotisserie, I heard Berta Benson, the leader of the café's corner-booth ladies. She was around the end cap nearest me, outside my line of sight but well within audio range. She was yakking it up with Joy Jacobson, also known as Tweety, her granddaughter and Grace's AWOL waitress.

I pulled up on my cart and listened.

"I'm calling Gustaf as soon as I get home," Berta grumbled. "He's the head of the county board, and he can order the sheriff to fire her, don't ya know. There's no way she was in the dark about Buck Daniel's plan to rob the pharmacy. She's his girlfriend." Berta's voice reminded me of a weed whacker, which seemed appropriate in some topsy-turvy way because her face resembled a noxious plant.

And Tweety? Well, according to Ole and the other men who kept vigil at the counter in the café, her body rivaled a "brick shithouse," but her voice sounded like Tweety Bird. Hence, the nickname. "Erin Connor ain't his girlfriend," she trilled.

"How do you know?"

"He dropped her like an old potato." I imagined Tweety's fists lodged against her ample hips, while her Madonna breasts—like the singer's, not the virgin's—jetted out before her. "He said she was too boring."

"You mean 'hot' potato."

"What?"

"He dropped her like a hot potato."

"Who did?"

"Never mind."

A request for a second checker, announced over the loudspeaker, interrupted them and the instrumental version of "Let It Be" that streamed through the store's sound system. In response, Berta amped up her volume. "Why'd she hafta come back to Hallock, anyways? We don't need no women cops 'round here."

"Well," Tweety replied, attempting to raise her voice but only succeeding in making it more grating, "from what I gather, she quit down there in Minneapolis because she got sick of doing nothing but crowd control."

"Oh, that's what she'd like you to believe. But I bet that wasn't the real reason. She probably got herself fired or something. That girl's been trouble her whole life."

"Uh-huh. But… umm… why do you… umm… care?" Obviously Tweety had gotten distracted.

"And why are you constantly checking your phone?" Berta wanted to know.

"I ain't. But if I was, it wouldn't be any of your beeswax."

Berta uttered something under her breath before reiterating, "No, I've never liked a single member of that family."

And I had never cared for her, either. In fact, I rarely spoke to her. Sure, I talked plenty behind her back, but I seldom said anything to her face. And given that face, no one could blame me.

"Rose is the worst, though," Berta added.

To which, Tweety replied, "She's not really a part of their family, you know."

"Uff-da. I don't care. Oh, she acted all hoity-toity in the café this morning just because she'd witnessed the robbery. Then we come to find out that she never even got a decent look at the guy."

"What the heck?" Tweety's voice might have climbed another octave, to glass-shattering range, and I momentarily feared for the one-gallon pickle jar in my cart. "Then how come everybody's so gall-darn sure it was Buck?"

"She spotted his tattoo. And he skipped town with Wilma's money. So the sheriff put two and two together and—"

"Well, who does he think he is?" Tweety whined. "Arnie Einstein? He's no math genius. He should just forget about Buck Daniel. Buck ain't from around here, anyways, so what does it matter?"

"Didn't you hear me? He stole his grandma's money."

"No, he didn't. His grandma put his name on her accounts, making it his money, too." She hedged. "At least, that's what I heard."

"Jiminy Christmas, Joy!" Berta never called her granddaughter by her nickname. She believed it was undignified. Tweety didn't seem to mind. She answered to most anything, particularly if a man did the calling. "That don't change the fact that he robbed the pharmacy."

"Allegedly," Tweety snapped.

"Well, excuse me, Perry Mason."

"Perry who?"

Berta let out a heavy sigh.

"As for him taking pills," Tweety ranted, "it ain't no big deal. He didn't have a gun or nothing, and the pharmacy's gotta have insurance. So if you tell Gustaf anything, tell him to make the sheriff mind his own business."

Other than griping about Berta now and then, I generally avoided speaking poorly of people, but that didn't stop me from having opinions, one of them being that Tweety was dumb. So dumb, in fact, she once claimed to be the smartest person in her graduating class because, unlike her classmates, she'd gone through several grades twice.

Since she was prone to that kind of thinking, I had a hard time believing she'd developed her defense of Buck Daniel all by herself. She must have learned it—as well as the word "allegedly"—from someone else. Most likely Buck Daniel.

"I will do no such thing!" Berta scolded. "I'm gonna demand that the sheriff keep working the case and that he fire Erin Connor, then throw her in jail. After all, it's as clear as day follows night that she was in cahoots with Buck Daniel."

◎ ◎ ◎

Hearing someone cough, I twirled around to find the sheriff in the produce section, where he had an unobstructed view of several crates of Honeycrisp apples, two barrels of Florida oranges, and me hanging on Berta and Tweety's every word.

Despite being miffed with him for his behavior in the café, I couldn't help but admire how handsome he looked in his brown bomber jacket and khaki uniform, his badge affixed to the breast pocket of his open jacket, and the county seal stitched to the front of his baseball cap. When I realized what I was thinking, however, I mentally slapped myself silly.

"I was just about to leave," I told him as he approached.

"Really?" The right side of his mouth ticked upward. "You didn't appear to be leaving. The truth is, you—"

"No, I'm leaving." Clutching the handle of my cart, I aimed to steer around him, but he blocked my path. I then stepped backward, only to have him grip the front of the cart and bring it to a halt.

"I want to apologize for teasing you in the café." He bent forward, invading my personal space. He smelled of pine trees and burning wood, and I suddenly got the urge to go camping and eat s'mores. "I'd have done it sooner, but you avoided me at the café."

"I don't know what you mean." With a shake of my head, I rid myself of all thoughts of the great outdoors, Hershey bars, and marshmallows. "I was busy in the kitchen."

"Is that right?" His tenor indicated he didn't believe me, but I assured myself that I didn't care. At least not a lot.

"How'd you even know I was in here?" I hoped he'd spent hours searching for me.

"I happened to see your car in the parking lot when I passed by."

"What made you so sure it was mine? Practically everyone in town drives a white SUV."

"Not with Rose O'Brian in it."

His lack of effort in locating me caused a stab of disappointment to pierce my chest, but I recovered with a healthy dose of sarcasm. "Impressive detective work, Sheriff."

"Yeah, well, I do my best. Anyway, I'm sorry I gave you a rough time about eavesdropping on Gustaf and—"

"I wasn't eavesdropping."

"Whatever." That's what Minnesotans say when they don't agree with a statement but aren't willing to debate the point. It was an appropriate response because Karl was familiar with my argumentative nature.

You see, we'd grown up together. He was two years older than me, and we dated my sophomore year of high school but broke up the night he graduated, after I found him in a lip-lock with his former girlfriend behind the concession stand at the drive-in theatre. I gave him the cold shoulder that entire summer, and in the fall, he went off to trade school, followed by thirty years in the army. He returned to Hallock six years ago, around the time Grace opened the café. He attended the grand opening but steered clear of me afterward.

All of that changed a month or two back, when he began visiting with me every chance he got. He didn't go so far as to stop out at the farm or ask me on a date, but whenever he spotted me in town, he found an excuse to engage me in conversation.

I wasn't sure how I felt about those encounters. Okay, that was a lie. I enjoyed them, even if I had no clue what to do about them. Notwithstanding my age, I was inexperienced with men. That's not to say I was a complete schmuck. I flirted with him some, but it didn't take long to realize I was in over my head. A mere glimpse in my direction and his dark-chocolate eyes would melt my resolve. "Fine. Apology accepted." See?

Fearing what I might say or do next, I opted for the coward's way out. "I better go. Like you said, Rose is in the car. She was too tuckered out to come inside. She insisted she'd be fine. The engine's running, the heater's on, and the doors are locked. There's also an afghan I knitted in the back seat. I mean it's lying in the back seat. I didn't knit it there. But that probably doesn't matter because I doubt she can reach it. Besides, I've been in here way too long. And that creep's still on the loose."

Glimpsing into my cart, I caught my breath before adding, "I'm done shopping. I had to pick up some buns and pickles for Grace and tater tots, canned corn, and cream soup for the hot dish I'm making for Vern Odegaard's funeral luncheon. I already have the hamburger. Grace won five pounds of extra-lean ground beef last Saturday at the Eagles' meat raffle. I'll have to use the stove and oven at the café because my new kitchen appliances aren't installed yet, but that shouldn't be a problem. Although that's why I got a rotisserie chicken for supper tonight. No stove."

Karl's eyes glinted with amusement, his crow's feet crinkling. "Doris, are you nervous? You're rambling."

"I am not rambling. I'm trying to have a conversation with you. But I'm done now. And I have my groceries. And I've accepted your apology. So there's nothing—"

He rested his hand on my forearm, ending my ability to speak. "Don't rush off," he said. At least that's what I think he said. Once he touched me, I also had difficulty hearing over the blood whooshing through my ears like water through a sump pump after a heavy rain. Eventually, though, some of his words cut through the noise. ". . . Erin's riding with me this afternoon. She's outside, visiting with Rose."

"Still, I should leave."

"Wait. I wanted to tell you that we've found neither hide nor hair of Buck Daniel."

"What?"

"Hide nor hair. It means—"

I groaned. "I know what it means. I'm not an idiot. It's just that in the café—"

"I said different because Gustaf's a rumormonger, and I didn't want to encourage him. But, yes, we believe that Buck Daniel is our man. Although we have a problem."

At the ominous sound of his voice, I swallowed hard, a lump lodging in my throat. "What is it?" I managed to ask over it. "Is Rose in danger?"

Backing against a shelf of canned soup, Karl crossed his arms over his chest. "We're pretty sure Buck Daniel is on the run. We've alerted the border patrol, and the highway patrol's on the lookout, but we don't know what he's driving. We found his motorcycle outside of town, near the distillery."

"Maybe he stole a vehicle. Since everybody around here leaves theirs unlocked and half of them leave them running, it wouldn't be hard."

Karl shook his head. "No one's reported anything, which makes us wonder if he had help."

"An accomplice?"

"It's possible." He straightened, his arms dropping to his sides. "I simply wanted you to know."

"What does this mean for Rose?"

He considered that for a couple of beats. "Probably nothing. Just keep a close watch over her. We're bound to catch him sooner or later. Most likely within in the next month or so."

"The next month or so?" I may have shrieked.

"That's not an issue, is it?"

Of course, it is! "Well… umm… no. Why would it be?"

My only concern should have been how a manhunt—particularly a protracted manhunt—might affect Rose's emotional well-being. Yet I also found myself speculating about how it could impact her temporary living arrangements and, by extension, me and my plans.

"I have no problem with her staying with me. Really I don't." Despite my true feelings, I didn't want Karl to think I was eager to unload her. "It's just that I'm sure she misses her own place."

Karl shoved his hands in his pants pockets and jingled his keys and change, a practice dating back to high school. "Erin mentioned that she and Buck broke up before all of this went down. Even so, I'll keep a close watch on her at work."

"Thanks." That's all I could say because my mind was stuck on "the next month or so." Admittedly, I'd neglected Rose, and for that I deserved to do penance. But wasn't "a month or so" a bit excessive? "Are you sure there's no way to catch him sooner?"

Karl canted his head. "Investigations take time. But I'm open to suggestions."

I had none, of course, and my frustration evidently showed on my face.

"Is there anything else going on, Doris? You look overwrought, as my mother likes to say."

Of course I'm overwrought! But how could I complain about caring for a ninety-year-old witness to a crime, who, over the years, had been nothing but kind to me and my family? "I guess this ordeal has me a bit jumpy. That's all."

"Are you sure?"

For a moment I contemplated reporting Berta's threat to get my daughter fired and arrested but decided against it. While I was certain that Karl knew I'd been listening in on her and Tweety, I wasn't ready to acknowledge it outright. Not after all of his teasing.

Wanting to get out of there, I said goodbye to Karl, aimed my cart toward the front of the store, and gave it a shove. It propelled forward on three wheels, the fourth stuck and refusing to budge. Listing to the left, it careened into a tower of toilet paper, and at least two dozen packages toppled to the floor. They landed in a heap under the bright, fluorescent tubes that hummed overhead.

I rushed toward the mess, hoping to prevent a spectacle, but so much for hope. A woman's voice once more interrupted the piped-in music. "Lloyd, cleanup in Aisle 1. Doris Connor just demolished the Charmin display you spent all morning creating."

"I'll never shop here again," I muttered, as shoppers gawked at me, Berta and Tweety among them.

Drawing near, Karl chuckled.

I didn't. Lloyd, you see, was a mentally challenged man, and I was mortified that I was responsible for wrecking his handiwork.

Meanwhile Emily Solberg stood at one of the three checkout counters, a microphone dangling from her hand and a sneer marking her lips.

"She hates me," I informed Karl. "It's because I'm Grace's sister. And, well, you know Grace."

Emily twiddled her fingers at me, while shoppers kept gawking.

"I'll help Lloyd." Karl scooped up an armload of bathroom tissue. "You go on ahead and check out."

Determined to take him up on his offer before he withdrew it, I gave my cart another shove, but it only jerked. A wayward package of Charmin was wedged beneath its wheels. I bent over to yank it free, and that's when I recalled that I was low on toilet paper at home. In that moment, however, I didn't care about my personal toilet-paper supply. Then again, toilet paper wasn't something you could be indifferent about. So I tossed the liberated package into my cart and nabbed two more from Karl's outstretched hands.

While I refrained from looking at him directly, I caught a glimpse of his face out of the corner of my eye. He had bitten his lower lip, apparently to keep from grinning, but he hadn't clamped down hard enough to get the job done. If my arms had been toilet-paper free, I'd have been more than happy to give him a hand—right across the mouth.

Chapter 8

Rose and I trudged through the back door of the café, weighed down by bags of buns and pickles. "We bought everything you wanted, Grace."

"Did you park in the alley?" My sister barely glanced up from the stainless-steel prep table in the center of the kitchen. She was elbow-deep in flour and bread dough, the sour smell of yeast riding the air. "If you did, you better hurry. The garbage truck will be here any minute."

"Why so late? I thought they emptied the dumpster early in the morning."

"Usually they do, but the truck broke down. It's fixed now, and they texted, guaranteeing they'd have us taken care of by three o'clock."

Rose and I placed the bags on the counter, and I stuffed my gloves in my pockets while checking the clock on the wall above the pass-through window. "It's almost three now."

"That's why you better hurry."

Lifting the lid from the pot on the stove, I breathed in

67

the flavorful aroma of chicken and Mexican seasonings. Tomorrow's lunch special: white chili.

I peeled back the layer of humiliation caused by the toilet-paper fiasco and the layer of depression brought about by Karl's speculation as to how long Rose may have to remain my houseguest, and lo and behold, there was my appetite. I retrieved two Styrofoam take-out bowls from the open shelf next to the stove. "First, a couple bowls of chili to go. We haven't had lunch."

Grace wiped her hands on the towel hanging from her shoulder. "Will you grab the garbage on your way out? Since Tweety was a no-show today, I've barely had time to breathe, much less take care of the garbage."

After ladling the bowls full, I fitted each with a plastic cover. "Speaking of Tweety, I saw her with Berta in the grocery store."

"I don't want to hear about it. I finally got myself calmed down. I'll deal with her tomorrow."

Just as well. I really wasn't in the mood for conversation. Mostly I wanted to go home and eat my chili and comfort myself by devouring the two "share" packs of M&Ms I'd picked up while paying for my groceries. I couldn't imagine any better way to combat residual shame and despair than downing plain M&Ms, followed by a peanut M&M chaser.

"Do you want us to stay and help you?" Rose asked my sister.

"No, just empty the trash."

I placed the chili bowls in a brown paper bag and passed the bag to Rose, who kissed Grace's flour-dusted cheek and toddled out the door. I tied the tops of two plastic garbage bags, heaved them from their rubber containers, and followed.

"Let me get the dumpster lid for ya," Rose garbled against the wind.

"No, I've got it. You just make sure you don't spill the chili." I set the orange bags on the pitted pavement and tucked my wayward hair behind my ears. Glancing down the alley, I spotted the garbage truck as it rumbled around the corner, belching exhaust into the air.

I yanked on the dumpster's metal door, glad Grace had rented the front-loading model. Its sliding door was far easier to navigate than the one with the lid on top.

As the door screeched open, the stench from inside nearly knocked me over. It wasn't as bad as in August, when heat shimmered off the asphalt, transforming the dumpster into an oven that roasted all of its contents, from rejected ranch dressing and banana cream pie to moldy cheese and meat gone bad. Yet it was pretty darn stinky.

I breathed through my mouth a couple of times before seizing the oversized garbage bags and absently chucking them inside, one after the other. They hit something I sensed didn't belong there, and I leaned in for a closer look. Right away I stumbled back and gobbled up fresh air before taking another crack at it.

The driver of the garbage truck honked his horn. No doubt my car was in his way. But he could wait. Grace had waited for him all day.

I scanned the interior of the dumpster. The few rays of light that had found their way inside created shadows that played tricks on me, leading me to squint to sharpen my focus. The truck's horn beeped again. And that's when I spotted what appeared to be a man.

I sucked in a lungful of foul air and coughed.

It was a man all right, sprawled on his back and halfway hidden under the bags I'd just added to the putrid mix. One of the bags had split open, leaving the man's bloody, misshaped head framed by wilted lettuce leaves and an empty egg carton. His lips were lax. And his black, lifeless eyes were pinned on me.

I threw up on my shoes.

"What in the Sam Hill?" Rose strained her neck for a look-see in the dumpster. "Well, I'll be." She pinched her nostrils and more or less honked, "I think that's Buck Daniel."

"How do you know?" I had no inkling where those words had come from. I was in shock, incapable of rational thought. And I was mourning my shoes. My brand new Allbirds. Nonetheless, I wiped my mouth with the back of my gloved hand and strung together another sentence. "You never got a good look at him."

"Considerin' the way his head's bashed in, it probably wouldn't of mattered."

Black dots danced in front of my eyes. "Why do you think it's him?"

"I feel it in my bones. And he has that snake tattoo on his left calf. See?"

No, I didn't see. I refused to look. And even if I had summoned enough courage to do so, I'd have been unable to zero in on anything because of the black dots. Just like I couldn't hear much beyond the growl of the garbage truck, the gnashing of my teeth, and Rose uttering, "Well, now, isn't this a fine howdy-a-do!"

Chapter 9

Several weeks had gone by since Rose and I had discovered Buck Daniel's body in the dumpster behind the café. Still, I had no desire to go out, and I definitely didn't want to curl, but Grace nagged me until I gave in. She argued that I'd surpassed the statute of limitations on trauma caused by finding the likes of Buck Daniel and would benefit from being around people. I suspected her competitive nature simply wouldn't allow our team to start the curling season with a forfeit.

"I'm headed to the wine bar with the others," she informed me after we were soundly defeated and back in the dimly lit warming room. "You coming?" She nodded toward a half-dozen people huddled by the door of the Quonset hut building. They were exchanging curling shoes for boots, a necessity brought about by the foot of snow dumped on our town during a two-day storm right after Halloween.

"Nah." I unbuttoned the Scandinavian cardigan I always wore when I curled. "I better go home and see how Rose is doing. She hasn't been alone since… you know."

"You sure?"

"Yeah, I curled like you wanted, but—"

"No, you didn't."

"What?" I plunked down on a faux-wood chair next to a faux-wood table and toed off my curling shoes. The odor of sweaty wool socks comingled with that of charred coffee to create an aroma unique to the fifty-year-old curling club. I wrinkled my nose.

"You played like a beginner." Grace propped her broom against the table and jacked up her voice to compete with the din around us. "You were awful. I certainly didn't want that."

"I told you I wasn't up to curling."

She motioned toward the three narrow sheets of ice on the far side of the scratched plexiglass that covered the upper half of the wall between the warming room and the curling area. "Trust me, no one mistook what you did out there for curling."

"Lay off." My eyelids burned, and I looked away.

But not before she noticed how emotional I was. "Hey, don't get all weepy." She kicked my stocking feet. "I always criticize your curling. It's what I do."

"Well, don't do it tonight."

"Why? You should be over that Buck Daniel business by now."

"Geez, Louise, Grace, it hasn't been that long."

"You didn't even know him." My sister breathed the words more than spoke them.

And I parroted her. "That's not the point. I found him. It was gross. And it made me distraught."

"As well as a lousy curler."

"Oh, shut up."

"I can't. I calls 'em like I sees 'em," she joked in an animated voice. "You actually fell over while sliding your rock. Not once, but twice."

I rubbed my left butt cheek. "I might have strained a muscle."

"Who are you kidding? You haven't had any muscles back there in years."

Laughter spilled from my mouth in spite of myself.

"What's so funny?" The question came from behind me.

I glimpsed over my shoulder to find the sheriff. "Just discussing my curling technique," I told him.

Grace pretended to choke.

He muttered, "That good, huh?"

Grace leaned toward him. "Let's just say no one will soon forget what they witnessed out there. No matter how hard they try."

Karl dropped onto the chair kitty-corner from me. "Doris, do you have a minute?"

"I guess that's my cue," my sister said, then padded toward her friends by the door.

For a second I reconsidered tagging along with her. Karl struck me as grim and maybe a tad prickly, and I wasn't up to dealing with the likes of that.

"How's Rose?" the sheriff asked once most of the curlers had left, making conversation much less of a shouting match.

"Shaky. Finding a dead body was hard on her. She's definitely too upset to return to assisted living anytime soon." And believe it or not, I was glad she'd asked to stay on with me a bit longer.

Ever since the dumpster ordeal, I'd been rattled by the prospect of staying home alone, especially after dark, which now occurred before six o'clock. And because I hadn't admitted my fears to anyone, Grace and my kids had maintained their normal routines. Thankfully, though, Rose was still at the house, where I pretended that she relied on me more than I relied on her.

"How do you feel about her continuing on as your houseguest?" Karl asked.

"I'm fine with it. Why wouldn't I be?"

"No reason." He sounded as if he knew something, causing me to wonder if I'd done a poor job of disguising my feelings about taking Rose in. I certainly hadn't mentioned anything to anyone lately. Since that fateful day, I hadn't ventured out of the house except to accompany Rose to Sunday Mass and the doctor's office and to drop her off at the senior center earlier that afternoon. Otherwise, we had spent all of our time at home, dealing with the electricians, watching *Columbo* and *Matlock* reruns, playing cribbage and Yahtzee, and agonizing over a one-thousand piece jigsaw puzzle that was spread across the dining room table.

"Really, it's all good," I insisted. "She ended up being an excellent guest. She's a whiz at Yahtzee, although I think she cheats at cribbage. And because she's practically deaf, she turns the television way too high. But she's pleasant. And she's not a picky eater. So I can't complain, can I?"

He shrugged yet said nothing, leaving me to fill the uncomfortable silence. "I'll admit I didn't care for the idea in the beginning, and I certainly don't want her to stay with me indefinitely. I have my own life." That sounded snotty, prompting me to add, "I'm sure she's eager to get back to her life, too. But right now, she needs me while she recovers from the trauma that she's experienced, and I'm happy to be there for her."

Indeed, I had misrepresented the situation, and a mere glance at Karl revealed that it hadn't been necessary because he wasn't listening to me, anyhow. In fact, several seconds ticked by before he even looked at me. And then it was with his serious cop face—a face I hadn't seen since the day after the air vents in Destiny Delovely's Ford Mustang were mysteriously filled with Uncle Ben's Long Grain and Wild Rice, Original Recipe, raw from the box.

"It's official," he uttered. "I received the autopsy report. Buck Daniel died from blunt-force trauma to the left side of his head. He apparently faced his killer, and the murder weapon was most likely a hand-sized rock, which means he was killed outside." He sniffed. "His system was also full of opioids."

Karl's cop face was all sharp lines and angles, and his eyes resembled two burning coals. Those unforgiving features, together with his tough-guy timbre, made me nervous enough to stutter when I asked, "W-when did the death occur exactly?"

"Well, let's see. He was alive when he robbed the pharmacy and dead when you and Rose discovered him in the dumpster, so…" No doubt about it, Karl was upset about something, and while I wanted to believe it had nothing to do with me, his tone suggested otherwise.

Nevertheless, I pretended everything was a-okay. "I guess I was asking if the coroner provided an official time of death."

"Between 11:00 p.m. and 5:00 a.m."

"And how about fingerprints? Or DNA? Have you had any luck with them?"

He scoffed, as if my questions were too dumb to answer. After some time, though, he begrudgingly stated, "Decent samples are tough to come by when the body's been lying in garbage, Doris. And regardless of what you see on television, the samples we did manage to lift will take time to process by the state crime lab."

Because I didn't care for his condescending attitude, I responded with a little attitude of my own. "Well, what about the backpack, the money from the bank, and the pills from the pharmacy? Or for that matter, Buck's phone, his keys, and his wallet? Have you found any of those things? From what I understand, you've struggled in that regard."

Angry red blotches formed on his neck and cheeks. I'd struck a nerve. Good!

"No, we haven't found a thing, although you'll be the first person I notify when we do. After all, we share everything, right?"

I had no clue what he portended by that remark. But since I wanted information, which he'd be reluctant to share if he was furious with me, I ordered myself to refrain from making any further jabs. I also pledged to do my darndest to dismiss his caustic manner. "So what happened, Karl?" I asked in a kind and gentle voice. Think Mary Poppins. "Do you have any theories?"

He cocked his head. "The state's Bureau of Criminal Apprehension is working on it. But I have a few theories. I am the sheriff, after all. Though some folks, like you, seem to forget that."

I guess my darndest was only around five seconds. "Okay, so why are you being such a schmuck?"

"Me?"

"Yes, you. What's going on?"

He propped his elbows on the table, laced his fingers, and narrowed his eyes. "I had to suspend Erin today."

"Suspend her? You gave in to Berta?"

"It had nothing to do with Berta. I suspended her because she lied to me." He perused the room, probably to determine if any stragglers were listening in. But rather than eavesdropping on us, the few remaining curlers had gone upstairs, where the liquor was kept. Their footfalls reverberated overhead, yet I couldn't hear their voices and doubted they could hear ours unless we yelled.

"Doris, do you recall the bruise Erin had on her chin?"

I delayed answering by studying my fingernails. "Yeah, ah, I guess."

"And how it got there?"

I scratched at the cuticle on my left thumb, pushing it to the quick. "Well, ah, Buck Daniel hit her."

"I knew it!" He spit the words out before going quiet for a ten-count. He obviously needed time to quash his fury. "You kept that from me!" He could have used another ten seconds. "I'm investigating a crime, and you withheld information!"

"Good grief, Karl. That bruise had nothing to do with the pharmacy robbery."

"What about Buck's death? Did it have anything to do with that?"

I slapped the table, stinging my hands. "I can't believe you'd even suggest such a thing."

"It's my job to examine crime from every angle. I also expect the truth from people."

"I didn't lie to—"

"You kept vital information from me. It's the same thing. No wonder..." He reined himself in, caution closing his mouth.

"No wonder what?"

He remained tightlipped. He knew better than to speak.

I, on the other hand, egged him on. "Come on. What were you about to say?" I wasn't sure why I felt the need to goad him. Maybe it was my way of dealing with the mounting tension—or the disappointment in his eyes.

"No wonder Erin lied to me," he muttered. "She comes by it naturally."

"That was uncalled for!"

"Well, for crying out loud, what am I supposed to think?"

I rammed my chair back, the legs screaming at the floor. "Think whatever you like. I really don't care." I shoved my feet into my boots. Any more force and I would have pushed right through the soles.

"Doris!" As I went to stand, he captured my wrists. "Your daughter dated Buck Daniel." His voice was barely above a whisper but lethal nonetheless. "They fought. He hit her hard enough to leave a good-sized bruise. She lied about it. And a few days later he was found murdered."

"You don't really suspect her of killing him, do you?" He hesitated a moment too long, and I pounced. "I can't believe you'd—"

"If nothing else, she should have disclosed the truth right after the robbery."

"She did nothing wrong!"

He let go of me. "It looks bad, Doris. Really bad. Especially if I confirm what I've heard about Tweety."

"And what's that exactly?"

"Let's just say girlfriends tend to get upset when their boyfriends step out on them. Some become so angry they even commit murder."

"Are you implying that Tweety hooked up with Buck Daniel while he was dating my daughter?"

"You weren't aware of that?"

"No." I sank back in my seat. "Then again, I didn't even know Buck was Erin's boyfriend until after they broke up."

"I wish I could believe you."

"Excuse me?" I clutched the sides of my chair to keep from lunging across the table and wringing his neck. Don't get me wrong, I relished the thought. But when in my mind's eye I caught a glimpse of myself in jail alongside a woman named Big Betty, I experienced a change of heart. "Let me repeat myself," I hissed, instead. "I don't give a tinker's da… darn what you believe."

"Hold on. Erin created this mess. I'm just the guy charged with cleaning it up."

I wrestled my jacket from the back of my chair and twisted my arms through the sleeves, all the while suppressing my tears with my pride. I was incensed. But along with my indignation, there was escalating fear for Erin. Gratefully my anger remained front and center, leaving me far less vulnerable than if the fear had taken over. "Well, don't let me keep you. Go right ahead and do your job, and I'll do the same."

He bucked to his feet, tipping over his chair. "What do you mean by that?"

I rose, too, but far less dramatically. Yes, I was the adult in the room, and I further demonstrated that by adopting a haughty tone. "Well, since it appears as if the local sheriff is out to get my daughter, I suppose I'll have to do whatever it takes to protect her."

He propped his fists against the table, his face only a foot from mine. "Do not interfere with our investigation."

I instructed my eyes to remain steady on him. I also prayed for my feet to stop quaking in my boots. My eyes listened, but my prayer went unanswered. "The past several weeks haven't been anything like I planned." My voice had lost some of its bluster. I suppose a person can fake haughtiness only so long, particularly when their knees are knocking. "And now I have to deal with this... hullabaloo." I again fell into the role of martyr, short only a stake and a match. "I don't see as if I have much choice."

"You always have a choice."

"Karl, you clearly have no clue about my life."

"What's that supposed to mean?"

I remained silent. My emotions were so close to the surface that I was afraid the tough-woman façade I had uncharacteristically adopted might crack if I so much as uttered a sound. And I couldn't fall apart. Along with caring for Rose and dealing with my own dumpster-related trauma, I now had to help my daughter. I needed all of my gumption.

Chapter 10

I didn't recall much of the drive home, but my senses sharpened when I spotted Erin's car in the driveway. Specifically, I saw red and heard myself ranting and raving although I never opened my mouth.

I angled my SUV into my new garage, then half slid, half limped along the icy sidewalk and entered the house via the front door, all while stuffing M&Ms in my mouth. I kept a stash in the glove box of my car for occasions like this, when chewing on something was better than grinding my teeth down to nubs.

I dumped my curling gear and jacket in the entry closet, kicked off my boots, and made my way through the foyer and dining room and into the kitchen. Erin and Rose were seated in the two chairs at my black drop-leaf table, a pan of chocolate-cherry cake and a spray can of Reddi-wip between them. The scent of chocolate filled the air.

"I wanted to frost that cake." I gestured toward the electric beater and bowl I'd left on the butcher-block countertop. "I tested out the new oven this afternoon, but I had to go before the cake was cool."

"Well, the new oven's none too shabby." Rose squirted more canned whipped cream on her half-eaten piece of cake. "And this here cake is pretty darn tasty without frosting."

Dragging a chair in from the dining room, I eyed Erin. She was dressed in her uniform, minus her badge and gun belt. "We have to talk." I sat down, groaned, got up, and hobbled to the living room.

The gas fireplace burned brightly, fingers of light tickling the artwork on the walls. Despite Rose's presence the past several weeks, I had managed to empty all of the moving boxes and the house almost felt like home again.

Choosing the thickest throw pillow on the sofa, I tracked my way back through the foyer, where the cuckoo clock startled me as it chirped ten p.m. I would have laughed at how I jumped, but I was too sore—and livid with Erin.

Entering the kitchen, I tossed the pillow onto my chair before lowering myself on top of it.

"What happened to you?" Rose pinched her features.

"Curling injury."

She again opened her mouth.

"Don't ask." My tone didn't invite any more questions. "Karl dropped by the curling club tonight," I informed my daughter before cutting my eyes back to Rose.

Erin answered my unasked question by saying, "I told her everything."

"What about me? Did you tell me everything?"

"What's wrong with you, Mom? I'm the one who got suspended."

I pitched my head back and communed with the

schoolhouse ceiling light until my eyes blurred. "I wasn't aware that Tweety was involved with Buck Daniel."

If Erin was shocked by what I had discovered, her voice didn't give her away. "I broke up with him as soon as I found out."

"When was that, precisely?"

She clasped her milk glass with both hands but never brought it to her mouth. "A week before the robbery. He came to my place after work one day."

"Huh?" Rose inclined her head. "What'd you say?"

Erin ratcheted up her volume. "Nana, you need hearing aids."

"No, you need to speak up and enunciate. Young folks don't enunciate."

With her brow furrowed, Erin proceeded—in a louder voice. "I told Buck I'd overheard a couple guys in the sheriff's office joking about Tweety and him going out behind my back. He laughed. Said it was no big deal."

My daughter's eyes glistened, and all pretense disappeared. She looked defenseless and frightened, like when she was thirteen and leapt off a moving tractor and nearly got run over. "I ordered him out of the house, but he wouldn't go. He tried to kiss me, and I shoved him away. He came at me again, and I slapped him. That's when he hit me. With a closed fist. Then he left."

She scraped her fingernails along her jawline. Although the bruise was gone, the effect on her psyche obviously remained. "Will happened by a few minutes later. I had borrowed his John Deere to mulch leaves, and he wanted it back. A lamp was overturned, and my chin was red." The memories clearly haunted her. "I had to tell him."

"You should have told me. Karl, too."

"I was humiliated. You know as well as I do that some people around here have longed for me to screw up ever since I got hired."

"You didn't screw up." Of course, she had. She'd lied to her boss. But agreeing with her would only make her feel worse.

"Mom, I dated an abusive man and fibbed about him hitting me. On top of that, he ended up being a thief. Not exactly an example of sound judgment from a woman who wants to be taken seriously on a police force full of men in a community that's never before had a female cop."

Yes, she fully comprehended the potential fallout from her actions. No need for me to belabor the point. "Don't worry, honey." Sensing I should say something profound but unable to come up with anything original, I went with the standard, "It's not the end of the world. We'll get through this."

"Really, Mom? By tomorrow afternoon everyone in town will know what happened. And if Berta and her minions get their way, I'll not only be fired for lying, I'll become the prime suspect in Buck's murder." She drew her knees to her chest and hugged her shins. "I'll never see the inside of the sheriff's office again unless I'm arrested and thrown in jail."

Rose harrumphed. "Don't be silly."

"Remember," I added, "everything happens for a reason."

Apparently Rose found my words of wisdom so lame that she felt it necessary to offer some of her own. "Sometimes, though, the reason bad things happen is you make bad choices, like bein' dishonest with your boss."

"But, Nana, this Buck Daniel thing was my mess, and I wanted to clean it up on my own."

"Erin, honey, I've seen your house. I doubt you could clean up much of anything on your own."

"Rose!" I motioned toward the clock above the sink. "Aren't

you up kind of late? The doctor recommended that you get plenty of rest."

"She doesn't have to go to bed on my account, Mom. It's true. I messed up. I've been messing up ever since I was a kid."

Rose burped and thumped her fist against her chest. "Excuse me." Another thump. "You were a great kid, Erin. A real firecracker. But bein' you left home right after high school, and you've only been back a year, it might take some folks a while longer to realize that you're now old enough—and wise enough—to carry a gun." She cut a second piece of cake and scooped it from the pan with fingers crooked and swollen by arthritis. After placing it on her plate, she topped it with another spritz of whipped cream. "They still think of you as 'little Erin Connor,' the fifteen-year-old who climbed the water tower on a dare."

Erin slipped into a slouch. "That was a dozen years ago."

"Be that as it may, it was epic."

"Epic?" I repeated. "She shaved ten years off my life that night."

Rose proceeded as if I hadn't spoken. "Or what about the time you outran the cops by drivin' through the floodwater along the Golden Grain Bridge? Oh, yah, Erin, you were a real corker."

Over the years, I had evoked numerous words to describe my daughter during her rebellious stage, but "firecracker" and "corker" were not among them. She was incorrigible and unrepentant and found trouble around every corner from her sixteenth birthday until Christmas of her junior year in college, when, out of the blue, she announced she'd given up "running around" to pursue a career in law enforcement. I had been as shocked as a bird on a live wire.

As the cuckoo in the foyer signaled the half hour with a tinkling chorus of "Edelweiss," I stared at the oblong pan on the kitchen table. I didn't need any more sweets, but I felt I deserved at least a small piece of cake after the evening I'd had.

My eyes wandered to the wooden plate rack on the wall, where the dessert plates were front and center. "We'll do whatever's necessary to clear your name," I assured my daughter as thoughts of chocolatey goodness overtook my brain. "Don't worry about being connected to Buck Daniel's death. Or," I absently added, "what Karl might think."

"Huh?" my daughter grunted, jolting me out of my sugar-longing daze. "Does Karl truly believe I had something to do with Buck's murder, Mom?"

"Well... umm... no, of course not." I prayed I sounded convincing, though Rose's face indicated I'd fallen short once again. Even so, I charged ahead. "But since he has townspeople yapping in his ear and the county board to contend with, it might be in your best interest if we quash any rumors that may be out there about you."

Evidently Rose had heard enough. "Oh, let's not make this a bigger deal than necessary. We just hafta visit with that nice Deputy Monson. He'll clear up everything."

"Deputy Monson?" I was ready to discard that idea out of hand. There was no way he was bright enough to fix this.

"Ya betcha," Rose answered. "He can confirm that after the robbery, Erin was with him the rest of the night, trackin' down Buck Daniel in hopes of arrestin' him. So she couldn't of been involved in the murder."

I was stunned. Not because I doubted Rose's ability to create a strategy for addressing our problem. Okay, that was a lie. Of course I doubted her abilities. She was ninety years old. Her synapses weren't supposed to be snapping anymore. Yet she had come up with a straight-forward plan.

Naturally, I felt foolish for not thinking of it myself. But at the same time, I was relieved we had a course of action.

I looked to my daughter in hopes of catching a glimpse of that same relief in her eyes. But it wasn't there. "Erin," I began in my stern-mother voice, "while I understand that you want to get back to work, you'll have to be patient. Karl's pretty angry that you lied to him. But while he's cooling down, we can put to rest any rumors about you being mixed up in Buck Daniel's death."

Erin dropped her head and studied the nubby yellow scatter rug beneath the table, as if seeing it for the first time.

"Oh, don't go and sulk there," Rose cautioned. "I love you, kiddo, but you brought much of this on yourself. You dated the scoundrel, then lied about what he did to you. True, you didn't—"

"It's not that, Nana."

"Then what is it, Erin?" I asked before Rose had a chance to admonish her again.

"I wasn't with Ed all night," she uttered.

And Rose grumbled, "What was that? He doesn't kiss right? Is that what you said? What's kissin' gotta do with it? He's your partner. Are you sayin' he's your boyfriend, too?"

Erin raised her head and shouted, "Ed's not my boyfriend! And he can't vouch for me because I wasn't with him the whole time."

Unlike Rose's hearing, mine was fine. But my brain must have been misfiring because I, too, was confused. "Wait a minute, Erin. Didn't you work with Ed until Karl got back to town? Isn't that why you couldn't come to the house with Rose and Grace and me?"

"Yeah, though I had to take a couple hours off." A flush darkened her cheeks. "To pull myself together."

"So you went home?"

She nodded. "Around eleven o'clock."

I massaged my temples. A monstrous headache was threatening. I could feel it approaching the back of my eyes. "And?"

"I meant to rest, but Buck showed up." She waved her hands. "I didn't kill him, Mom. He wanted me to help him get out of town, and I agreed to do it."

"What?" I shrieked.

Erin flinched. "I said I had to get my car keys. I planned to grab my gun and arrest him. He had humiliated me, and I was furious. Most of the deputies were laughing behind my back. But when I got back to the door with my pistol, he was gone. He must have realized that he couldn't trust me."

"Any guess as to where he went?"

"I assumed Tweety's place. When Ed picked me up later, we checked. Her car wasn't there, although we discovered it at Rowley's retirement bash at the distillery. That's probably why Buck came to my house. Tweety wasn't home. Or he decided she wasn't smart enough to help him get out of town."

The refrigerator hummed along with the steady tension inside of me. "Did you talk to her at the distillery?"

"Yeah. She insisted she knew nothing about Buck's whereabouts, but she could have been lying."

"And you never mentioned to anyone that Buck was at your house? Not even Ed?" I found that hard to believe. I told Grace everything. Then again, Ed was no Grace.

"No!" As opposed to Erin's other words, that one was accompanied by an exclamation point that almost goosed Rose right off her chair. "I wanted to bring him in myself. I thought it would go a long way toward proving myself to the guys at work. But after he vanished, I decided to keep quiet.

I was afraid people might think I was an accessory after the fact."

The worthless platitudes that had occupied my brain had finally given way to other thoughts, but none of them comforted me. "Erin, while I'm no police officer, it seems to me that you don't have an alibi."

"You're right, Mom. I don't."

Despite the sunny outlook the newly painted "cheery yellow" kitchen was supposed to arouse, I felt beaten down and longed to bang my head on the table. But I settled for my drug of choice: cake steeped in whipped cream, right out of the pan. Dessert plate be damned.

Chapter 11

The following morning, under a gloomy sky, Rose and I made our way to the assisted-living wing of the medical center. Her goal was to pick up more clothes. My goal was to get through the day without my head exploding. After Erin's confession, I couldn't sleep, and I woke with the same horrendous headache that had plagued me at bedtime.

Rose flipped on the light in her apartment, illuminating the beige walls and laminated-wood flooring. "I should go ahead and move back in here."

I followed her inside, wiping my boots on a plastic welcome mat that declared, "Kiss me, I'm Irish!"

Because her place smelled musty from being closed up the last several weeks, I propped open the door to the building's main hallway before setting her empty suitcase on the floor in her honey-oak kitchenette. "You can't be alone right now, Rose. You're having nightmares."

She eased onto a padded metal chair at a bistro table positioned against the wall. "I won't be alone." After removing her gloves, she unbuttoned her car coat. "Staff people are all around."

"It's not the same. At my house, I can get to you in an instant when you have a bad night."

"Bein' I'm on those pills now, it shouldn't be long before the nightmares are a thing of the past. Plus, if I move back, I can go to Bible study next week."

"I thought your Bible-study group disbanded. Something about Erma Donaldson causing too much ruckus." I plopped down on the chair opposite her, smothering the hummingbirds in the fabric seat cover.

"Yah. As her dementia got worse, her swearin' did, too. It got so bad that Vera Lowendowski refused to come to any more meetin's. She said God promised that the meek would inherit the earth, and she intended to stay in her room until that happened—or Erma quit the group."

"And Erma finally dropped out?"

"In a manner of speakin'. She died."

"I'm sorry."

"Vera Lowendowski isn't. She called yesterday. Said our group's startin' up again. She was happier than a butcher's dog." Rose clicked her dentures. "Anyways, Erin needs you."

"I'm not sure I can help her." The room was warm, hot air spewing from the ceiling vents. I shrugged out of my corduroy barn jacket and cuffed the sleeves of my cable-knit sweater.

"Wait a minute, Doris. Last night you said—"

"That was before she admitted she didn't have an alibi for around the time of Buck Daniel's death."

"All the more reason for you to be there for her."

My shoulders drooped. "Rose, most of the time she thinks I'm an idiot."

"That's not true. She's just strivin' to make her own way in the world. But she's countin' on your help, even if she can't come right out and ask for it. And if I wasn't around, you'd have more time for her. No doubt about it, I'm an added bother."

"Don't be silly. You're not a bother."

She tilted her head and flashed me side eyes. "I know for a fact you had other plans for when you moved to town and no longer had to contend with that no-account husband of yours."

"Rose!"

"May he rest in peace." She made a haphazard sign of the cross.

"You shouldn't talk like that."

"Why? It's the truth. And it's nothing I didn't tell him to his face when he was alive. He was my nephew, after all. My own sister's son. And a horse's behind. Always out carousin'. Leavin' you to care for the kids and practically everything else on the farm, includin' his own parents." She tsked. "Doris, I haven't mentioned it often, but I'll be eternally grateful for the way you helped with my sister at the end there."

I felt as if she had hugged my heart. "Thank you."

Rose got up from the table, her coat puddling on the chair. She toddled to the kitchen sink. She was dressed in a purple polyester sweatsuit, and she reminded me of the bunch-of-grapes guy in the Fruit of the Loom commercials.

Filling a plastic pitcher, she spoke over the running water. "After gettin' everything straightened out for Erin, you'd have time to enjoy yourself some, too. You could go places. Do things. Maybe even date some."

I almost swallowed my tongue. "I'm not the least bit interested in dating."

"Oh, fiddlesticks." With the pitcher in hand, she skirted the coffee table that separated the flower-print sofa and coordinating club chairs. Reaching a tiered plant stand in front of a petite picture window, she brushed back the foliage on a vine, its leaves crunchy. If not already dead, the plant was well on its way. And no wonder. Dry heat blew into the room like Chinook winds. "Grace says neither of you is past your 'best used by' date, though she claims you're kind of a fuddy-duddy."

"I am not a fuddy-duddy. I'm always busy. Later this morning, for instance, I have to make a cornbread hot dish for another funeral luncheon. And after—"

"Well, excuse me. You're a regular social butterfly."

"Oh, be quiet. And stop listening to Grace. She's nuts." I picked up the laminated placemat in front of me and fanned myself until the birds pictured on it appeared to fly.

"Yah, she reminds me of me when I was younger, while you—"

"I know. I know. I'm more like our mother."

"Hold your horses. That's not a bad thing." After watering her dead and near-dead plants, Rose set the empty pitcher on the Formica counter and returned to her chair, groaning as she sat. "Your mother was my best friend from the time we came to this country until the day she died. Together with my sister, we were the Three Musketeers." She blinked back tears. "I miss them both something fierce."

"I know you do."

"But that's neither here nor there." She slapped the table, as if to shutter all further memories as well as the emotions that accompanied them. "We're talkin' about you and how you're watchin' over me, which you sure as heck didn't expect to do."

"And you didn't expect to witness a robbery. And none of us expected the robber to get killed, or that he'd be Erin's abusive ex-boyfriend. And we certainly didn't expect his killer to be on the loose or Erin to end up in hot water over the whole thing."

She waved her hand dismissively. "Regardless, it's unlikely that Buck Daniel's killer gives a hoot about me. Buck Daniel might of, if he thought I saw him in the pharmacy. But his killer can't possibly have anything against me. So I shouldn't fret none about movin' back."

"I'll say it again, Rose: It's not a good idea. At least not yet. And certainly not just so you can go to Bible study. We can read the Bible at my house."

Rose leaned forward and spoke in a conspiratorial tone. "Well, just so you know, I've overheard you tell Grace more than once how you can't wait for your days to be your own again."

And that answered the question about how discrete I'd been with my griping. "I've changed my mind. In fact, I've decided that because of everything our family's gone through lately and everything we still might face, we should stick together. Be there for each other. And you're a part of our family."

She blinked at the moisture in her cloudy eyes. "That's awfully kind of you to say."

I wrung my hands. It was the second compliment she'd offered me in the last few minutes and two more than I was comfortable receiving, particularly since the latter was earned under false pretenses. Sure, Rose was "one of us," but that wasn't the only reason—or even the primary reason—I wanted her around. As I may have mentioned, I was anxious about being alone. "Anyhow," I continued, in an effort to further perpetuate the fraud, "you should plan to remain at my house until we get this mess with Erin cleared up. It would be good for you—and her."

"But at breakfast this morning you complained that I was too hard on her."

"Yet for some reason, she loves you." Before I realized what I was doing, I added, "We all do."

Rose plucked a wadded tissue from beneath the cuff of her sweatshirt sleeve and dabbed the corners of her eyes. "I love you, too." She returned the tissue to her cuff and reached across the table to squeeze my hands.

Being Scandinavian, I had never felt at ease with overt displays of affection—verbal or physical. Voicing words of love and showing tenderness weren't in my family's wheelhouse. The closest I usually came to telling my kids that I cared was when I warned them to watch for deer while driving at night. As a result, I was confounded by my emotional outburst and wasted no time in moving on. "Anyhow, I also realized that I spent almost a full year working through everything after Bill's death, and—"

"You didn't even like him all that much."

"Rose!"

"Sorry." She didn't appear the least bit sorry. "I didn't mean it." She hesitated. "Okay, I meant it. I just didn't mean to say it out loud."

I tried to keep from smiling, but I didn't try very hard. "I was going to say that Bill's death was different than witnessing a robbery or finding a body, yet all are traumatic events and recovering from them may require some... umm... assistance."

"Assistance?" She scrunched her face until it appeared as if it warranted a good ironing.

"Uh-huh. Like discussing what happened with someone."

"But we never discuss what happened, Doris."

"I don't mean with me. I'm no good at that sort of thing. That's why you should consider seeing a counselor, like Dr. Osgood recommended."

Rose's jaw dropped.

Fearing her dentures might slip right out of her mouth, I chucked her chin. "I know it's ironic that I'm suggesting it." I wiggled around on my chair, uncomfortable even broaching the subject. "But while Grace can sometimes make me wish she were a piñata, she was right about the benefits of therapy. Though if you tell her I said that, I'll deny it, then convince her you have dementia, and we'll put you in the nursing home."

Rose pretended to zip her lips and throw away the key, only to unzip them again a second later. "Well, don't worry none. I won't mention it because I'm not gonna do it. I'm too old."

"No, you're not. And you've been through a lot. A few sessions might actually go a long way toward stopping your bad dreams."

"Doris, I can't divulge my secrets to a complete stranger. Heck, at my age, I can't even remember most of them." She patted the white sausage curls on her head. "Anyways, you probably need therapy more than me."

"This isn't about me."

She placed her hands on the table and steepled her fingers, as if preparing to negotiate. "I'll tell you what. I'll stay with you a while longer. And I'll keep takin' the medicine Dr. Osgood prescribed. But I won't see a counselor." She waited a beat. "And you hafta promise to do whatever you can for Erin."

I closed my eyes so tightly I saw flames on my eyelids. "I was kind of hoping her situation would resolve itself." Then I opened them and blinked until there was only one Rose again. "Karl has to settle down at some point, and no one will take anything Berta says seriously, right?"

Peering at me over the top of her glasses, Rose said, "Doris, your daughter lied to the sheriff, and she got mixed up with a criminal who ended up murdered after hurtin' her. There's no gettin' past it. Her name has to be cleared. And since she doesn't have an alibi, clearin' it means findin' Buck Daniel's killer."

"In that case, I better hire a private investigator."

"What kind of investigator's gonna come all the way up here to work a case? No one worth their salt, that's for gall-darn sure. What's more, bringin' in an outsider will only make folks more suspicious. The way I see it, you'd be better off pokin' around yourself."

My heart did a stutter step. "I'm a retired farmer. I don't know the first thing about investigating a crime. I only said what I said last night because I didn't want Erin to worry."

Rose proceeded as if she hadn't heard me. "Yah, after livin' in this town your whole life, you know the people. You could do some snoopin', and if you come up with anything good, you could alert Karl. And even though Erin's suspended, she could help. The same goes for Grace and me." She arched her eyebrows. "We'll be like Charlie's Angels."

"Or the Keystone Kops."

"Oh, come on, Doris. You gotta give it your best shot. Otherwise, I'll come back here to my apartment, and you'll be in a bind." A smirk took root among the folds in her face and slowly sprouted. "See, I know you don't like spendin' time alone anymore, particularly at night."

"Huh? Then why were you talking about moving—"

"I had to make sure I was doin' the right thing by stayin' on with you."

"Well…" I felt equal parts embarrassed and loved. "You're pretty cagey for someone who applies her lipstick outside the lines."

Her hands shot up to her lips. "I'm not wearin' lipstick, am I?"

"Gotcha."

Chuckling, she again clasped my hands in her touchy-feely Irish way. "So, what's it gonna be?"

There was no point in arguing. She was stubborn. And more than likely right. "Okay. I'll dig around and see how it goes. But if things aren't settled in a week, I'm calling a real investigator."

"Fair enough. Although bein' you're nosy, you might be better at this whole investigatin' thing than you think."

"I'd almost have to be. And I'm not nosy."

"Whatever."

Chapter 12

Voices rose from the hallway outside Rose's open apartment door. Two men were discussing assisted-living bingo at high volume. One complained that Helga Foston cheated, while the other confessed that he couldn't imagine how such a thing could be accomplished.

"You know what, Doris?" Rose began after the men moved on down the hall. "I'm pretty sure that things will not only get better for Erin but for you and me, too."

"What are you talking about?"

"Well, you finally went out last night."

"Curling. That's all. And only because Grace nagged me. Besides, you played whist yesterday afternoon at the senior center, so I had no choice. I had to try."

Rose stood with a grunt and shuffled to the refrigerator, where she grabbed two mini bottles of water and a bag of Hershey's Kisses. "Speakin' of the senior center, I was thinkin' of going back there again today. Though I can stay home if you want. We can work on the jigsaw puzzle." She returned to her chair, handed me a bottle, and dropped the open candy bag in the middle of the table. "Who would of thought a puzzle of the Last Supper would be so blasted hard?"

I guzzled my water. When the bottle was empty, I unwrapped a candy Kiss and popped it into my mouth. "You don't have to babysit me. If I'm to get past this ridiculous fear of mine, I better get on with it."

Rose glanced toward the doorway, as if to ensure that no one was lurking. "I wanna tell you something else, too." She tapped the tips of her paddle-shaped fingernails against her plastic placemat. "Even though I complain sometimes, I really do appreciate everything you and Dr. Osgood have done for me. With the nightmares and all."

"Thanks. But most of the credit has to go to Dr. Osgood."

"Yah, he's not half bad, even if he is too young to be seein' patients on his own."

I spoke around the chocolate melting over my tongue. "Rose, he's in his thirties. He's been through years of schooling. Fact is, you might want to consider him for your own doctor."

"Oh, no." She shook her head so hard her neck waddle wiggled. "I like Dr. Betcher just fine. He's always been good to me and my friends."

"But don't you think he's awfully arrogant? And kind of strange? Socially awkward, you might say?" The furnace kicked in once more, and I reclaimed my placemat.

"Oh, for heaven's sake, Doris, everyone's socially awkward at times. After ninety years on earth, I still have no clue where to look or what to do when people sing me 'Happy Birthday.'"

Neither did I. But that was beside the point.

"Dr. Betcher doesn't patronize us," she went on to say. "He treats us like the adults we are."

"Really?" My hand went limp, and I dropped the placemat. "I got the impression that most people only went to him because he's often the only doctor around."

"No. Some folks really like him. And not just old people. Your son, for instance, is—"

"What? Will?" I sat up straighter, as if improved posture would improve my comprehension. "Will and Dr. Betcher don't know each other."

"Yah, they do. Before I came to stay with you, I saw the two of them visit several times right here in the medical center."

"Are you sure?"

"Doris, I may be old, but I'm not blind. And Will always stopped in to see me afterward."

I attempted to place that information among everything else I knew about my son. It didn't fit. There was no reason for Will to meet with Dr. Betcher. "If that's true, Rose—if the two of them really are acquainted—how come I've never heard about it?"

She cocked her head. "You would of had to visit me to find out."

◎　◎　◎

"Hey, you two, what's all this talk about Dr. Osgood?" The question came from Dr. Betcher as he barged into Rose's apartment from the main hallway, where he'd obviously been listening to us.

Granted, I was in no position to judge anyone for eavesdropping, but Dr. Betcher was a professional. I expected better of him. Besides, whenever I was discovered taking in someone else's conversation, I had the decency to get flustered. It didn't prevent me from doing it again the next time, but at least I felt a certain modicum of shame. That clearly wasn't the case with Dr. Betcher. And that's why I didn't feel particularly bad that he may have heard me urge Rose to replace him with another physician.

"Oh, Dr. Betcher," Rose squealed. "You're back. How was your vacation?"

"It wasn't a vacation." He used his left middle finger to slide his glasses up his narrow, rodent-like nose. "My mother's health is failing. I went to St. Paul to make arrangements for her long-term care. And it took longer than I anticipated."

Like the other times I'd seen him, he wore a white dress shirt and a conservative tie under an open lab coat. And once again his dark dress pants were belted just below his chin.

"Now, what's this about you consulting with Dr. Osgood?" Betcher asked.

And Rose answered, "I only went to him because of that business with Buck Daniel. I started havin' bad dreams, and Doris insisted I see someone, and you were gone." She sounded like she was pleading with him to accept her apology for having an affair. As I may have mentioned, I had no first-hand knowledge of how that sounded, although I had imagined such a conversation on numerous occasions over the years.

"Well, I'm glad you didn't permanently drop me. You were one of my first patients here, Rose, which means we've been together more than three decades."

"Oh, Doctor, I'm not going anywhere."

"Good. Now why don't you make an appointment with me, so I can check on how you're really doing?"

The question earned him a series of enthusiastic nods from my sidekick.

"I'm also happy to see you back in your apartment." He swung his arms like he was Monty Hall and her apartment was the prize behind door number three. "I'm sure you were fine at Doris's house, but this is where you belong."

Irritation festered in me like a pesky infection. Aside from my initial trepidation, I'd done pretty well by Rose and didn't appreciate him characterizing our time together as merely "fine."

"Actually, Doctor," I said, "she's still at my house and plans to stay a while longer. She's only here to pick up some clothes. Now if you'll excuse us, we have to get her packed. She has plans this afternoon, and I have a hot dish to make."

"In that case, Rose, why don't you go and select the clothes you want to take with you and lay them on the bed?" His request dripped with so much sweetness that my teeth ached. "I have to speak with Doris privately for a minute."

"Ya betcha," Rose replied before I had a chance to object.

◎   ◎   ◎

As soon as Rose padded into her bedroom, I put the doctor on notice that I had no intention of arguing with him again about where she should live—even temporarily.

"Okay, we won't argue." He eased onto the chair Rose had vacated, folding her coat over his lap. "I certainly don't want to upset you." He flashed a smarmy smile and reached for my hands, but I yanked them from the table, silently thanking God for my quick reflexes.

He seemed unfazed. "I'm sorry for how I acted after the robbery, Doris. I realized later that you only wanted Rose close by because you care for her, which is wonderful. A number of people in assisted living have no one." Okay, maybe I'd been too critical. Maybe I'd allowed Grace to influence my opinion of him. "I simply didn't gather how dear she was to you since you so seldom visited her." Then again, maybe I hadn't been critical enough. He was a dolt. A dolt who looked like an albino rat. "In any event, Doris, to make amends, I'd like to take you out to dinner."

"What?" My pulse spiked to the rate usually reserved for pap tests.

"Dinner," he repeated, bending toward me. The heavy scent of his musk cologne mingled with his coffee breath and the sweltering heat, making me woozy. But not in a good way. "It's precisely what the doctor orders." He snickered at his own joke. "I can make a reservation at the steakhouse here in town. Or better yet, let's drive to Winnipeg for seafood. Your passport's up to date, isn't it? And I'm sure you like seafood. What do you say? Bill would have wanted you to date."

Hearing my deceased husband's name, I swallowed a heaping helping of emotions. I never voluntarily discussed Bill or my marriage and didn't appreciate when others did, either. Yes, I had to cut Grace some slack. She was family. And Rose was like family. But Dr. Betcher was neither. I hardly knew the guy, and he had no idea what had transpired between Bill and me or how it had left me reeling.

Admittedly I'd been eager to get married, even though Grace had argued that, at twenty-two, I was far too young. She also went ballistic when she discovered I intended to convert to Catholicism, at Bill's request. But most of all, she hated the notion of me changing my name. On numerous occasions, she called long distance to lecture me that by doing so, I would "perpetuate inequality by participating in a practice that harkened back to a time when husbands deemed their wives to be their property." That's right. She really used the word "harkened."

During those conversations, I could almost see her with the phone in one hand and a joint in the other, her unsupported boobs bouncing beneath her tie-dyed tank top as she pontificated. Sure, I listened. It was hard not to. She practically screamed. And she repeated everything a zillion times. But I didn't take any of it to heart. I was young, in love, and all set to live a fairy-tale life.

Not long after the wedding, however, I came to realize that Bill's interest in me hadn't been predicated on love but rather the desire to engage someone in the care of his aging parents. He also wanted a woman who'd split farm chores with him and produce a few children, who, eventually, could offer assistance of their own. Once I grasped all that, I wasn't so happy.

The reality of my situation dawned on me one night following an argument over Bill's inattentiveness. He stormed out, and while I waited for him to return, I stewed—and ate the top tier of our wedding cake. I uncovered it in our basement freezer, where it was stored in a box waiting for our first anniversary, some three months away. After licking my fork clean, I patted my aching belly and made a valiant effort to convince myself that his love for me would develop over time. I couldn't. And it didn't.

During our marriage I had suffered a number of miscarriages—five during the eleven years that separated Will and Erin—and Bill's resentment of me grew with each one. He called me a failure and claimed my status as such reflected poorly on him. To make himself feel better, he argued he "needed" to spend evenings out. And for the most part, I pretended not to care.

But once his parents passed away and our kids graduated from high school and moved out, he seemed to change. He valued me more, or so I thought. We chatted over supper, shared dreams about the farm, and even went on a couple of winter vacations together.

I concluded that my head-in-the-sand strategy had worked. He'd caused me tremendous heartache, but our marriage appeared as if it would survive. Maybe even prosper. That's why I went a little crazy when I learned about Destiny Delovely. Only then did I fully comprehend that my husband hadn't changed at all. He had merely become more skillful at deceit.

"Earth to Doris." Dr. Betcher pulled me from my depressing musings, only to return me to the dismal subject at hand.

While I shuddered at the prospect of dining with the doctor, I didn't want to antagonize him, either. He had attempted to save my children's father. And he was Rose's doctor, a relationship unlikely to change since she regarded him as a god—a god I'd see more frequently now that I'd pledged to be a better friend and guardian.

Even so, I said, "Andrew?" My right eyelid began to twitch. "While I appreciate your offer, I'm not up to dating anyone right now."

He winced, as if I'd slapped him. "I swore someone at the hospital mentioned they'd seen you with the sheriff on occasion, including at the curling club just last night."

I held my eyelid to ensure he wouldn't mistake my twitch for a wink. I knew first-hand how confusing eye movements could be. "Karl and I are friends. Nothing more." Recounting our curling-club argument, I quickly amended that statement. "In fact, we're not even friends. More like acquaintances."

"Good! Then you're free to go out with me."

The intensity of his expression prompted a tightness in my chest that felt a lot like indigestion. "As I said, I'm not up to dating anyone at the moment."

He pushed to his feet and towered over me, his body imposing in Rose's small apartment. "Doris, I'm the most eligible bachelor in town. You'll never find anyone else like me."

I can only hope. "Even so..."

"You're making a terrible mistake." With his left hand, he adjusted his crotch, and I whipped my head around to consider the robin featured on my plastic placemat.

"That may be," I muttered to the bird. "Still, my answer's no."

The bird didn't appear to care one way or another. But Andrew Betcher warned me, "I'm afraid you'll regret your decision, Doris. Really, I am."

Chapter 13

While Rose visited with friends in the assisted-living section of the medical center, I schlepped her suitcase out to my SUV, one of many parked in the lot in front of the building. While the wealthy farmers in the area never hesitated to purchase $700,000 combines or $70,000 pickups, they refused to drive fancy cars. BMWs, Porsches, and Mercedes were just "too darn showy" for reserved Scandinavians, me included. Thus, after my Irish husband died, I traded in his Lincoln Town Car for a white Ford SUV. It was "good enough."

Once back in the medical center, I headed down the corridor, my mind a smorgasbord of thoughts about Dr. Betcher, some of them creepy, others kind of scary, none of them good. I rounded a corner and slipped, kicking over a placard that read, *Caution: Wet Floor*. I caught myself on the railing that lined the wall.

While gathering my composure and assuring myself that nothing was broken, I smelled cinnamon and heard Dr. Les Osgood. He was speaking with my daughter in his office, which happened to be directly ahead of me. And wouldn't you know? The door was cracked open an inch or two.

"What brought all this on, Erin?" Dr. Osgood's baritone voice was edgy.

"Now that I'm suspended, I have more time to think."

"About Buck Daniel? He's been dead for weeks." He left unsaid but implied, *Why are you only thinking about him now?*

"I'm well aware of how long he's been dead. You don't have to remind me." Obviously, my daughter could get snotty with people other than Grace and me. Good to know. Not particularly nice of her, but it made me feel better.

"The drug angle has niggled at me from the start," she said, as I imagined her sitting in one of his upholstered chairs, wrapping wayward hair around her fingers. "Buck's motorcycle accident happened a year before he moved here. He popped pills once in a while. More during the last month we dated. He claimed they were for lingering pain. I never asked what kind of medication it was or where he got it. But following the pharmacy incident, I wondered."

"Why didn't you come to me about this earlier?"

"I spoke with the sheriff regarding my suspicions the morning after the robbery. He assured me that he'd take care of it. I suppose he didn't want me involved since I had dated the prime suspect. Then later in the day, Buck was found dead in the dumpster behind the café."

"And?"

"I don't believe the sheriff ever acted on my hunch. He probably dismissed it since the robbery suspect was dead."

"But Buck Daniel didn't die from an overdose. So why the interest in a 'drug angle?'" Dr. Osgood made my daughter's suspicions sound downright silly.

And I was shocked when she didn't call him on it. She merely said, "I suspect there's a connection between the robbery and the murder. Since major crimes are unusual around here, when two occur close together, they're more than likely related. Plus, Buck's system was full of opioids when he died. And a lot of opioids were stolen from the pharmacy."

"So what do you want to know? If I prescribed him pain pills?"

"Well, actually, I want to know if Dr. Betcher did."

"Dr. Betcher?" Surprise resonated in Dr. Osgood's tone.

"Yeah. I have it on good authority that Dr. Betcher was seen with Buck Daniel on numerous occasions here in the medical center."

"Lots of people are seen with Dr. Betcher. As for Buck Daniel, I'm sure he and Dr. Betcher routinely discussed his grandmother's care. She has Alzheimer's and resides in our memory-care unit."

"But Dr. Betcher has a reputation for prescribing medication when other doctors won't, and—"

"And what makes you think he overprescribes meds, Erin?" A chair squeaked and I envisioned Osgood rising from his seat, the morning sun shining through the window behind his desk and backlighting his profile.

"It's common knowledge. You've only been here a few months, but—"

"I'm about to start my tenth month."

"Then I'm amazed you haven't heard about it already."

My stomach growled, and I folded my arms over my midsection to muffle the noise. Because I'd overindulged on cake the night before, I had allowed myself only a cup of Greek yogurt topped with berries for breakfast, and I was hungry. I also had a slight headache, possibly because it was the first day in I don't know how long that I hadn't topped off breakfast with chocolate. The measly candy Kiss devoured in Rose's apartment before Dr. Betcher arrived didn't count.

"Doctors have different approaches to the practice of medicine," Osgood stated, signaling that my stomach pangs had gone undetected. "Older physicians, like Dr. Betcher, are often more comfortable treating patients with medication right off the bat, while we younger ones have been trained to explore other treatment options first, like lifestyle changes. But that doesn't mean one approach is right, and the other is wrong."

"That's very diplomatic of you."

He chuckled. "Erin, while I admire your tenacity, I covered for Dr. Betcher while he was out of town recently, and I didn't see any evidence of him writing excessive prescriptions."

"Well, maybe he got the pills some other way. Maybe he stole them from the pharmacy or sold the samples he received from pharmaceutical reps. Or maybe he's involved in a drug-company kickback scheme."

"You have an active imagination."

"No, I have good instincts." Finally, she had gotten testy.

And in response, Dr. Osgood lost his good humor. "Drug protocols have tightened over the years. Samples are no longer handed out like candy. As for kickbacks—"

"But he's the chief of staff! He can do whatever—"

"Erin, he runs a tight ship."

"He has a checkered past. He only came here because no clinic or hospital in the Twin Cities would hire him after what he did."

"What happened down there had nothing to do with fraudulent prescriptions or missing pills or anything along those lines. On top of that, it was thirty years ago."

"Well," my daughter growled, "tigers don't change their spots."

"You mean leopards."

"Whatever."

A couple moments passed before Erin concluded with an air of defeat, "You won't tell me anything, will you?"

"There's nothing to tell. On top of that, you're a suspended law enforcement officer seeking privileged information."

Another squeak and I suspected that Dr. Osgood was back in his chair, his feet on his desk, his hands folded behind his head, and the tails of his white coat trailing at his sides. I really had no way of knowing if he routinely sat like that, but that's how I pictured him. "Now how about the truth? Why are you hellbent on crucifying Dr. Betcher?"

"I'm not." Erin sounded exasperated. "I'm merely attempting to make sense of what happened."

"But what you're suggesting doesn't make the least bit of sense. If Buck Daniel was getting drugs from Dr. Betcher, he wouldn't have robbed the pharmacy. And while you claim the robbery was connected to the murder, you haven't offered any reason for why Dr. Betcher would want Buck Daniel dead."

"Buck was out of control! He could have blown the lid off of Dr. Betcher's entire operation."

"Like I said, you have quite an imagination."

While I desperately wanted to hear what my daughter said next, I couldn't stick around. Two nurses dressed in scrubs that featured cartoon turkeys and pilgrims were headed my way. And even though their outfits made them appear friendly, I doubted they'd take too kindly to catching me with my ear practically pressed against Dr. Osgood's office door.

Chapter 14

Following lunch at home, where I craved sweets but feigned excitement over baked chicken and raw spinach, I made a cornbread hot dish while Rose napped.

When she woke up, we got back in my car, and I drove to St. Patrick's Catholic Church, where I dropped off the funeral-luncheon hot dish before taking her to the senior center. She planned to play whist, then join other seniors for the monthly birthday supper, scheduled to begin at four o'clock sharp.

Even though she'd gone to the senior center the day before, she appeared nervous. Or, maybe, she was just worried about me staying home alone. I didn't ask. We'd already explored our feelings enough for one day. Maybe enough for the entire month.

While I maneuvered the slippery streets, pleased that the potholes were snow-packed because it made them far less hazardous than during the summer, Rose repeatedly repositioned her purse on her lap. And when we reached the senior center, she asked several times if I was sure I didn't want her to stay with me.

After convincing her that I'd be hunky-dory on my own, she said she'd arranged a ride home with Elsa Olson. In spite of being ninety-three, Elsa possessed a driver's license and, purportedly, decent night vision, an enviable combination that propelled her popularity among the geriatric set. From what Rose said, Elsa wasn't particularly nice, but folks willingly forgave her transgressions in exchange for a ride.

Leaving the senior center, I bumped across the train tracks and, at the intersection, waited for three semitrucks loaded with sugar beets to pass. I extended each driver a finger wave, which only required raising one index finger from the steering wheel. Not a complicated gesture, but failure to offer it could result in getting labeled "kind of snotty" or "none too friendly."

Once the road was clear, I headed downtown because, contrary to what I'd insisted to Rose, I didn't feel "hunky-dory" about going home to an empty house. I also wanted to stop by the café and share with Grace what had transpired at the medical center.

Inching my way along Main Street, I spotted a burrito truck in front of the gas station-turned-brewery. As if mocking the cold, a number of people milled about outside with beer mugs in their hands and their jackets open or missing altogether.

Vehicles lined both sides of the road, making my search for a parking space all the more difficult. I suspected there was room in the alley, next to the dumpster, but I was apprehensive about parking back there and probably would be for some time.

The second time around the block I spied a white crossover pull away from the curb in front of the gazebo, and I rushed to claim its spot. I swung out of the car and dashed past the wind-whipped buildings and down the alley. Along the way I encountered two young men in orange hunting jackets, although they didn't seem to notice me. No surprise there.

As I approached the rear entrance of More Hot Dish, Please, a wind gust slapped my hair across my face, obstructing my view and causing me to slip on a patch of ice. I almost did the splits, which, if not so painful, would have been amazing since I'd never succeeded at doing them before, not even as a cheerleader in high school.

When I entered the café, Grace removed her cell phone from her ear, its usual location when she wasn't cooking. "Perfect timing. I'm finally done in here. Tweety's still cleaning out front. But let's have our coffee anyway."

I stomped snow from my boots and winced from groin pain before limping to the prep table. "You look drained, Grace."

"In addition to everything else, I made thirty take-out lunches for deer hunters today."

I carefully sat down on a stool. "I'd never go deer hunting. If for no other reason, it's too darn cold."

"But no mosquitoes."

"True enough."

Grace returned to the counter alongside the stove, speaking over her shoulder, "Did you happen to see Otto Anderson's pickup?"

A strange question, causing me to hesitate with my answer. "Nooo, why?"

"Well, it seems that on the way to his hunting shack this morning, he got an eight-point buck—with his truck. It went right through the windshield. Other than a few cuts, he's okay, but the truck's in rough shape. They towed it into town earlier."

"Didn't he hit a deer last year, too?"

"No. A moose. Out of season."

"Oh, yeah, it was you who hit a deer."

Grace turned on me, nostrils flaring. "That wasn't my fault. That deer intentionally leaped in front of my car. I'm pretty sure it was clinically depressed. It was a long winter."

After tossing her apron on the counter, she joined me at the prep table, a coffee pot and two mugs in one hand and several napkins and a pan of blueberry streusel bars with lemon-cream filling in the other.

I reminded myself of my pledge to forego sweets and, in an effort to remain true to my intentions, concentrated on her t-shirt rather than the bars. Today's shirt read, *Be happy being yourself, unless you can be a mermaid. Then, by all means, be a mermaid.*

Grace settled on the stool kitty-corner from me, while I pondered life as a mermaid. I couldn't get past the no-legs thing.

"How's your day been?" she asked, ending my mermaid musings. "Has it improved any?"

My day had started at 5:00 a.m., when I got up to use the bathroom and found Grace dressing for work. While she wiggled into her clothes, I recounted for her every excruciating detail about Erin seeing Buck Daniel after the robbery.

Now in the café, after shrugging out of my jacket and leaving it to dangle from my stool, I summarized Erin's conversation with Dr. Osgood, finishing with, "Although Dr. Osgood seems doubtful, Erin apparently considers Dr. Betcher a suspect in Buck Daniel's murder."

"Well," Grace said, "I have to agree with Dr. Osgood."

"How come that doesn't surprise me?"

"I mean it." She filled our mugs with coffee, steam curling through the air. "Why would Buck Daniel rob the pharmacy if Betcher was supplying him with pills?"

I stared at the bars, one of my favorite non-chocolate treats. While uncertain how my eyes had made their way over to the pan, I allowed them to remain there as I explained my daughter's theory, as colored by my own thinking. "Well, once Buck got addicted and started acting crazy, Betcher probably cut off his supply. But it was too late. Buck was hooked. In his mind, he had no choice but to rob the pharmacy, which left Betcher no choice but to stop him before he got caught and ruined everything."

"I'm still not convinced."

The coffee's rich aroma filled my nose and almost—but not quite—persuaded me that I didn't need sweets to be satisfied. "That's what Erin seems to think, and since she's a cop, she's bound to be more knowledgeable about those kinds of things than either of us."

"Unless she's grasping at straws. Considering she's caught in the middle of all this madness, she may lack objectivity." Grace cut a bar, and I drooled a little, like Pavlov's dog. "The same goes for you."

"That's harsh." I licked spittle from the corner of my mouth.

"Believe me, I'd love to see Betcher in trouble. But your take on the situation isn't logical. He almost lost everything once before. Why would he risk it all again? He's well off. He lives in one of the nicest houses in town. And he drives a Humvee. Yes, it's a stupid vehicle, but it's expensive, and some people are impressed by it." She stopped for a heartbeat. "He's also a doctor. Do you really believe he'd kill someone?"

"You don't think doctors ever commit murder? Besides, it could have been an accident. Maybe he ordered Buck Daniel to leave town. Buck refused. They fought. And Dr. Betcher accidently killed him."

I heard the clank of a mop in a bucket, followed by the swish of water.

"Tweety must be about done cleaning out front," Grace said.

121

That prompted me to hurry along. I wasn't interested in anything Tweety had to say about this or any other subject. "Anyhow, Erin believes the robbery and the murder are connected because they happened one right after the other."

"That only makes them coincidental."

"According to the police on TV, coincidences are not to be believed in criminal situations."

"Well, if they say it on TV, then it must be true."

Ignoring her sarcasm, I cut a bar of my own. I couldn't help myself. I hadn't eaten any sweets all day except for that one candy Kiss. And I was certain more sugar would help me think.

"You have to be careful," my sister warned while sipping her coffee. "You can't go around implicating Betcher in a crime—or crimes—without solid evidence. He's the type of guy who'll sue you in a heartbeat. That is, if he has a heart."

"But with his past—"

"Having inappropriate relations with a female patient is different than pushing drugs."

I bit off a good-sized chunk of my bar and instructed myself to eat it slowly, though a couple seconds later, I was all done chewing and swallowing. "Grace? I'm confused. Why are you sticking up for the guy? I thought you hated him."

Grace lifted her chin, her eyes fixed on me from over the end of her turned-up nose. "Call me crazy, but I won't accuse anyone of murder without proof. Not even Andrew Betcher."

"That still doesn't answer the question. Why do you hate him?"

"Me?" The knot of hair on top of her head teetered. "You're the one who accused him of murder."

"I never said that exactly. And quit evading my question." I wadded up my napkin and threw it at her. "Now tell me!"

"He's a sleazoid!" She pitched the napkin back at me. "Yet I made the mistake of going out with him once, shortly after I moved back here."

"And?"

Grace inspected her left index finger. It was wrapped in a fresh bandage. Grace's hands were marked by an array of fresh wounds and old scars from kitchen burns and cuts. She'd never make it as a hand model. "We had dinner in Grand Forks," she muttered. "And afterward he took me to the drive-in—against my wishes."

The old drive-in theater was a couple miles south of town. It was no longer operational. Hadn't been for decades. The screen was torn, and broken speakers dotted the cracked parking area like spent candles on a dried-out birthday cake. But after dark, it remained a destination for young people in search of a place to drink, smoke weed, or make out.

"Just us and a half-dozen teenagers." Her eyes flitted between me and the bat-wing doors that separated the kitchen from the dining area—and Tweety. "He actually thought we'd play kissy face… at the very least. But as soon as we got there, I insisted I had to go home because my stomach ached."

"Smart move."

"Not really. He's a doctor. Right away he volunteered to examine me. Of course, I declined the offer, but he kept on making passes." Her voice grew so quiet that I had to lean over the table to hear her. "His hands were everywhere. I finally had no choice but to… umm… punch him in the balls."

"What?" I halfway screamed.

She pressed her bandaged finger to her lips and shushed me. "I clawed my way out of the car." She continued to whisper. "Then I ran all the way home."

I copied her tone. "No one offered you a ride?"

"Are you kidding? I was mortified. Whenever I spotted someone, I hid in the ditch."

"Did you report him to the police?"

"No!" So much for whispering. "What part of 'mortified' don't you understand?"

It struck me then. "You never told me."

"You were in one of your short-lived, marital-bliss stages at the time. I didn't want much to do with you."

"But it's been six years."

"I handled it. He couldn't walk upright for a week."

Not sure what to do about my bruised ego, I checked the bat-wing doors, then said, "He asked me out."

"Huh?"

"Betcher. He invited me to dinner."

"No!" Grace's bun toppled over her forehead.

"That's what I said, but he didn't care for that answer. He actually got pretty cross."

She pulled her hair from its binder and redid the knot. "The slightest thing can set him off. The night we went out, he yelled at the waitress for bringing us the wrong bottle of wine. She ended up in tears."

With her hair once more mounded on her head, she abruptly switched gears. "Enough about him. He's not worth any more of our time. Let me tell you about Dr. Osgood, instead." If her ears hadn't been in the way, her smile would have wrapped itself around her entire head. "Just before you got here, I made an appointment with him for a complete physical." She did that Groucho Marx thing with her eyebrows. "You should do the same. It might be a lot of fun."

My eyes rolled of their own accord. "You just got done relaying a story about a doctor who took—"

"That was totally different. I told him no."

I sighed long and hard. "Well, I'm not interested in Dr. Osgood in any capacity. Although I did suggest that Rose start seeing him—professionally."

"And?"

"She loves Betcher."

"I guess there's no accounting for taste."

Grace then went on to sip her coffee, thinking God only knew what, while I reflected on my own thoughts: My sister had kept a secret from me for years. It was almost impossible to believe and definitely too much to consider when I had so many other things on my mind.

So, instead, I contemplated Dr. Betcher. Grace was right. He was a sleazoid and, according to my daughter, a likely murderer. And it was up to me to assist Erin in proving that. But, thus far, I hadn't done anything useful to that end. In fact, I had no clue where to begin. Unless... "Grace? You really don't believe Dr. Betcher was connected to the robbery or murder in any way?"

She swallowed the last of her bar. "It feels off. That's all."

"So... umm... I'd be crazy to call and tell him that I changed my mind about going out with him?"

Grace coughed and sputtered, and a smattering of coffee shot out of her nose. "Didn't you hear a word I said?" She grabbed a napkin. "Why on earth would you go out with him?"

"It's not like I want to. But I have to do something. And he's our only lead."

Chapter 15

Tweety trudged into the kitchen, bringing with her a mop, a bucket, and the strong scent of disinfectant. She also brought an end to our discussion of Dr. Betcher.

"I set the barrel of used grease out back," she informed Grace while emptying the water bucket into the utility sink on the back wall.

"Thanks. I don't consider myself weak, but I can't budge those barrels once they're full."

Tweety stored the mop and bucket in the closet next to the walk-in cooler. After that, she loosened her stained apron and strategically pulled it over her mammoth bust, revealing a short-sleeved button-down shirt with one too many buttons undone.

"Want some coffee?" Grace asked.

"No," she answered. "I gotta go. I hafta get ready for my date."

"Oh? Going someplace special?" Grace posed the question in a teasing, sing-song voice.

As for Tweety, she styled her yellow, straw-like hair with a shake of her head. "Supper and a movie in Grand Forks."

"Anybody I know?"

Tweety chewed her thumbnail. "We've only dated a while, and we're keeping it on the down-low."

"Why?" Grace wanted to know. "He's not married, is he?"

Notwithstanding how Grace portrayed herself, she was as nosy... I mean, as inquisitive as me. I knew it. She knew it. And she knew I knew it. Yet she pretended it wasn't so.

"No, he's not married." Tweety tossed her apron into the plastic trash can used for laundry and closed the closet door. "We just don't plan on getting serious. We're only out to have fun."

She then slid her hand into the pocket of her skinny jeans— if a size sixteen can be called "skinny"—and peeled from it a wad of crumpled bills. "Oh, before I forget, here's my rent money."

"December first isn't for two weeks," Grace reminded her.

"Yeah, well, I have the cash now. So either take it or leave it."

Grace appeared flummoxed. Still, she grasped the ball of money. "Boy, tips must be good. Or did you get a second job? You never pay your rent early."

"No other job. I guess folks are just in the Thanksgiving spirit. It's less than a week away, you know."

Grace dropped the bills onto the prep table and began ironing them with her fingertips. Soon she was so immersed in the task that I was certain she wouldn't mind—wouldn't even notice—if I butted into her conversation on my daughter's behalf. So that's what I did.

"Tweety," I began, a faux smile attached to my lips, "I gotta say I'm surprised you're already dating someone new. Buck Daniel's body is barely cold."

Tweety shifted her attention my way. "I only went out with him a few times. Right after he broke up with Erin."

"Oh, really? Is that when it was?"

She angled her square jaw and jutted her chin, reminding me of a bulldog. It wasn't a good look. "Irregardless of what you think, Doris, I don't go out with guys that are taken."

"I'm sure you don't." We both knew I didn't believe her. It was evident in my tone and her angry eyes. "But you were dating him at the time of his death, right?"

"There's nothing wrong with seeing someone once in a while."

"I didn't say there was." I lost my smile. It was too difficult to keep it affixed to my face when none of the muscles around my mouth really wanted to assist. "But when you begin dating again only a few weeks after your boyfriend's murder, people wonder."

Tweety narrowed her eyes. With their mascara-laden lashes, they resembled a pair of giant spiders. And I imagined squishing them.

"Just 'cause you stay cooped up in that big old house all the time," she said, "don't mean I have to."

"I don't stay cooped up—"

"That's probably why you went cuckoo last year." She twirled her finger alongside her head.

"Hey!" I pushed off my stool.

"You know, Doris, people need people."

"And who in the heck do you think you are? Barbra Streisand?"

Grace snagged my arm. "Don't let her get to you."

To Tweety, she added, "You better leave."

"Oh, no." I shook off my sister's hand. "I have a couple more questions for her before she goes anywhere."

I'd worked with Tweety off and on at the café for the past several years, but we didn't really get along. She was a big flirt, a personality trait I didn't appreciate. She also enjoyed playing the role of victim because all too often it got her exactly what she wanted—namely, the attention of men who couldn't resist a damsel in distress.

I found both her and her act tiresome and normally dismissed them, but I refused to do that this time. There was too much at stake. "Tweety," I said, "speaking of Buck Daniel, did you happen to see him after he robbed the pharmacy?"

The question seemingly came out of nowhere. But somewhere in the recesses of my mind, I'd been contemplating Erin's hunch that Buck Daniel had gone searching for Tweety after the robbery to ask her to assist him in getting out of town. If Erin was right, Tweety might know why he never made it beyond the dumpster.

"Of course I didn't see him." Tweety's eyes volleyed between Grace and me. "Where did you come up with that?"

I played dumb. It was easier than I would ever care to admit. "Just wondering."

"Well, if someone said they seen me with Buck Daniel that night, they lied."

"How about beforehand?" I posed. "Did he mention to you that he planned to rob the pharmacy?"

Tweety opened and closed her mouth like a guppy. "Why would he?"

"Because he was your boyfriend."

She stomped her foot. "We only went out a few—" She cut her sentence short as a far-away look commandeered her face. Several seconds ticked by before she blinked back to me. "See here, Doris Connor, you're not gonna pin anything on me. Just because your daughter's a suspect in Buck's murder and—"

"What?" I splayed my hands on the prep table. "Erin is not a suspect."

"Well, she got herself suspended, didn't she?"

"That had nothing to do with Buck Daniel's death."

"Oh, really? That's not what I heard."

"Well, you shouldn't listen to your grandma. She doesn't have a clue."

Tweety arched her heavily penciled brows. "What about your son, then?"

That remark caught me off guard. "What are you talking about?"

"If Erin didn't kill Buck, maybe Will did."

My breathing faltered. She had me rattled, but I did my best to hide it. "What exactly are you suggesting?"

Tweety braced herself against the opposite side of the table, her arms rigid, her massive cleavage on parade. "Buck dropped by my place a few days before he got himself murdered. He was beat up pretty good. Said Will done it. Said Will swore he'd finish the job next time he seen him."

Even if what she said was true, I couldn't let her get away with saying it. "I don't believe you. You or Buck would have reported Will to the sheriff."

"Buck wanted to take care of it on his own, and I didn't want to get involved."

"And why was that?" Grace had been silent for so long that I was startled by her voice.

"Well..." Tweety eyed the back door. She obviously wanted out, but I doubted it was because she was running late for a date. "You've been good to me, Grace." She went back to gnawing on her thumbnail. "When Mom died, you gave me a job and a good deal on the apartment upstairs."

"Your mother was my best friend."

"Yeah, so maybe I wanted to return the favor by keeping quiet about what I knew."

131

I didn't buy it. Not for a second. "Grace has been good to you. Way better than you deserve. But I'm not Grace, and you've never liked me."

Tweety scoffed. "You're right about that. I've never liked your... umm... 'holier than thou' attitude. That's what Grandma calls it, you know. She says it's no wonder your husband ran around. No matter what he did, he wasn't good enough in your eyes."

That did it! I charged around the prep table. I wasn't sure what I'd do once I got a hold of her, but I suspected it would include a fair amount of slapping, scratching, and hair pulling. While she was bigger and stronger than me, I was confident that I had the edge because I intended to unload all of the wrath that had built up inside of me due to women like her and Destiny Delovely.

Grace had other ideas. Sliding in front of me, she pressed her hands against my ribcage. "Don't, Doris."

"But—"

"Tweety!" she barked across her shoulder, "Go! Now!" Despite being six inches shorter than me and sixty pounds lighter than Tweety, my sister meant business. It was evident in her tone.

For her part, Tweety shot both of us a squinty-eyed glare. "Fine. I'll go. But just so you know, the sheriff called, and I'm meeting with him tomorrow night. He has a few more questions for me. And I'm gonna tell him everything."

⊚ ⊚ ⊚

After Tweety stormed out, Grace and I resettled on our stools before she uttered, "That didn't go very well, did it?"

"What are we going to do?"

"Oh, let's not get ahead of ourselves. She hasn't spoken with Karl yet."

132

"But she will soon enough, Grace."

"That doesn't mean she'll mention Will."

"Why wouldn't she? She's furious with us. And she hates me. She'd love to see me suffer, especially if she could do it by way of my kids. She knows they mean everything to me." I got the chills and had to slip my jacket back on.

"Tweety never has any money," Grace volunteered in the tone reserved for sharing secrets. "She requests advances on a regular basis. Yet she paid November's rent on time and in cash, and now she's paid December's rent early and in cash."

"So?" Still shaken from the scuffle, I had difficulty following her.

"So I suspect the real reason she hasn't said much to the sheriff is that she doesn't want to implicate herself in a crime."

"A crime?"

She rolled her hand, as if to encourage me to keep up. "Not that long ago, her new boyfriend emptied his grandmother's bank accounts, requesting the withdrawal in $100 bills. And since then, she's paid two months' rent in $100 bills." She spread December's rent money across the table. Six $100 bills.

Like her, I whispered, but only because my words seemed too preposterous to say out loud. "Tweety stole the money Buck withdrew from Wilma's bank account?" My mind took another—even wilder—turn. "Do you think she killed him, too?"

"I don't know. When you say it out loud, it sounds outrageous. Still, she hasn't asked for an advance or complained about tips for weeks."

"She did say that with Thanksgiving coming up, tips have been better."

My sister looked at me as if I had a room-temperature IQ. "Have you ever received a $100 tip while waitressing in here?"

My eyebrows may have collided with my hairline. "I barely receive any tips when I waitress here."

"Okay, you're not the best person to ask. Just trust me when I say that no one gets tips of $100 bills. Not even Allie. Remember, most of our customers are Scandinavian. When it comes to tipping, they're the first to put their hands in their pockets and leave them there."

I burrowed deeper in my jacket. "I'd really like to believe you're onto something, but Erin thinks that Dr. Betcher's responsible for Buck Daniel's death, and I trust her instincts."

"Well, maybe Tweety and Betcher were in on it together. Didn't Karl mention the possibility of more than one person being involved?"

"Uh-huh, although you didn't believe Betcher could—"

"And I still have my doubts, Doris. But whether I'm right or wrong, we can't do much about Betcher tonight. We can, however, see if Tweety's connected to any of this." She aimed her eyes at the ceiling and Tweety's upstairs' apartment.

My mouth went dry. "Oh, no. Please don't be thinking what I think you're thinking."

Grace's voice remained steady as she pointed out, "She'll be gone all evening on a date seventy miles away. And because I'm her landlord, I have a key to her place. Let's just take a look. Maybe we'll uncover the rest of the money or the backpack the money was in or some other incriminating evidence."

"Grace, we cannot search her apartment."

"But I've got a strong feeling about this."

"So do I. It's so strong, in fact, I may throw up."

My sister flashed me the stink eye. "How can you think this is a bad idea when you're willing to go out with Dr. McFeely?"

"Going out with him isn't illegal."

"Well, it should be!"

I hugged my chest in an effort to keep my heart from banging right through my ribcage. The racket was so loud

I had difficulty hearing myself. Nonetheless, I was almost positive that I said, "Grace, I will not be a party to this. I will not break into Tweety's apartment."

Chapter 16

Around eleven o'clock that night, Grace and I broke into Tweety's apartment. Okay, Grace used her key, but considering we were clad in black and each carried a flashlight, it wasn't much of a stretch to say we broke in.

Grace insisted we refrain from turning on any interior lights. She said lamplight might be seen from the street, whereas light from a flashlight posed no such threat. When I claimed that made no sense, she replied, "Then take it up with the folks on those police shows you're so fond of because that's what they do. In the meantime, use your damn flashlight."

So I shined my flashlight around the efficiency apartment, and while it didn't help me determine if Tweety was a criminal, it did lead me to conclude that she was a slob. The entire space served as a dumping ground for everything from dirty dishes and half-empty takeout containers to discarded clothes and Coke cans.

"I'll have to fumigate if she ever moves out," Grace complained. "It smells like sour milk and sweaty socks and something I don't want to think about."

She motioned toward the kitchenette. "You check over there. I'll start with her closet."

"You actually want me to go through her cupboards?"

"Well, yeah. She's not going to leave evidence lying out in the open."

"Fine. But I refuse to look in her fridge. God only knows what kind of fungus is growing in there."

Shuffling to the kitchen, I tripped over a pop can.

Grace shushed me, and I snarled, "For Pete's sake, we're the only people in the building."

"I don't care, Doris. We shouldn't be loud."

I offered up my most sardonic laugh. "What are you talking about? We shouldn't even be in here."

"Quit your bellyaching. You agreed that it would go a long way toward clearing both Erin and Will if we found something in here to tie Tweety to the crimes."

The kitchenette was small, the sink, stove, refrigerator, and cupboards all along one wall. I opened the upper cabinets but didn't spot anything incriminating—just mismatched plates and bowls, an economy-sized bag of a knock-off brand of Froot Loops, and two packages of Double Stuf Oreos. While the cereal didn't do anything for me, I had to use all of my willpower to keep from stealing a handful of cookies.

"Well," Grace grunted, "her closet only has a few skanky outfits on hangers and a pile of clothes and shoes on the floor. I wouldn't be caught dead in most of her stuff, but I really like these wedges. What do you think?"

I peered over my shoulder. Her flashlight was aimed at a pair of rope-strapped sandals with a three-inch cork heel. Size nine or ten. "Plan on growing your feet?"

She shrugged. "They're cute. That's all." She pitched them back into the closet, their landing cushioned by a mound of shirts and jeans. "Guess I'll move onto the bathroom. Do the dresser when you're done in there. And don't forget to check under the bed."

"Tweety's dumb, Grace. But even she's not dumb enough to hide ill-gotten gains under her bed."

"Oh, really? Weren't you the one who told me she was the reason shampoo bottles came with instructions? And remember, she paid two months' rent with $100 bills that she claimed were tips from waitressing in a small-town diner. My food's good, but not that good."

Unable to argue with that, I returned to the cupboards, making a cursory scan of the silverware drawer. Finding only a few miscellaneous knives, forks, and spoons, along with a naughty-looking corkscrew, I redirected my efforts to the bottom cabinets. Because the one directly below the sink was warped from what appeared to be a leaky pipe, nothing was in it other than a full bottle of dish soap.

I shifted to the next cupboard over, and that's when a thud sounded from somewhere behind me. "Whoa, Grace! Now who's being loud?"

Grace curled around the bathroom door. "It wasn't me."

"Yeah, right." Refocusing on my search, I nudged aside a George Foreman grill and, in my flashlight beam, caught sight of a package of paper napkins, an ice cream pail full of sugar packets, and another with tiny tubs of coffee creamer. Everything but the grill was from the café.

As I spun around to inform my sister of my discovery, I heard another thump, followed by some shuffling.

Grace again appeared at the bathroom door. "Oh, shit!"

I raised my flashlight, nearly blinding her. "That wasn't the water heater clanking, was it?"

She shielded her eyes. "Someone's coming up the stairs."

My stomach sank to my knees, leaving its usual location vacant, and my nerves immediately moved in. "I knew this was a mistake." I spoke as emphatically as I could while barely making a peep. "Now what?"

"We gotta hide," she warned me, like that wasn't obvious. "I could get sued for snooping in my tenant's apartment."

Out in the hallway, the footsteps, chatter, and giggling grew louder.

"Do you hear that?" I asked. "She brought her date home with her." I frantically scanned the room. "Quick! Under the bed."

"Under the bed?" Grace hissed. "Are you kidding? That's the first place they'll look."

"Why? They don't know we're in here. Besides, there's no other place. Now move."

Without another word, Grace dropped to her knees, then onto her back, and I copied her. We extinguished our flashlights and slithered beneath Tweety's queen-size mattress, Grace groaning from back pain and me practically gagging from the stench of the dirty underpants I tossed aside.

In the hall, Tweety had difficulty unlocking the door. The key clattered for long moments, but neither she nor her date seemed to mind. Instead, they found the entire situation hilarious.

"They're drunk," Grace needlessly said.

"Good. Maybe she'll pass out, he'll leave, and we can sneak out."

"From your lips to God's ears."

The door swung open, the overhead light blinked on, and from my vantage point, I watched as the bottom halves of two people tumbled into the room.

Tweety hushed her companion. "Be quiet. You'll wake the neighbors."

"Huh?" the guy grunted. "You don't have any neighbors."

"Oh, yeah." Tweety giggled like a ninny. "I forgot."

The guy's voice was vaguely familiar, but I was stymied as to his identity because I couldn't see his face.

Tweety switched on a table lamp, snatched a red blouse off the floor, and tossed it over the shade. "For ambiance," she purred before adding something about "slipping into something more comfortable."

For his part, her date replied in the voice of a Vegas lounge singer, "You don't have to slip into anything, if you know what I mean."

I threw up a little in my mouth.

The guy went on to suggest that he douse the overhead light, but before he flipped the room into semi-darkness, he flung his jacket and shirt onto her vinyl recliner. They slid onto the floor, and he bent over to pick them up. And that's when I caught a glimpse of his face.

I covered my mouth to keep from crying out. The guy, you see, was Deputy Ed Monson. And without his shirt, he wasn't nearly as nondescript as I had initially thought.

The deputy cut the overhead lights, pitching the room into a muted pink glow, before Tweety led him to the recliner, shoved him into the seat, and straddled his lap.

"Wait." He gestured toward the bed. "Let's move this over there."

"What?" Tweety squawked. "You want to rearrange furniture? Now?"

I rolled my eyes so far back in my head that I caught sight of my toes, while Grace's entire body shook with silent laughter. And Ed? He merely clasped Tweety's hand and guided her to the bed, apparently thinking that she was too dumb to find it on her own.

Dropping onto the mattress, they rooted and grunted until I prayed that God strike me temporarily deaf. But again, my request went unanswered, which really irked me. After all, it wasn't like I'd asked for world peace or even a cure for hot flashes. I only wanted to be deaf for a while, and I deserved that since I hadn't missed Mass in God only knew how long, and I'd put my new life on hold to care for a quasi-aunt and keep my kids out of jail.

No question about it, I was in the middle of a pretty good pity party when Ed unfastened his belt buckle, its clatter signaling the start of another kind of party. And at that point, I went from full of self-pity to full-blown panic. I had to get out of there, and since God evidently wasn't in the mood to rescue me, I'd have to rescue myself. Of course, that meant wiggling out from under the bed and exposing myself and possibly getting arrested. But considering that the deputy would be "fully exposed," too, perhaps he wouldn't take me in.

Deciding to go for it, I squirmed toward the light, although I didn't get very far because Grace had a hold of me. Specifically, she had sunk her teeth into my shoulder to keep from guffawing at all the craziness.

I intended to elbow her in the ribs, in hopes of loosening her jaw, but Ed stopped me when he said, "Now, Tweety, tell me more about Buck Daniel."

The bed ceased rocking. Grace and I went statue-like.

"Why are you so interested in Buck?" If her tone was any indication, Tweety was none too happy. "You've asked me a hundred questions about him tonight."

Ed hemmed and hawed. "I guess I want to learn about my competition. He was your last boyfriend, you know."

"But we didn't date long. And he's dead."

142

"Which can make measuring up even more difficult for me as the new guy."

Tweety wiggled to the edge of the bed and dangled her bare legs over the side, way too close to my face. "What do you mean, the 'new guy'? Didn't you just wanna have fun? Isn't that why you said I couldn't tell nobody about us?"

"Maybe I've changed my mind. Maybe I want more." Ed dropped his legs alongside hers.

I was grateful to see his socks and jeans. Had his hairy legs and calloused toes stared me in the face, so to speak, I'd have gone into convulsions.

"What brought about all of this?" Tweety wanted to know.

Ed shifted closer to her. "Oh, come on, you aren't suspicious of me, are you?"

"Well, you are a cop, and you're asking lots of questions, so I can't help but wonder if you're more interested in Buck's murder than in me. You don't think I'm dumb, do ya?"

Ed wisely elected not to answer that question, posing one of his own instead. "You know I like you, right?"

Tweety kicked her legs, almost swatting me in the nose with her heel. "I don't know what to think."

Ed then tentatively uttered, "So, Tweety, let's just say that I... umm... did want to learn more about the robbery and Buck's death. Not that I do, mind you. But if I did, what information could I get from you exactly?"

I wasn't much of an investigator, but I'd never been trained. Ed, I presumed, had. Yet he made me look like that lady on *Murder, She Wrote*. Not literally, of course. She was older, shorter, and somewhat heavier. But you get my point.

"Ed!" Tweety sprang from the bed and stomped her feet, her red toenail polish flashing like warning lights. "Get out of here!" Yep, even Joy Jacobson, aka Tweety, who finished forty-eighth in her high-school graduating class only because there weren't forty-nine students, had figured out what he was up to.

"I was kidding, Tweety."

"No, you weren't, Ed. Now make like a tree and go."

"You mean leave."

"What?"

"Never mind."

Ed sucked in a deep breath but remained where he was. "I don't want you to end up on the wrong side of the sheriff. That's all," he said. "But it could happen if you withhold information or say something you don't really mean."

Her toes curled. "How do you know I'm meeting with the sheriff?"

"It's a small office."

"Well, I am kind of scared. Sometimes he looks at me like he can see right through my head. Like it's empty or something."

Once again, Ed withheld comment, and I had to give him credit for that. If I'd been face to face with Tweety, I couldn't have done it. Heck, even holed up under the bed, I had difficulty keeping my mouth shut.

Ed patted the mattress. "Now come on over here and tell me everything. It'll be off the record."

"Off the record?" Tweety shuffled closer to him. "You mean like pillow talk?"

"I mean exactly like pillow talk."

With that, he yanked her onto the bed. The wooden support slats beneath the mattress vibrated. And my sister sank her teeth deeper into my shoulder.

As for me, I was more determined than ever to escape. I again twisted toward the light, towing Grace, by way of her jaw, along with me. But when I was almost free from beneath the bed—or what I had deemed a perfect metaphor for hell—one of the wooden mattress supports cracked.

Craning my head, I attempted to assess the damage. I spotted the splintered slat as well as a shoebox. The shoebox was on its side, among the dust bunnies and next to a lace bra. And in it—the shoebox, not the bra—appeared to be money. Several small packs of money.

Setting aside all thoughts of the gyrating gymnasts above me or what might happen if any more supports broke, I wormed my arm along my body until I pinched one of the thin paper-banded stacks. I drew it to my face for closer inspection. Sure enough, $100 bills. Ten of them bundled together.

Grace inhaled sharply, and I was certain that she, too, was fixated on the cash. But that wasn't the case at all. She had Tweety's bra in her hand. And she sounded quite impressed when she murmured, "38DD. I never would have guessed."

Chapter 17

The next morning, I regretted opening my eyes. They felt gritty, like I'd rubbed them with sandpaper. While I didn't remember doing that, I did recall wanting to scrub my brain with bleach after returning from Tweety's apartment. I just couldn't determine how to get it done.

Thank goodness the sheriff had phoned Ed on police business before he and Tweety had a chance to consummate their magic. Even so, I'd suffered considerable emotional distress under Tweety's bed but decided it was worth it because, by finding the money, my kids were undoubtedly one step closer to exoneration in Buck Daniel's murder.

Still, when I closed my eyes and huddled under my quilt, try as I might, I couldn't rid myself of the mental snapshots of my time in Tweety's den of iniquity. The worst picture featured her strutting naked to the bathroom after Ed's departure. In the shower, she sang show tunes at the top of her sizeable lungs. Her off-key vocals damaged my eardrums as well as any appreciation I may have had for Broadway musicals. Even so, they provided Grace and me with the opportunity to tiptoe out of her apartment and hightail it to my house.

Once back in my kitchen, we'd eaten M&Ms while discussing our next move. I'd granted myself dispensation from abstaining from sweets for two reasons: First, breaking and entering carried significant jail time. And since I doubted snacks were served in the big house, I figured I was entitled to mine now. Second, I had witnessed Tweety in all her naked glory. Enough said.

Naturally, Grace and I were disappointed that we'd been unable to garner evidence to prove definitively that the money we discovered under Tweety's bed belonged to Buck's grandma. It wasn't in his backpack or accompanied by a note that read, "Money from Wilma Daniel's bank accounts." Yet we were pretty sure of its origin and presumed that Sheriff Ingebretsen would make the necessary connection.

Of course, to get him to do that, we'd have to disclose our actions. Not a pleasant prospect. But we had no choice. Because of Erin's suspension and deer-hunting season, the sheriff's office was short on staff. That's right. In this neck of the woods, a few things—namely, the fishing opener and deer season—took precedence over everything, even a murder investigation. And while Ed Monson, the newest deputy, remained on duty, neither Grace nor I ever wanted to see any part of him again.

Halfway through our bag of candy, however, Grace decided that I should meet with Karl on my own, claiming a one-on-one conversation was preferable under the circumstances. In truth, she was afraid he'd kill her because of what we had done but suspected he'd only maim me. I wasn't so sure.

You see, before leaving Tweety's place, my sister had argued that we were obliged to take some of the money with us to prove our story. But once we got home, a pack of cash nestled in the waistband of my leggings, she wondered out loud if we had made a mistake. When I reminded her that there hadn't been any "we" in that decision, she claimed she didn't recall me objecting. She supposedly couldn't hear my ranting above Tweety's shower rendition of "I Enjoy Being a Girl."

After making an effort to blur the visions from the previous night with a shake of my head, I turned onto my side, my legs getting tangled in the sheets. I switched on my bedside lamp and opened the top drawer of my nightstand. Sure enough, there it was: a pack of ten $100 bills, paper-banded together. That confirmed it. I was a full-fledged criminal. I had committed breaking and entering and had absconded with evidence.

Scrunching into the fetal position, I yanked my quilt over my head.

◎ ◎ ◎

Two hours later, when I crawled out of bed, I was much calmer. I'd worked it all out in my head. Despite Grace's concerns to the contrary, Karl was a reasonable man, our curling club encounter notwithstanding. Once I explained everything, he'd understand and might even be grateful for the effort Grace and I had made to prove Erin and Will's innocence.

Shuffling downstairs in my flannel pajamas and fuzzy slippers, I paused in the foyer to wind the cuckoo clock, the gears grinding as I pulled on the dangling chains. When I was done, I passed through the dining room and into the kitchen, where I jumped at the sight of my daughter.

Living in a small town, I enjoyed the freedom of never having to lock my doors. But I also never had any idea who I'd come across at my table.

Sure, we had deadbolted every door and locked every window after bringing Rose home the night of the robbery. But as soon as Buck Daniel's body was discovered the following afternoon, we went back to our old ways, regarless of Erin's disapproval. As a cop, Erin always locked her doors. Although most people didn't see the point. In the matter of Buck Daniel, for instance, folks believed his killer was intent on murdering him and him alone.

Erin had a casserole dish on a hot pad in front of her. The dish was a quarter full of leftover chicken tetrazzini bake that Grace had brought home from the café. "I just heated this up," Erin said. "Want some?" She extended a forkful of chicken and noodles.

"For breakfast?" My voice was as rusty as an old hinge.

"It's after eleven, making it more of an early lunch."

"Where's Rose? She was in bed when Grace and I got home from the café last night." It wasn't exactly a lie. Grace and I had been at the café or, at any rate, in the apartment above it. "Because we were going to be late, I got Sophie to come over and keep her company. According to Sophie, they had a good time. Rose is teaching her to knit."

"Why don't you do something like that, Mom? You say you don't feel connected to Sophie. It might help if you spent more time with her. Taught her a craft or something."

"I'm not patient enough." I retrieved my favorite mug from an array of mugs hanging from hooks beneath the shelf that was home to the coffee maker.

"You just don't like her." Erin snickered. "No woman will ever be good enough for your Willie."

"Oh, shut up and eat."

Erin filled her mouth but kept right on talking. "Anyway, Rose already left. She went to late Mass with Elsa Olson. And after Mass they're off to the senior center for bingo. As for Grace, she's at the café, working on something."

No, Grace is hiding until she finds out if I survive my meeting with Karl.

"Wait a second." I performed a conversational backtrack while adding water to my coffee. I enjoyed strong coffee, but when Erin made it, I had to cut it with a knife rather than stir it with a spoon. "Elsa isn't Catholic."

"Yeah, but she's sweet on Frank Beckerman, and he's ushering this morning."

My daughter's eyes drilled into the back of my head. And when I spooled away from the sink, I felt compelled to confess, "I couldn't go to church today. I'm coming down with something." I coughed pathetically. Add lying—about God no less—to all my other sins.

Claiming the seat across from her, my knee joints creaked, much like the dried-out rungs on the chair. "So what are you doing here, Erin? And why am I making excuses to you about my church habits? You're a heathen."

Erin smiled as she scraped the dark edges along the sides of the casserole dish. "You're making excuses because you feel guilty. As for why I'm here, I was hungry, but I have nothing in my refrigerator, and I'm low on cash."

The mention of cash reminded me of the money in my nightstand, though I had no intention of sharing with my daughter how it had come into my possession. Something positive had to happen with it first. Otherwise, Grace and I would look like nothing more than a pair of senile fools. And that wouldn't be good. My daughter questioned our judgment enough as it was.

With her fork, Erin impaled several small pieces of chicken. "I've developed a theory about the robbery and murder. Want to hear it?"

"Sure." No need to let on that after listening in on her and Dr. Osgood, I already had a good understanding of her thinking on the subject.

"I spoke with Les—Dr. Osgood—yesterday, and while he insisted there wasn't any reason to suspect Dr. Betcher of involvement in either crime, I'm not so sure."

"Dr. Betcher?" I used my surprised voice and thought it was quite convincing.

"I realize he did his best to save Dad and all, but he's the most logical suspect. Nothing ever happens around here. Then we experience two major crimes one day apart. And he's like central to both."

"How so?"

She fed herself the chicken before using her fork to check off her reasoning from an invisible list in the air. "Buck robbed the pharmacy at the hospital. Betcher is chief of staff there. And Buck was seen with Betcher on numerous occasions before the robbery."

"How do you know?"

"I asked around. And Rose mentioned it. Of course, she didn't realize it was Buck Daniel at first. But after she found out what he looked like, she said she'd often seen him at the medical center."

I wondered if Rose had also mentioned that Will had visited Dr. Betcher on occasion.

"Betcher's known to play loose with prescriptions, too," Erin continued without any comment about her brother. "And years ago, he almost lost his license for engaging in an inappropriate doctor-patient relationship. As a result, we know he's not opposed to breaking rules. What's more, Buck got killed within hours of the robbery, long before most people had any idea what had happened or that Buck was involved. But Betcher knew."

"Still, plenty of folks may have a hard time believing that Betcher's a killer," I said. If Grace was any indication.

"Mom, everyone's capable of murder under the right circumstances. And I'm not necessarily suggesting that Buck's murder was premeditated."

"Oh, don't get me wrong. I find your theory compelling. I'm merely reminding you that some folks might take issue with it. For instance, you said Dr. Osgood wasn't impressed."

"Yeah, but I didn't go into a whole lot of detail with him because he didn't seem open to the possibility that I was on to something." She paused. "He may be covering for Betcher."

"Huh?"

Erin poked at the pasta left in the casserole dish. "Betcher hired Les, and since Les has to keep this job for five years to get his student debt cleared, he's not likely to say anything critical of him."

"What concrete evidence do you have regarding any of this, Erin?"

"I'm getting it as we speak. Or I should say, Ed is. He's re-interviewing the assisted-living residents. We had Betcher do it initially, remember? We assumed the residents would be more comfortable speaking with him, but now we wonder if he bothered to talk to them at all."

"Ed's at assisted living?" I envisioned him walking the halls bare-chested. The image of him in that state of undress while mingling with the elderly led me to rub the heels of my hands against my eyes.

"He'll stop over here once he's done."

I yanked my hands away, leaving me fuzzy-eyed.

"You don't have a problem with that, do you?" she asked.

"Ah, no. Of course, not."

"If we're right and Betcher lied about questioning the residents, Ed will discuss next steps with Karl."

With a clang, she dropped her fork into the baking dish. "Anyway, on the night of the robbery, Betcher disappeared shortly after Ed got done with his inventory of the pharmacy."

"Oh?" I replayed in my mind my time at the medical center that night. "You're mistaken, Erin. I spoke with him in the hallway just after you and Deputy Monson left Dr. Osgood's office."

"That's when we went to the squad car to discuss the possibility of Buck being a suspect. Once we finished, we went inside again to ask Betcher a few follow-up questions. You had just left with Rose and Grace. We couldn't find Betcher anywhere, and the nurses didn't seem to know where either he or Dr. Osgood had gone."

"You think that's when Betcher went looking for Buck?"

"Most likely. And after Buck left my place in search of Tweety, he probably ran into him."

Or Tweety steered him in the doctor's direction. Yes, the idea of Tweety and Betcher being partners in crime was outlandish, but the evidence—specifically the money hidden under Tweety's bed and, now, Erin's revelation about Betcher's disappearance after the robbery—pointed in that direction. Still, I wasn't ready to discuss Tweety's possible role in the crimes with my daughter. Though I could assist her in another way. Even if Grace considered that "other way" tantamount to lunacy.

I downed a long drink of hot coffee to ready myself. "Erin, should I meet with Dr. Betcher? See what I can learn from him? He asked me out, so I—"

"What?" Erin was incredulous.

"I turned him down, but I can call and say I changed my mind. Granted, you'll have to prep me beforehand to ensure I pose the right questions." I only hoped she was more conversant in that process than Deputy Monson. If not, Betcher would be on to me before we finished our appetizers.

"Wait a second. Why on earth would Dr. Betcher want to go out with you?"

Coffee splashed over the side of my cup. "Excuse me?"

Erin blushed a dark shade of embarrassment. "I didn't mean it like that. It's just…"

"Oh, I don't know." I nabbed a napkin from the counter, and wiped up my spill. "Maybe he has a brain tumor and is doing the unthinkable. First, he killed Buck Daniel. And now he wants to go out with the likes of me."

"Mom, don't be so touchy. I'm only wondering what he's up to. Like, is he trying to use you to get information?"

I threw my wet napkin in the trash basket under the sink and reclaimed my chair. "I don't have any information to give. If I did, it would have come from you. But since you're suspended, you don't know much, either. And by now, he and everyone else in town are well aware of that."

Of course, I didn't mean to suggest that my daughter was ignorant. But since she had implied that I was the gunk at the bottom of the barrel where men went scraping, I didn't rush to clarify myself.

It didn't matter. She was oblivious. "Mom, did Dr. Betcher happen to say anything about Karl?"

"Karl?"

"Yeah, lots of people think you two are good friends. Maybe even more than friends."

"That's ridiculous." For some dumb reason, my face grew warm.

"Well, you did date—"

"A hundred years ago." I slurped more coffee. Hot coffee wouldn't cool my face, but hiding behind my cup held appeal.

"At any rate," Erin continued, "Dr. Betcher may think you learn things from Karl."

My daughter had started to irritate me. No, that wasn't right. She had gone well beyond "started." "Erin, do you want my help or not?"

She crossed her arms over the lynx logo on her basketball jersey. "I appreciate the offer, and I'd like to take you up on it, but I'm worried it's a setup." She chewed her bottom lip. "Before you call him, let's see what Ed finds out at assisted living."

With that, she got up, ambled around the table, and awkwardly hugged me. "Thanks."

I'm sure I showed surprise.

"Sometimes I can be a little hard to..." She ended her sentence right there. She routinely struggled to admit to bad behavior. And while I wanted to believe that inability was the result of a defective gene inherited from her father, I was well aware that I, too, could be unyielding.

A knock at the front door put an end to our Hallmark moment, such as it was, and Erin headed out of the room. "That must be Ed."

I trotted after her, although when we reached the foyer, I veered off to the staircase. "I have to get dressed," I said as I ran for cover on the second floor.

Chapter 18

I remained squirreled away upstairs while Erin and Ed visited in the kitchen. I attempted to listen to them through the heating grate on my bedroom wall, but when I couldn't hear anything beyond the rattle of the furnace and the hum of their voices, I gave up.

Moseying into the bathroom, I showered, shampooed, and shaved. Because it was November and I'd be clad in pants for the next six months, my hairy legs would go unnoticed. But I wasn't a slob, so I shaved. Though only up to my knees. No point in being obsessive.

When I climbed out of the shower, I checked the bite marks on my shoulder. Grace had been a biter when we were young, too. Some things never changed.

Back in my bedroom, I dropped my towel and slipped into my "power" underwear. They didn't feature Wonder Woman or Ruth Bader Ginsburg, but the bra and panties matched, all the hooks were accounted for on the former, and the elastic was intact on the latter. In other words, the underwear trifecta.

The kind of underwear that made me feel confident, which was imperative since I was about to text Karl and ask him to stop by.

Crawling onto my hastily made bed, I caught sight of myself in the full-length mirror next to my closet door. My saggy-skinned, middle-aged body shocked me, like it always did.

I climbed off the bed and pulled on a pair of freshly laundered jeans. Then failing to convince myself that the small muffin top bulging over the waistband was due to the clothes dryer and would disappear as my pants stretched, I added an oversized sweatshirt. After that, I once more sat among the throw pillows on my bed and composed and edited my text message. At the same time, I polished off the snack-sized bag of M&Ms that I'd found earlier at the back of the drawer in my nightstand.

When Ed and Erin left the house, I was well-groomed, my message had been sent, and I'd pledged to eat better the rest of the day. Naturally, I would have preferred knowing what Ed had learned at the medical center, but the urge hadn't been strong enough to coax me downstairs. Erin would have to fill me in later.

Back in the kitchen, I lunched on lettuce topped with tuna and grated cheese and mentally patted myself on the back for being healthy. I then made easy ravioli hot dish for supper. Because the kitchen was in working order again, it only made sense that I prepare our Sunday meal since Grace had cooked at the café all week.

As the name implied, the ravioli dish was simple to make, which was perfect because I would never be mistaken for Julia Child. Growing up, I had assisted our father, a third-generation Red River Valley farmer, in the fields, while Grace split household chores with our mother. I loved farming and knew my way around all of the machinery and equipment. The kitchen was another matter.

Following my wedding, Mom had taught me enough about cooking to keep Bill, his parents, and our children fed. But I possessed neither the knack nor the interest to do anything beyond the basics. One more area where Bill found me lacking, and I guess others agreed that it was a serious transgression.

The Sorenson sisters, for example, once expressed to some of my friends that my ineptness in the kitchen likely translated to ineptness in other rooms of the house, as well. That, according to the Sorenson girls, explained, if not fully excused, Bill's philandering. I hated the Sorenson sisters. Okay, that wasn't nice. I didn't hate them. But if they ever caught fire, and I had a bucket of water, I'd drink it.

Turning my attention back to the ravioli, I layered the ingredients in a large casserole dish while reflecting on the questions looping through my mind: Do I actually dare go out with Dr. Betcher to gather information about his relationship with Buck Daniel and Tweety Jacobson? How angry will Karl get after I confess what Grace and I have done? And why on earth did Will repeatedly visit with Dr. Betcher?

Each question caused me more angst than the last, and I soon found myself digging out what remained of the two-pound bag of M&Ms from the night before. After placing the ravioli in the oven, I sat at the kitchen table and popped the candies into my mouth one after another. I mulled things over better when I munched. And that's how my son, Will, found me—mulling and munching—when he trudged into the house around half past three.

I'd called him the day before, after my confrontation with Tweety but prior to Grace and me doing our Lucy-and-Ethel impersonation in her apartment. I said I needed to see him as soon as possible, but I added that he probably wouldn't want Sophie to be privy to our conversation. So he agreed to stop over after Sunday's Vikings game, while Sophie visited her folks in Fargo.

A grin spread across his face as his eyes skipped from me to the bag of candy and back again.

I lied. "I'm about to bake M&M cookies."

He patted the bag. "A small batch, huh?"

"Oh, shut up."

He chuckled while grabbing a glass from the cupboard and the milk jug from the fridge.

"Who won the game?" I watched him fill his glass and place the jug on the counter.

He was dressed in his usual late-fall attire: a plaid flannel shirt under a Carhartt jacket, faded blue jeans, battered work boots, and his favorite Minnesota Twins baseball cap.

He sat opposite me, extending his legs and crossing them at the ankles. "Who do you think?"

While I wasn't a big football fan, even I knew the Vikings were experiencing another rough season. Before leaving the café one day a while back, Will had asked Grace, a diehard fan, "What's the difference between the Vikings and a dollar bill?" His answer? "You can get four quarters from a dollar."

"Oh, before I forget," I said, pointing toward the dining room, "take your lanterns home with you. They're on the floor, next to the patio door."

"That's okay, Mom. Keep them."

"No. You have more use for them out on the farm than I do here." I motioned toward the pendant light above us. "Our electricity's all hooked up."

"I bought a few extra, so at least keep two. You never know when they'll come in handy." He downed his milk, set his glass on the table, and yawned.

"You look all done in, Will."

"No more than at the end of any harvest."

I squinted my skepticism.

"Fine. Being in charge of the farm was definitely more challenging than I thought it would be. I'm glad we're done for the year."

"I think it was the first harvest I've sat out in forty years."

"What about when Erin and I were born?"

"I took you with me."

He screwed up his lips. "I understand why you moved to town, Mom. But I still don't get why you quit farming."

While I was certain he had heard about his father's dalliances, I had never mentioned Destiny Delovely or any of the others to him. Nor would I ever confess to him that they—in collaboration with his father—had spoiled farm life for me. "It was time to retire. That's all. Time for a simpler way of living. But, so far, what's passing for my new life is crazier than my old one."

He grabbed a handful of candy from the bag. "If this is about Erin, don't worry. She'll be back to work before you know it. Everyone lies sometimes. Even to their boss. And no one really believes she had anything to do with Buck's death. Karl's just being a hard-ass."

"It's more than that. Everything's so different, Will."

His face wrinkled like a wadded newspaper. "You aren't getting depressed again, are—"

"No. Just floundering a bit."

"Maybe you should call that therapist."

"I don't need more counseling."

He crinkled the candy bag, clearly uneasy. Which wasn't surprising.

Will had never been good at dealing with emotions. While Erin had often become furious with her father for his behavior and me for failing to "fix" our family, Will preferred to pretend that everything was fine. And when he couldn't pretend, he'd pick a fight with some poor, unsuspecting soul. Not that Buck Daniel was a poor, unsuspecting soul.

"Will? Did you threaten Buck Daniel's life?"

"Where did that come from?"

"Just wondering. So when you beat him up, did you threaten him?"

"Well, yeah." His tone made it clear that he thought his answer should have been obvious to me. "I swore I'd kill him if he ever touched my sister again."

Shivers skidded down my back. "And a week later he was dead."

"So?"

"Tweety's scheduled to meet with Karl tonight. She plans to tell him that Buck claimed you promised to kill him."

Will removed his cap and wiped his brow with the back of his hand. "Buck admitted to me that he went out with Tweety behind Erin's back. He laughed about it. Said Tweety was as easy as a TV Guide crossword puzzle, while Erin was pretty to look at but kind of boring." He replaced his cap along the sunburn line that bisected his forehead. "I told him to break up with her then. But that only made him laugh harder. He said it was good to keep 'two in rotation whenever possible.' That's when I let him have it." He shook his left hand. "My knuckles hurt for a week."

"Sore knuckles may be the least of your problems after tonight."

"I'm surprised he told anyone that I got the best of him." He again crinkled the candy bag.

"Well, since he was dating Tweety at the time, I suppose it makes sense that he'd confide in her."

"Not really, Mom." More crinkling. "He didn't especially like her. He said she could get real mean. Said he couldn't trust her as far as he could throw her."

"Trust her?"

"Uh-huh. A day or two before I canned him, he was yammering about how he had to 'take care of business' but didn't trust Tweety to help him." Still more crinkling. "I never paid much attention because I was pissed that he wasn't concentrating on his work. At the time, I didn't know that he was probably strung out on pain pills."

I grabbed the candy bag to put a stop to the noise. "And you didn't think to tell Karl any of this after Buck got killed?"

"Given my fight with the guy, I've done my best to steer clear of the sheriff and his investigation."

"Because of Sophie?"

"That's not an issue. Not anymore."

"In that case, Will, talk to Karl. Preferably before Tweety meets with him tonight. Maybe you could give him a call."

He stood. "I'll think about it."

I reached for his arm. "I have something else on my mind." I gave myself to the count of three to collect my thoughts. "What's this about you chumming around with Dr. Betcher?"

"Huh?" He frowned, his expression wary.

"Rose mentioned that she saw you visiting with him at the care center several times when she was still there."

"And how old is she?"

I gave him a couple shakes of my head. "Don't go there. Over the past few weeks, I've learned a lot about Rose, and I know darn well that she isn't senile. Hard of hearing? Definitely. Goofy? Sometimes. But not senile. Now tell me the truth. How did you become friendly with Betcher? It's not like Sophie sees him for her prenatal care."

He resettled himself on his chair.

"Are you sick? Is that it?" I didn't wait for a reply. "If you are, you have to tell me. I can't be kept in the dark. I lived that way far too long."

"No, Mom, I'm not sick."

"Then what is it?"

As the sun dipped toward the horizon, a shaft of light cut through the window above the sink and crossed Will's shoulder. While I waited for him to answer me, I watched the dust motes flit around on it, their movements mirroring my nerves.

"You can't tell anyone," he finally said.

Oh my God! What has he done?

"I'm… umm… in anger-management therapy."

"What?" His response was so far from anything I had expected, I couldn't comprehend it.

"I've been in group counseling for going on four months now."

"But you fought with Buck just a couple months ago. Right before he died."

He hitched his shoulder, slicing the sunbeam. "I guess counseling's not a cure-all. Anyways, that's why I wanted you to keep quiet about the fight. I didn't want Sophie to know that I'd slipped. But on my way home, after we talked in the café that day, I decided you were right. I had to tell her before someone else did. So I confessed everything."

"Anger management," I repeated, still attempting to wrap my head around the idea.

"Yeah, Sophie insisted on it after the brawl I was in last year. I put it off, but once she got pregnant, she made me sign up. I don't think it's necessary, but she swears it is."

I discovered two M&Ms in the corner of the candy bag and popped them in my mouth. The smell of garlic drifting from the oven didn't mix particularly well with the taste of chocolate, but that didn't stop me from checking the bag for more. "Well, I think it's good." The bag was definitely empty. "Although I don't understand what it has to do with Dr. Betcher. He's not in charge of your group, is he?"

Will sighed. "No, he's not in charge. He's a member, like me."

"What?" I almost choked.

"You okay?" He came around the table and slapped me on the back.

I waved him away. "Betcher's in counseling with you?"

Resting against the counter, he crossed his chest with his arms. He appeared apprehensive but said, "He verbally abused a nurse a while back. He entered the program to keep her from lodging a formal complaint against him. You can't tell anyone—not even Grace. Our group's confidential. I shouldn't have shared any of this with you, but I didn't want you more stressed than you are."

"So that's what you were doing with Betcher? Discussing anger issues?" I waited for a response.

Will merely rolled his head, like his neck was stiff. "I won't say anything more about it. And neither will you."

"Of course not. Although I can hardly believe Betcher—"

"Mom, enough."

Chapter 19

A few minutes after Will left, Rose called to say she wouldn't make it home to eat. She was on her way to the café in Lancaster with some other women for "Sunday Senior Supper." They needed to go, she said, because they had discount coupons that were about to expire. But she assured me she'd be back by eight o'clock, and we'd catch up then, while we worked on the puzzle. She was bound and determined to finish Jesus's robe.

As for Grace, she remained cowering in the café. Consequently, I ate ravioli by myself. When I finished, I ran the dishwasher, ambled into the living room, and flipped on the gas fireplace as well as all the lamps. Yes, it would be a while before I again was comfortable alone after dark.

I searched for my reading glasses but couldn't find them on the mantel, which was in desperate need of dusting. Or on the end tables. But I eventually discovered them on top of my head.

Snuggling into the corner of the couch, I covered my feet with an afghan and flipped through the television channels, hunting for a show to keep me company while I crocheted. I found nothing of interest. Sunday nights were like that.

I hit the off button on the remote and tossed it aside, then picked up my hook, my yarn, and the bulk of the yellow-and-white baby blanket I was making. A couple more hours of concerted effort and my future grandbaby would have his—or her—first blanket.

While I reviewed my pattern, the wind rattled the windows. Because I was used to the sound, it didn't frighten me. Though it did remind me to check into buying new windows.

I began to crochet to the tick-tock rhythm of the cuckoo clock. As I stitched, I considered what Will had said. Maybe he was right. Maybe this Buck Daniel chaos would be resolved sooner rather than later, and neither Will nor Erin would be blamed for any wrongdoing. If that happened, Grace and I would deserve some of the credit. After all, we'd located the money.

A smile teased the corners of my mouth. Sure, I felt foolish for sneaking into Tweety's apartment, and I hoped and prayed that my kids would never find out. Still, I was pretty sure I had all but cleared them of any connection to Buck Daniel's murder. And that was a pretty big deal.

A knock sounded at the front door, and my crochet hook and everything else went flying. "Oh, fudge!" I gathered my wits, which, like my yarn and pattern, were scattered all over the place.

Easing off the couch, I stepped on my crochet hook and voiced another "fudge!" before picking it up and hobbling through the foyer and into the entry. I flipped on the porch light and saw Karl in the window in the door.

Stepping aside to let him in, my right foot found a puddle left behind by snowy boots, and I grumbled, "Ah, sh… sugar."

"Nice to see you, too."

"I stepped in water." I showed him the heel of my sock.

"Yeah, well, I didn't think you'd invite me over to apologize, then curse me once I got here."

"I didn't curse."

"Not with your mouth. But in your mind." He grinned. "Some things never change."

I shut the door on the sharp smell of winter. "What did you mean about apologizing?"

"Come on, Doris. I know you have trouble admitting when you're wrong, but I'm here, so just do it. Then we can move on."

"Really, I have no clue—"

"Okay, I'll meet you halfway. I was a jerk, too."

"When? You'll have to be more specific." As soon as I realized how that probably sounded, I backpedaled. "I didn't mean you're always a jerk. It's just—"

"Hold on." He adjusted the brim of his baseball cap, as if that might help him understand me, but, believe me, it would require far more than a tweak of his hat. "Didn't you ask me over to apologize for how you acted Friday night at the curling club?"

Because the entry was small—only big enough to shed boots and coats before heaving them into the closet—we stood way too close, leading me to opt for another step in reverse. And wouldn't you know, this time my left foot edged into the puddle. "Me? Why would I apologize? You were the one who was out of line."

"I admitted I was wrong, Doris, but so were you. You kept information from me—information pertinent to an investigation."

I shook my wet foot like a dog. "You already said that—over and over."

"And?"

"I was protecting my daughter. And I won't apologize for that. I shouldn't have to."

He scowled, and I got worried. If he started out angry, where would he end up after hearing about my visit to Tweety's apartment?

"Fine," I begrudgingly acknowledged. "Maybe I could have been more forthcoming."

The corners of his mouth curled. "Now was that so hard?"

"But Erin did nothing wrong."

"I've been sheriff for five years, and I think I've served this county pretty darn well. But what's your opinion? Am I okay at my job?"

"Of course you are." Though I couldn't say the same for some of his recruits. Case in point, Ed Monson. As for my daughter, she was inexperienced, while several of the other deputies were close to retirement and seemed more interested in marking days than actually "protecting and serving." Karl's top deputy, Randy Ryden, had relocated to the Twin Cities a few years back to be closer to his girlfriend, Emerald Malloy, an up-and-coming newspaper reporter there. So the sheriff was short on reliable help. But he was a good sheriff. Possibly the best we'd ever had.

"Then can you trust me to do my job?"

I tiptoed into the foyer and motioned for him to follow. "Let's talk in here. My feet are cold. I need to get rid of these wet socks."

"I don't want to intrude. You're probably getting ready for supper."

I dismissed his concern with a grunt. "I already ate. Remember, we're over sixty. We can eat as early as four, and no one can make fun of us."

Stepping onto the area rug in the foyer, he gazed at his boots.

"Don't fuss about tracking in snow." I peeled off my socks and cringed at the static sound my dry feet made.

He leaned into the newel post at the bottom of the staircase and twisted his lips between his thumb and forefinger. Like in the grocery store, he knew better than to snicker. But as I mentioned before, he was lousy at schooling his features.

I swallowed my irritation. "Are you hungry?" In addition to wishing to remain on friendly terms, at least until after I confessed my most recent misdeed, I had an obligation, as a "nice" Minnesotan, to offer him food. After all, he was my guest. Even if he aggravated me. "I ate ravioli for supper, and there's plenty left. Both Rose and Grace canceled."

"No, I'm fine. I had a late lunch."

"Are you sure? I'm not a great cook, but it's not half bad, if I do say so myself." According to the unwritten but religiously followed rules on how to be a proper Minnesotan, every offer of food had to be extended more than once.

"No. But thanks just the same."

"How about some coffee, then?"

"Don't go to any bother, Doris."

"It's no bother. The pot's half full."

The same with drinks. One invite wasn't sufficient. In fact, it was out-and-out rude.

"That's okay. I can't stay. I have an appointment."

"Oh?" Being fully aware of the nature of his appointment, I had no choice. I couldn't put it off any longer. I had to disclose what Grace and I had discovered and how we had made that discovery. I only hoped that we could avoid dwelling on the latter. "Yeah, well, about that, Karl, I have some information that may be pertinent to your appointment as well as the Buck Daniel investigation."

He inched toward me, as if interested, but narrowed his eyes and rubbed the back of his neck, as if leery, which may have summed up his thoughts about me in general—interested but leery. "How do you know about my meeting? And what information do you have?"

"Well, before I say, just keep in mind that I'm helping you out here."

"Doris." He found me exasperating. It was evident in his tone.

"Fine. Just don't get angry."

He pressed his lips together until they formed a tight, colorless line.

I had to move along. "Okee-dokee. Stay right here. I'll be back in a jiffy."

I scampered up the squeaky stairs and thirty seconds later came back down, slippers covering my dry feet and a single stack of $100 bills in one hand, my crochet hook still grasped in the other. I stopped on the second-to-the-last step to maintain direct eye contact with him. I needed every advantage I could get.

"Grace and I found this." I waved the slim pack of bills in front of him while retaining a firm grip on it. "Tweety had it. We think it's part of the money Buck Daniel withdrew from his grandma's bank accounts just before the robbery. The money you couldn't find." That last comment was merely another reminder of my assistance, in case he harbored any thoughts of giving me a hard time.

"Where did you get it?"

"Like I said, Tweety had it."

"But how did you end up with it?"

I shuffled from one foot to the other, and the step beneath me groaned. At least I think it was the step. But it may have been me. "Is that really important, Karl? Isn't it enough that

I'm handing it over? And I know where the rest is, too. Well, that's not quite true. Tweety spent some. That's how Grace and I became suspicious. She paid Grace her November and December rent in $100 bills. But we counted six other packets, for a total of $7,000, including this. And—"

"Doris, you're rambling again."

"No, I'm explaining."

"Just tell me where you found it." I'm pretty sure he ground his teeth.

"Well…" Deciding to go with the bandage approach, I drew in a lungful of air and ripped the words from my throat. "We found it in a shoebox under her bed, but we left the rest of it there, so you could locate it on your own to make everything official."

His face screamed, *You've got to be kidding!* But his actual words were restrained in timbre. "What were you doing under Tweety's bed?"

I sensed my response to that question was extremely important, prompting me to ask, "In your professional opinion, what would be a good reason—a justifiable one—for us being there?"

His face contorted, giving the impression that he might be passing a kidney stone.

"Karl, are you all right?"

He ignored my concern. "You didn't have permission to be in her apartment, did you?"

"Well, not technically, although Grace is her landlord."

"Doris, we're investigating Tweety. I have a deputy assigned to her."

I harumphed. "If you mean Ed Monson, you better thank Grace and me because he's not going to get anything from her except a communicable disease."

"Whoa! How did you find out about Ed?"

Because I couldn't wring my hands since they were otherwise occupied, I wiggled my toes in the fleece that lined my slippers. "Well, you see, we happened to be in Tweety's apartment when she brought him home with her last night."

"Under the bed?" Was he mocking me?

"Yes, under her bed." I wanted to come across as smug, but I didn't quite land it. "That's how I learned how pathetic your deputy is at interrogation. I don't want to get him in trouble or anything, but aren't cops supposed to know how to do that? Question people, I mean? It makes me wonder if he wasn't trained as well as you assumed when you hired him." I gave him a second to consider that. "Whatever the case, he wasn't about to get any information from her, so you may want to thank Grace and me."

"Thank you?"

"Yeah. Now you only have to come up with a legitimate reason to go into Tweety's apartment, confiscate the rest of the money, and arrest her."

"Why, Doris?"

The man could be incredibly thick-headed. "Because she most likely had something to do with Buck's—"

"No! I mean why did you break into her apartment?"

"We didn't break into it. Grace had a—"

"Doris!"

I closed my eyes and silently counted. Losing my temper wouldn't be good.

At thirteen he interrupted me. "Doris?"

I peeked with one eye. "Tweety was passing $100 bills off as tips, and we had to find out why."

"How come you didn't come to me?"

I opened both eyes wide. "Because you wouldn't have let us sneak into her apartment."

"But why did you have to sneak in last night?"

The questions were coming fast and sidestepping them was draining. "Because she was scheduled to meet with you tonight."

"How did you know that?"

"She told us! She also said she planned to implicate Will in Buck's murder." My voice faltered. "Buck claimed it was Will who beat him up."

"I suspected as much."

"Huh? You knew that Tweety intended to frame Will?"

"No, I suspected that Will beat up Buck Daniel." He was miffed. His eyes were razor-focused on me, and his jaw was hard-set. "How long have you known?"

I couldn't dodge the question unless I ran for the hills, and I couldn't do that because Kittson County had no hills. Not a single one. "Since the night of the robbery," I mumbled.

"Did Will tell you?"

I wasn't about to reveal that Erin was the one who had confided in me. She was in enough hot water already. "Will let him have it because he hurt Erin. He also threatened him and ran him off the farm."

"He threatened him?"

I mentally thumped my forehead. I hadn't meant to say that. "Well, yes, but he didn't kill him."

"How can you be so sure?"

"What?" My fatigue slid over to make room for righteous indignation. I clenched my fists, the crochet hook digging into the palm of my hand. "That's the other reason we searched Tweety's apartment before coming to you. We knew that if we didn't find evidence to the contrary, you'd believe the worst

175

about Will, just like you do about Erin. But Tweety has the money, and that proves she was in on the robbery. Not my kids. In fact, she may have killed Buck. Or, at least, conspired with someone. Erin actually has a theory. She thinks—"

"Stop right there!" Karl rocked back on his heels. "Erin's suspended. She's not supposed to have anything to do with this investigation."

"And she doesn't," I lied. "We were just pitching ideas. And we think it might be worth checking—"

"Doris, stop! I don't want to hear it!"

"But you can't suspect Will."

Karl scrubbed his face. "I follow the evidence."

"Meaning?" My anger went to war with my fear, and the sheriff had a good chance of becoming collateral damage. "What evidence do you have against him? Tell me. I have the right to know. I'm his mother." My hands juddered through the air until my crochet hook sliced within an inch or two of his chest.

He glowered while watching me lower my arms. "First off, Doris, you don't have the right to know diddly-squat. Will's his own man. He's almost forty. But because I'm such a nice guy, I'll tell you this: The murder victim worked for your son. He and Will had a physical altercation. Will fired him. And now I've learned from you, no less, that Will threatened the guy." He ticked off each point on a finger, using his thumb—the only digit left—to add, "Not to mention, a week later the guy was found murdered."

"But what was Will's connection to the robbery? The two crimes had to be connected, right?"

"Not necessarily."

"But Erin—" I stopped myself. My mouth definitely was moving faster than my brain, and that routinely caused me trouble. "I mean, what are the chances that two serious crimes occurred a day apart without any connection? Especially here, where serious crimes almost never occur?"

"Doris—"

"Fine. Then explain Will's motive to me. Murderers have to have motives, don't they?"

"I really haven't given it much thought."

"I don't believe you. You rattled off your evidence against him way too quickly for someone who hasn't 'given it much thought.' You used all the fingers on one hand, for God's sake. So what's your theory?"

Karl examined the ceiling while the wind howled outside and I stewed.

"Well, let's see," he began. "Buck hit Erin. And Will, her overly protective brother, couldn't abide by that, so he went after him."

"That only explains why he beat him up. It doesn't account for why he'd wait another week to hunt him down and kill him."

"I think I better leave."

"No!" I shifted the crochet hook to my left hand—the one holding the money—and grabbed the sleeve of his leather jacket with my right. "Is Erin still a suspect, too?" I was frazzled, furious, frightened, and felt like lobbing another f-word his way, and it wasn't "fudge." But I went with sarcasm. "Or do you think that Erin and Will teamed up with Buck to rob the pharmacy? Then they killed him and gave the money from Wilma's accounts to Tweety out of the kindness of their hearts? As for the stolen drugs, Erin's now selling them on the street because she's suspended and has a lot of free time on her hands. And she and Will are splitting the profits—with me."

He tugged the money out of my hand, and the crochet hook fell to the step. "I should get back to work. The county board wants an arrest—soon."

I yanked his jacket sleeve. "And my kids are easy marks, huh?"

"Do you really think I'd do that?"

I didn't answer. Tears had gathered behind my eyes, and speaking would surely open the floodgates.

"Sometimes I can't believe you, Doris. Sometimes you still act like you're sixteen." And with that, he stalked out of the house.

As for me, I picked up my crochet hook, desperately wishing for something–or someone–to stab.

Chapter 20

Monday morning Rose and I arrived at the café right after eight. Erin was already there. Grace had called us in because Allie was home sick and Tweety was a no-show.

"Don't get ahead of yourself," I cautioned my sister as she folded omelets on the grill. "Remember, Tweety skips work all the time."

"This feels different."

"Of course it's different. She was furious with us when she left here Saturday afternoon."

Grace glanced at Rose, and I answered the question my sister, the person who knew me best, didn't even have to ask. "I gave Rose the lowdown on our visit to Tweety's place, and I filled her in on Karl's suspicions regarding Will. But Erin still doesn't know about either. I'm not sure how much more she can handle."

Grace nodded understanding before returning to the matter of her missing waitress. "She won't answer her phone. I even went upstairs and pounded on the door but nothing."

"Did you... ?" Again, finishing wasn't necessary.

"I decided I better not make a habit of that, Doris. But I talked to Berta." She bobbed her head toward the front of the café, where Berta and her minions no doubt sat in the corner booth. "She hasn't spoken to Tweety in a couple days. I phoned Karl and asked him to check with Deputy Monson. Ed hasn't seen her since Saturday night. So I requested a welfare check, although Karl wondered if I might be jumping the gun."

"He refused to do it?" Rose had settled on the wooden chair next to the back door, where she switched her snow boots for a pair of thick-soled walking shoes.

"No, he came by for the key to her apartment about five minutes ago. He's up there now."

"You mean he's here, in the building?" My voice was chock-full of venom.

"I'm mad at him, too. I can't believe he'd suspect Erin or Will of anything criminal. But what else could I do?"

Erin peered through the pass-through window and whistled to get our attention. "Can I get some help out here in the dining room?"

"Yah, for sure," Rose replied. "Put a stool behind the counter, and I'll take care of the till." She toddled toward the swinging doors. With her white hair and Kelly-green sweatsuit, she reminded me of an elderly leprechaun. "I'll handle the coffee for the crew at the counter, too." She raised her voice, clearly intending for everyone to hear her. "But I won't take any guff from Ole." That got a lot of folks laughing.

"Erin, here's your omelet order." Grace stepped past me with a plate of food that was ripe with the scent of onions and peppers. "Hash browns, bacon, and wheat toast on the side."

My stomach growled an order of its own, and I obeyed by snatching two pieces of crispy bacon from the paper towel on the counter while en route to Rose's vacated chair.

At the same time, the sheriff banged through the back door and almost knocked me over. Either he didn't notice or didn't care.

"Well?" Grace posed as he lumbered her way.

After toeing off my boots, I followed him in my stocking feet, chomping on my bacon and glaring at his back.

"Yep, she's gone." He handed Grace her key.

"And the money under the bed?" I swallowed.

"Gone, too."

"Any idea where she went?" Grace asked.

He shook his head.

"Did she say anything when you met with her last night?" That was me again.

"She never showed. She didn't answer her phone, either. And her car was gone. I'd planned to stop in here later this morning to question her. Then, if necessary, I'd request a warrant to search her place. But Grace called first."

"Ed probably scared her off." I wiped my greasy fingertips on my jeans. "The way he interrogated her Saturday night was less than tactful."

A frown clouded Karl's face. "Or she may have checked under her bed, realized her stash of cash was short, and made a break for it, knowing someone was on to her."

"Or, like I said, Ed scared her off." I wasn't about to accept responsibility for her disappearance without solid proof that it was my fault. "What now?"

He contemplated his well-worn hiking boots for a couple beats. "I'll carry on with my investigation, which now includes hunting down Tweety. And for a change, you two will mind your own business."

If his aim was to irk me, he'd succeeded. "This is my business! You see, the local sheriff thinks my kids are complicit in Buck Daniel's death. I know it's hard to believe. Outlandish, even. But that's what he thinks."

Karl stared at his boots some more before muttering under his breath and heading through the swinging doors.

I tied my tennis shoes, pulled an apron over my fleece sweatshirt, and delivered plates of Grace's buttermilk pancakes to the mothers' table.

It wasn't the mothers' normal meeting day, but because it was Thanksgiving week, they had altered their schedule. That meant I was forced to serve seven screaming kids when all I wanted to do was listen in on the sheriff and Berta, who now occupied a booth by themselves.

By the time I got the kids' orders sorted out, my apron and sweatshirt were caked with maple syrup and Karl was on his way out the door. He said nothing to me, although he did shake his head, as if infuriated, and I, in turn, thought about bribing the kids to squirt a little syrup his way.

After I made my way to the service counter, Erin tugged on my sleeve. "Ed didn't learn anything new at assisted living yesterday." She examined her sticky fingers before wiping them on a dishcloth. "No one but Rose witnessed anything at the time of the robbery. I meant to call and fill you in last night, but I fell asleep. I haven't gotten much rest lately."

"Well, maybe Betcher wasn't lying."

"It's possible, though that doesn't mean he's innocent." She cleared a few plates from the counter and set them in a plastic tub. Once the tub was full, one of us would schlep it to the kitchen and stack and run the dishwasher. "He's in the clinic today. At least that's what Dr. Osgood said."

I scanned the room for the younger doctor.

"He already left, but he'll be back later. He invited me to supper in Grand Forks. He said I had to get out of town for a few hours, and he promised to let me bend his ear about what's been happening." She paused. "He's a nice guy." For a second, she almost appeared happy.

"Anyway..." She turned somber again. "I thought about interviewing Dr. Betcher at the clinic but decided against it. He'd never confess anything of importance to me. I'm not that well acquainted with him. And since everyone in town already seems to know that I'm suspended, I can't use my position to get him to open up."

In other words, she needed my help. "Now you want me to talk to him?"

"I always did. I just didn't trust his motives. And I certainly didn't want you to go out with him. Or be alone with him. I still don't. So if you speak with him, make sure it's in the hallway."

"Erin, I can't very well ask if he murdered Buck Daniel while standing in the hallway."

A woman at the far end of the counter motioned for a coffee refill.

"Well, if you end up in his office, keep the door open." My daughter retrieved the pot from the warmer behind us. "And don't come right out and accuse him of murder."

"Don't worry. I'll be fine." Hopefully.

"I almost forgot. There's something else I should tell you. So wait right here." She then stepped away, poured coffee in several cups, and dropped a bill at the booth nearest the front door.

"Anyway," she said upon her return, "Dr. Betcher supposedly had it out with Gerti Bengston right around the time of the robbery and murder."

I angled my hip against the edge of the counter in an effort to relieve my sciatic-nerve pain. "What does that have to do with anything?"

"Well, I guess they argued about the misuse of pain medication. It got really heated. And afterward, Gerti threatened to file a grievance against him."

"For misuse of meds?"

"I'm not sure, but it sounds that way."

"Hmm. I've lost touch with Gerti, but I can't imagine her yelling at Dr. Betcher. She's been his head nurse for decades. And she's one of his few true friends. But if she got after him for misappropriation of medication, she might be aware of something that would bolster your theory."

I waved to a trio of women from the nearby insurance agency as they slid off their stools at the counter and headed for the door. Because of the sun glaring through the plate-glass windows, I couldn't see their faces, but I knew who they were. They occupied the same three stools every workday morning. "Where did you hear all of this, Erin?"

She gestured toward the corner-booth ladies, their heads almost touching as they gossiped. "They were discussing it earlier. I recalled hearing a bit about the argument right after it happened, too, but it didn't make much of an impression on me at the time."

"How come I don't remember anything about it?"

"I don't know."

I glanced at the old ladies. "Why on earth would they spend time gnawing on something from months ago given everything that's happening right now?"

She picked up a dishcloth. "I'm not sure. But, like I said, it might be worth checking out. Particularly since you know Gerti, and you'll be at the clinic to see Betcher, anyway."

The women at the mothers' table prepared to leave. After skidding their chairs away from the table, they dipped their napkins in their water glasses and scrubbed their kids clean, then wrangled them into their jackets. For a second, the scene made me nostalgic. But only for a second. After that, I felt relieved that those years were behind me.

"Okay, Erin," I said, reaching for a dishcloth of my own. "As soon as I leave here, I'll drop Rose off and head up to the clinic."

◎　◎　◎

Erin lugged the tub of dirty dishes into the kitchen, while I wiped the mothers' table and claimed my $2.00 tip.

As I wondered what I'd do with my newfound wealth, Ole motioned for me from where he sat on his usual stool, his back a lazy "C."

I ambled his way.

At the same time, Rose railed from her stool behind the till. "See here, you old goat, you've already downed enough coffee."

Ignoring her, Ole warbled, "I have another joke for you, Doris. But first, refill my cup. That other one won't do it."

I glimpsed at Rose, "that other one," and she canted her head, signaling she wanted me to play along.

"I don't know, Ole." Faux trepidation coursed through my tone. "I have no desire to become the subject of Rose's wrath."

"Oh, don't fret about her none." He waved his age-spotted hand like he was shooing a fly. "I think she's kind of sweet on me."

I had to bite my lip. "Really? She has a funny way of showing it."

"Which probably explains why she never married."

Swallowing my laughter, I grabbed the coffee pot and poured him a cup.

"Thanks." He dipped his head. "Now here's my joke: How do you make a tissue dance?"

185

I returned the coffee pot to the warmer before pitching my elbows on the countertop in front of him. "I don't know. How?"

His grin wrinkled his face, calling to mind a grapevine wreath. "Put a little boogie in it."

He was alone that day. No buddies on either side. But that didn't stop him from slapping the counter and chortling.

"Ole, that was the dumbest joke of all time."

He pulled a hanky from his pants pocket and sniffled while wiping his nose. "No, it ain't. This one's way worse." He stuffed the hanky back into his pocket. "What did General Washington say to his men at the Potomac River, just before they got in their boat?"

"I don't know. What did he say?"

His milky-blue eyes twinkled. "Men, get in the boat." This time, his laugh was mostly wheeze.

Yep, that joke was worse, and I was about to inform him of that when the bells on the door jingled and Gustaf Gustafson waddled in, leaving the door open for way longer than anyone appreciated. He looked haggard. Bad enough to scare the blind, as Rose would later say.

"You know," I murmured to Ole, while everyone else craned their necks to see the person guilty of letting in the Arctic blast, "I used to think he was the biggest blowhard in town, but that honor may belong to you."

"Hey, that there is mean." The old man pouted. Then again, with the deep ditches that framed his mouth and meandered across his forehead, I couldn't really distinguish his pout from his happy face. "I'm nothing like Gustaf Gustafson," he said. "He's so dumb that when someone went into the bank last week and asked him to check their balance, he tried to push them over."

I actually laughed out loud. "Okay, that one was pretty good."

"Thanks. But I really do hate the guy. He thinks the sun comes up just to hear him crow. But he's nothing more than a drunk and a gambler. So's his wife. Word is, she spends more time at the casino in Mahnomen than at home. Heck, I see her every time I'm there."

I refrained from commenting on the irony of that statement and, instead, considered speaking with Gustaf. Naturally, I would have rather stuck a fork in my eye. But later, when confronting Dr. Betcher at the clinic, I'd feel less panicky if I was armed with the latest on the robbery and murder investigations. And Gustaf was just the guy to fill me in.

Before I could coerce my feet into moving, however, Erin approached me and said, "Grace and I decided earlier that if Gustaf came in, she'd question him. We think it's the best approach since he's always had a thing for her, and he hates your guts."

"But Grace finds him almost as repulsive as I do."

Erin fluttered her eyelashes. "What can I say? She loves me."

As if cued, Grace sauntered in from the kitchen sans her baseball hat and her cooking smock. Her tight t-shirt read, *I've been told I have ADHD, but—Hey, look, a squirrel!*

Chapter 21

With her mug in one hand and her chest leading the way, Grace snagged the coffee pot and strutted toward Gustaf, her hips swishing from side to side like windshield wipers during a rainstorm. "Care if I join you?" she asked. "It's finally slow enough that I can take a break before gearing up for the lunch rush."

Gustaf's mouth fell open, and several seconds ticked by before he managed to sputter, "Ah, yeah, s-sit down. T-take a load off."

Sliding into the booth on the bench seat opposite him, Grace placed her cup on the table while filling his cup to the brim. A moment later, Erin appeared and whisked the pot away.

Gustaf was clearly gobsmacked by Grace's presence. In fact, it appeared as if he might pass out. His face glinted with sweat, and his man-boobs rose and fell at an alarming rate.

"I'm not resuscitating him," I warned my daughter when she sidled alongside me in my new location near the pass-through window. That spot would put me close enough to hear

Grace and Gustaf while still providing cover. And by "cover," I meant that Erin and I could pretend to review the meal tickets stacked on the ledge in the window while listening in.

"Gustaf, you look like you're coming off a rough night," Grace said to start their conversation in earnest.

Gustaf replied while kneading his ham-hock hands, "Well, you know how it is." As if that explained everything.

"Yeah, I have problems of my own." Grace inhaled deeply, fully inflating her chest. For a self-proclaimed feminist who routinely preached against using feminine wiles to get ahead, she seemed oddly comfortable. "I'm sure you've heard that Erin was suspended from the sheriff's office for lying."

Gustaf ogled Grace's t-shirt, but I didn't believe for a second that he was the least bit interested in doing any reading about attention deficit hyperactivity disorder. "Y-yeah, I heard."

"Well, I don't know what to do about it."

They both had lowered their voices yet again, leaving me no choice but to abandon Erin and move once more.

I picked up a tray of empty salt and pepper shakers and lugged them to the booth directly behind Gustaf. There, I'd fill the shakers—while listening.

As I set the tray on the table, my sister sent me a withering look. It was undeniably meant to put me on notice that because of her efforts on my daughter's behalf, I'd be indebted to her for a long time to come. A very long time.

Thankfully, when Gustaf said, "While I'd like to help you, Grace, I hafta support the sheriff," she was forced to blink back to him.

"Oh, goodness gracious, I don't expect you to intercede on my behalf." Evidently she had chosen to play the part of a southern belle—a belle with a heaving bosom. "Erin lied to her boss, and she has to be punished for it. I understand."

"You do?"

"Of course. My only concern is that some people believe that the suspension is insufficient. They're intent on implicating her in the pharmacy robbery—and even Buck Daniel's death." Grace discreetly pointed toward the corner-booth ladies.

"Well, just so you know, I don't believe Erin had anything to do with either." Gustaf was whispering even softer now, his discretion both surprising me and forcing me to kneel on the bench seat behind him in order to hear. "Sure, she was a hellraiser when she was young," he added, "but the sheriff says she has real potential as a deputy."

Grace nodded. "Still, some—"

"Yeah, Berta phoned me." Gustaf shifted in his seat, and the vinyl burped. "She said Buck was Erin's boyfriend and claimed that Erin killed him because he jeopardized her job when he committed the robbery. But you know what?" He didn't wait for a response. "I told her that the way I heard it, her granddaughter was actually dating Buck at the time of his death. So as chair of the county board, I should probably order the sheriff to take a closer look at her."

Grace batted her eyes. "Well, I certainly do appreciate you sticking up for my niece."

"Oh, it was nothing." Gustaf flapped one of his porky palms. "I always try to be nice. I'm just that kind of a guy."

I almost retched.

Grace, conversely, managed to keep her gag reflex in check and go right on talking. "Gustaf, do you think Tweety's really a suspect?"

"Oh, I don't know. The sheriff doesn't say a whole lot. It's one of the complaints against him. Some of the county board members would like him to keep them better informed."

"Well… umm… speaking of county board members, what do you think of Andrew Betcher? He's been on the board with you for some time, hasn't he?"

It was a clumsy segue, but Gustaf didn't seem to mind. He answered without hesitation. "To tell you the truth, I don't think much of him. Even though I'm the chair of the board, he acts like he's in charge. And that really burns my buns, being he's only on the board because no one else would take the job. You see, ten years ago, during a town meeting, he excused himself to use the toilet, and while he was gone, he got voted into the job."

"So have you heard any rumors about him lately?"

"What kind of rumors?" Gustaf jiggled, and again the seat burped. Or so I thought. I soon realized, however, that it was neither the seat nor a burp.

Grace scrunched a napkin against her nose, and when she spoke, she honked like a goose. "For instance, have you heard that he might have had something to do with the pharmacy robbery, considering he's in charge of the medical center, and he has a reputation for pushing pills?"

Gustaf threw his head back and laughed. "Andrew Betcher would never allow himself to get mixed up in something so… tawdry. Not after what happened in the Cities. The fact is, he's a real pain in the keister on the county board. He won't let us take any action without first checking to make sure we dotted every 'I' and crossed every 'T.' No, sir-ree. Can't cut any corners with Betcher around."

"What about his proclivity for pushing pills?"

"Oh, I can't fault him for that. If he didn't have me on a dozen pills or more, I'd be a goner. I have a bad ticker, you know."

"Betcher's your doctor? But you said—"

"He knows his medicine." Gustaf whipped his arm through the air like a weatherman pointing out a storm front. "And look around. This town isn't exactly crawling with doctors to choose from."

I glanced around the café. Gustaf was right. There wasn't a doctor in sight. Or hardly anybody else, for that matter. Even Ole and the corner-booth ladies were gone. Grace would have to hurry if she was to get anything useful out of Gustaf before he left, too.

She must have been thinking the same thing because she was quick to ask, "You aren't the least bit concerned about Betcher's temper?"

"Huh?" Gustaf grunted.

Grace made an effort to clarify herself. "It's just that he can get pretty ornery, from what I understand."

Okay, okay. I'd shared with her everything Will had confided in me about Betcher being in his anger management group.

"Oh, sure, he flies off the handle," Gustaf confirmed. "But he's taking steps to get that under control. Though no one's supposed to know."

"So you don't think he could have lost his temper after Buck Daniel robbed the pharmacy and..." Grace apparently couldn't bring herself to finish her sentence.

Gustaf had no such problem. "And murdered the guy?" He snorted a laugh. "Where'd you get an off-the-wall idea like that?" He sounded as if Grace's naïveté was cute in a dumb sort of way. "Trust me, Gracie, I can't stand Andrew Betcher. He has a big mouth, and his social graces make me look like Emily frickin' Post. But he's no robber. Or killer. Not that the death of Buck Daniel was a big loss."

"What?"

He sucked in air like he was striving to reclaim his words. "I probably shouldn't have said that. I really didn't know him all that well." Pulling a napkin from the dispenser at the end of the table, he patted the top of his glistening dome. "I only met with him a few times as his grandmother's banker." He tossed the wadded napkin aside, and it fell to the floor.

"Well, I have no idea what to do about Erin." Grace's voice was full of whine. "Even though she had no part in Buck Daniel's death, I'm afraid what will happen to her if the real murderer isn't found–fast."

"Oh, don't worry, Gracie. The sheriff's on it."

"That doesn't mean he'll succeed. From what I gather, he's being pushed to make an arrest."

"Yeah, that's true. The board members who are up for re-election next year are afraid that they'll take heat from the voters if the case goes unresolved for too long."

"What about you?"

Gustaf puffed himself up. "I have another three years on my current term. On top of that, I know how to handle these kinds of situations."

"Yet you can't help me. And I was counting on you."

Grace's whimpering, along with the pleading look in her eyes and the aforementioned breasts, proved too much for Gustaf. He gave in with a sigh. "Well, the truth is, Gracie, I am aware of a few things relative to the murder investigation, but I probably shouldn't repeat them."

"Why not? You always repeat things."

Gustaf dug in his ear with a finger that resembled a ballpark frank. "You wouldn't like this. And I don't wanna upset ya."

"Oh, please tell me, Gustaf. Pretty please. Pretty please with sugar on it."

He squirmed.

"I'll be eternally grateful." She fluttered her eyelashes. "Really, I will." I didn't even want to hazard a guess as to what she meant by that.

"All right," Gustaf answered as if in a trance. "If you insist." He then used his hot-dog finger to scratch through the half-dozen hairs that comprised his pathetic combover. "According to the folks at the sheriff's office, your... umm... nephew is the number-one murder suspect."

"What?" Grace shrieked. "Will?"

I gasped and dropped an open shaker, spilling pepper all over the table. I pinched my nose but nevertheless sneezed uncontrollably.

Not surprisingly, Gustaf jerked his head around to see who was causing the fracas. But because his head was so big and his neck, so thick, he gave up at around forty-five degrees. "Well, you hafta admit that he likes to fight," he said, refocusing on Grace. "And now the whole town knows that he beat up Buck for hitting Erin."

"Then waited another week before killing him? That doesn't make a lick of sense." Yes, Grace and I had also kicked around the absurdity of that theory.

"Hey!" Gustaf lifted his hands slightly above his head, stretching his roly-poly arms as well as the seams of his flannel shirt. "Don't kill the messenger. I'm only repeating what folks are saying."

"Well, I just can't believe—"

"Don't worry, Gracie. By tomorrow everyone will have a different suspect in mind. That's how these things go, don't ya know." He reached for my sister's hands, but she yanked them off the table. Yes, we Anderson girls had quick reflexes.

Although Gustaf wasn't dissuaded. He merely employed a different tactic. "If you want, Gracie, I'll keep you posted. I'll let you know everything I hear. Just give me your cell phone number."

"What?" Grace shrieked. "My phone number? No! Not that. I'd never give you my number."

Then, evidently, she remembered her goal: to obtain whatever information Gustaf had—or could obtain—that might possibly help my children. "I mean..." She inhaled a deep breath and let it out slowly. "I mean, I never have my cell phone with me. Mostly I forget it at home. Or it's not charged. So you'd be better off to stop by here."

Chapter 22

Before Gustaf or Grace left their booth, I rushed into the kitchen to place a call. Settling on the chair along the back wall, next to the door, I blew a tissue's worth of pepper out of my nose, then retrieved my phone from my purse and punched in Will's number.

"Hello?" Will's words were garbled, like his mouth was full.

"What's going on?" I had to speak up because the dishwasher was clamoring, as if the dishes inside were arguing over soap or some such thing. "What are you doing, Will?"

"I'm eating lunch. Leftover chicken-and-stuffing hot dish. Sophie made it last night. She's a great cook, Mom. You might want her to teach you a few things."

I swallowed my pride as well as my response. Now was not the time for that particular discussion.

"Will, you better hire a lawyer." I clutched my purse so tightly that my fingers ached.

"What are you talking about?"

"Umm… it seems that Tweety isn't the only person in town who thinks you might be responsible for Buck Daniel's death."

"Well, they're wrong." He slurped what was most likely a drink in a tall glass full of rattling ice.

"The sheriff might be one of them, Will. And that's probably my fault."

"Your fault?" He sounded relaxed, which was inappropriate under the circumstances and out of character for him at any time. "You're not making any sense, Mom."

I looked to the ceiling in search of the words to explain myself, but all I saw was a water stain in the shape of Wisconsin, with a spider crawling around Madison. The stain was probably the result of Tweety's leaky sink, although I had no idea where the spider had come from. "You see, Karl came by the house last night, and I kind of let it slip that Tweety claimed you had threatened Buck."

"Why on earth did you do that?"

I shook my head, as if he could see me. "I don't know. I'm awfully sorry."

"Calm down."

"I don't think you understand the seriousness of the situation."

"Mom, I spoke with the sheriff last night, just like you wanted. I ran into him at the Cenex station when I was gassing up my truck. He said Buck Daniel was killed from a blow to the head."

I uh-huhed. "Blunt-force trauma. Probably a rock."

"That's right. He also said the perpetrator was right-handed."

"How does he know—"

"By the angle of the wound or something." He must have stuffed his mouth with more hot dish because his words were mushy when he added, "Anyways, it couldn't have been me because, as you know, I'm left-handed."

Since I was used to him speaking with his mouth full, despite all of my harping, I deciphered his words just fine. But because they left me both relieved and confused, I was rendered temporarily speechless.

"Mom? Are you still there?"

I managed a grunt.

"He even tested me. Saw for himself that I'm practically useless with my right hand. I also told him the guys on my baseball team would swear to it. So I'm in the clear."

"Really?"

"Anyway, you can't say anything about the whole right-hand, left-hand thing. I guess it's an important part of the investigation."

"I won't say a word." Why did I ever bother to make such a promise? Everyone knew I'd blab to Grace. I couldn't help myself. She, on the other hand, was good at holding onto secrets, as I'd only recently discovered.

"Everything's good, then, Will?"

His fork clattered against his plate. "Oh, I wouldn't go that far. The sheriff doesn't like me much. Though he may be sweet on you."

The back of my neck heated up. I glanced over my shoulder and through the window in the door. No, I couldn't blame the sun. The sky had clouded over, and it looked as if it might snow. "Yeah, right. I make him nuts."

"I'm not so sure. He seemed awfully protective of you."

"As I've explained before, we dated in high school. And because of that, he might be nice on occasion. But he certainly wouldn't go out of his way for me."

"Whatever." He crunched on something. Probably ice. "Still, I told him that if he was really concerned about you, he'd ease up on Erin. But he didn't like that. He's definitely upset with her."

"Does he actually believe that she was involved in the robbery or Buck Daniel's murder?"

"I got the impression he doesn't want to, Mom. But he's worked up about something. I just couldn't figure out what it was. And he wasn't sharing."

I hung up, then placed another call.

◎ ◎ ◎

After I left the café, I dropped Rose off at the senior center before detouring to my house to change my syrup-laden sweatshirt and use the bathroom. While I was determined to have it out with Dr. Betcher, my digestive tract wasn't so sure that was a good idea.

Fifteen minutes later, I was ready to head out again, a clean navy sweatshirt under my jacket, but I was unable to locate my purse. I checked everywhere before spotting it on the toilet tank. Slinging it over my shoulder, I trotted downstairs and opened the front door. Then I yelped.

Dr. Betcher, you see, was on my porch. "Sorry, I didn't mean to frighten you, Doris."

"What are you doing here?" Tendrils of dread curled in my stomach, even though I assured myself that he had no way of knowing I considered him the prime suspect in a heinous crime—or two.

"I saw I missed your call. But on my way home just now, I noticed your car." He pointed to my SUV, which was parked in front of his black Humvee.

I opened my mouth but couldn't speak. My scaredy-cat digestive tract was apparently connected to my larynx. I didn't recall that from high school anatomy, yet it appeared to be the case.

"I'm glad you phoned." He motioned toward the open door behind me. "Shall we?"

"No!" My larynx had freed itself.

"Pardon me?"

Stepping onto the porch, I tugged the door shut behind me and huddled in my jacket. The temperature was below zero, and the wind was brisk, but we were not going inside. "I'm on my way out." The wind chimes jingled manically, like my nerves.

"Is anyone else at home?" With his beady rat eyes, he scoped out the yard, as if he might find Erin and Rose making snow angels.

"What?" My spidey senses tingled.

"I want to say hello."

"You just visited with Rose at assisted living yesterday."

He furrowed his brow, obviously speculating as to why I was acting like a crazy person. "Has she scheduled an appointment with my office?" His glasses slid down his nose, and he withdrew his hand from his coat pocket to nudge them back into place.

"She might have said something about it this morning."

"She's not here to ask?"

I was slow to respond because I was busy scolding myself for choosing to live on the edge of town. I could have picked a more central location. But, nooo, I had to have privacy. I wanted seclusion, and I got it. The empty road running perpendicular to my driveway confirmed how little traffic passed by my house, even at the end of a workday. And regardless of Dr. Betcher's failure to adhere to the notion that a nondescript SUV was "good enough," no one would see his outrageous Humvee unless they drove by.

"Actually, Rose is at the senior center." I edged toward the steps.

"How about Erin, then? Is she home?" With a shuffle, he was in front of me again.

"What difference does it make if she's here or not?"

His face was a picture of confusion. "Well, as you know, Doris, I've been out of town. Thus, I haven't had a chance to express how sorry I am about her troubles. True, I'm not very familiar with her, but we have a few things in common." He pursed his lips. "For instance, I'm fully aware of what it's like to be at the center of unfounded rumors. It can permanently damage your reputation as well as your career. From then on, some people will suspect you whenever wrongdoing occurs."

Because I was one of those people, at least in this instance, I wasn't sure how to reply. On top of that, I was frightened. Consequently, I said nothing. Yeah, hard to believe.

"You see," he continued, "I don't think your daughter was complicit in either the pharmacy robbery or Buck Daniel's murder. I'd stake my reputation on it."

He had set the bar awfully low. Still, I remained mum. Yep, just call me Miss Restraint.

"I'm an excellent judge of character, Doris. And shortly after Erin arrived at the medical center on the night of the robbery, I determined that she was as dedicated to her work in law enforcement as I am to my profession. Since then, I've concluded that she must be innocent and, like me, simply the victim of a smear campaign."

"You deduced all of that from seeing her one time?" To my way of thinking, it was far more plausible that he was certain of Erin's innocence because he was entangled in one or both of the crimes himself. Although, again, that didn't seem like something he'd want to hear.

"I'm a keen observer," he boasted. "I also spoke with Berta Benson. She called to insist that I, as a member of the county board, order the sheriff to fire Erin, then arrest her. From what I gathered, Gustaf had refused to do her bidding. But, for once, he and I were in sync because I refused her, too."

"That was kind of you."

"Yes, it was. Though it probably won't be long now before my name is bandied about in connection to the Buck Daniel investigation. Berta was quite upset, and she can cause a host of problems."

He stopped speaking while four snowmobilers buzzed through the ditch along the highway, heading for the bridge that crossed the river. I didn't care for snowmobiling. It was too jarring. Yet in that moment, I longed to be on the back of one of those machines, bouncing far away from here.

"But more than that," he went on to say once the snowmobiles were out of sight, "the robbery occurred in my medical center, and I briefly treated Buck Daniel."

"What?" Stunned by his admission, I jerked my head around to face him and, in doing so, almost somersaulted backward over the wooden porch railing and into the snow that banked the house's foundation. "Umm… how can you come right out and admit that?"

He shrugged. "He's dead, Doris. I don't anticipate him objecting. Now, about Erin…"

"She's not here!" If I'd had any neighbors, they would have heard me. But, as I may have mentioned, there was no one nearby. "Although…" I ordered myself to settle down. I didn't want him to see my fear. "I expect her any minute." That was a lie. She was in Grand Forks, on her first date with Dr. Osgood. I just wanted Dr. Betcher to believe otherwise—in case he had designs on killing me.

"I'm sorry to hear that."

"You're sorry she's coming over?" My heart beat faster, like after a hard workout. True, I couldn't remember my last workout. Still, I was pretty sure of the feeling.

"No, Doris. I'm sorry because I'll miss her. I need to get going. I have plans tonight."

"Really?" *Thank God! He's leaving.*

Then again, I needed answers for Erin. "Wait!" And regardless of my apprehension, I was bound and determined to get them. "Before you go, Andrew, I have a couple of questions." Even with the cold, sweat formed above my upper lip. "So... umm... how long was Buck Daniel your patient?"

He shrugged. "Only a few months. Right after he moved to town."

"Why did you quit seeing him?"

He studied my face, as if attempting to read my mind.

I wasn't worried. I was so discombobulated that he'd have a tough time making sense of anything he happened upon in my head.

"Why are you so interested, Doris?"

I had to think fast, which was difficult on a good day, and this was far from a good day. I certainly couldn't say, *Because I have a hunch that you killed the guy.* So I went with, "Well, like you pointed out, my daughter's name and reputation are getting dragged through the mud because of him. Therefore, I'm out to learn everything I can about the guy. That's why I called you. Since Wilma Daniel was your patient, I thought you might have known her grandson. I didn't realize he, too, was your patient."

"As I said, not for long. He was addicted to opioids. Once I recognized that, I rebuffed all further requests for prescriptions. Naturally, he became furious. And that's when I suggested he find another physician or, better yet, seek treatment."

"Instead, he robbed the pharmacy."

Dr. Betcher bristled. "That wasn't my fault, although I wasn't terribly shocked. He wouldn't admit he had a problem, which usually signals trouble ahead."

"When was the last time you saw him?"

He smirked. "You sound like your friend, the sheriff."

"Yeah, I imagine the sheriff's spoken with you many times. But, as I mentioned before, we are not friends."

"Nonetheless, Doris, I'll tell you the same thing I told him. I didn't see Buck Daniel for a month or more before the robbery. Not even to confer with him regarding his grandmother."

"Really?" I had assumed he would stonewall me, yet that didn't appear to be the case. Yes, he may have lied, but there was no evidence of that. Although I'd always had difficulty recognizing lies. Case in point: my entire marriage.

"Now," he repeated, "I better go."

"No!" While I had nothing else to ask concerning Buck Daniel—at least at this time—I had several questions about Tweety, the most important being, "First, tell me how well you're acquainted with Joy Jacobson?"

"Excuse me?" His face went from pink to ruddy red. "Where did that come from?"

"Just wondering."

He blinked uncontrollably. "You mean the waitress? The waitress at More Hot Dish, Please?

He was stalling. Hiding something. But I didn't push. Erin had warned me against that. Rather, I simply said, "Yep, she's the one."

Reaching between the bottom two buttons of his overcoat, he adjusted himself. Some men scratched their heads when anxious. Apparently Dr. Betcher fiddled with his junk. "Is that why you refused my dinner invitation, Doris? You thought I was dating Tweety?"

"Huh?"

"I can assure you that I'm not interested in her." He grinned, revealing way too many veneered teeth. "We went out a few times, but she means nothing to me."

I made an effort to muster the energy necessary to correct his apparent—and totally erroneous—assumption, but there wasn't nearly enough of it left in me. Questioning Andrew Betcher was grueling work. "Just tell me when you were with her last."

"I can hardly believe you're jealous."

"Jealous?" Nope. I wasn't even going to go there. "Just answer the question."

He pulled his sunken shoulders back and lifted his head, providing me with another close-up view of his hairy oversized nostrils. "I'd normally be flattered, but you're acting somewhat aggressive. And that's not becoming. Particularly for a woman your age."

"What?"

"A woman at your stage in life should be grateful when any man shows interest, particularly a man of my stature. I suspect it doesn't happen very often."

The hair on the back of my neck stood straight up, like little soldiers—angry little soldiers.

"Oh, wait." He tilted his head. "I get it now. You've changed your mind about going out with me but aren't sure how to tell me. Well, in that case, your jealousy is kind of cute."

In my mind's eyes, I fisted my hand, pulled my arm back, and aimed for his jaw.

In reality, a car door slammed, diverting my attention and saving him, at least for the time being.

Chapter 23

Karl trekked around his patrol car, his hiking boots crunching the brittle snow along the edge of the driveway. He made his way up the sidewalk and onto the porch, bringing with him an apple and a large helping of tension. The former occupied his right hand and occasionally his mouth. The latter made the porch feel crowded.

I let my fist drop to my side. I should have been happy to see him. He'd arrived in time to stop me from committing an assault—or worse. Nonetheless, I was irked. I had confirmed that Betcher was Buck Daniel's doctor and that Tweety and Betcher knew each other—quite possibly in the biblical sense—but I hadn't had the opportunity to ask about the money Grace and I had discovered in Tweety's possession. However, punching Betcher in the face probably wasn't the best way to go about that.

"Spotted your car," the sheriff grumbled to the doctor. "Anyone sick or hurt here?"

While Andrew Betcher and the Karl Ingebretsen were the same height, Karl had him beat in stature. Not that it mattered. It wasn't a contest. Even so, next to Karl, Betcher was an empty suit.

"I stopped by to check on Rose." Dr. Betcher blinked like he was sending a Morse code SOS.

"Is Rose okay?" The sheriff asked me the question while yanking his cap from his head, only to replace it again after raking his fingers through his hair.

"Yeah. She's at the senior center."

"So she's not even here?" Karl's hostility toward the doctor was almost palpable when he turned to him to add, "And you don't seem to have your medical bag, anyway."

Betcher inched toward the steps. "It's in my car. But I have to go."

"No!" I shouted. "We were in the middle of a conversation."

"It will have to wait. I have another engagement." And with that, Dr. Betcher practically tripped off the porch and down the sidewalk.

As for Karl, he bit into his apple, juice spraying from his mouth. "He doesn't care about Rose."

"What?" I sniffled and did my best to wipe my runny nose with my gloved hand without him noticing. Because it was late afternoon and the sky was growing dark, I was pretty sure I succeeded.

"Doris, he was here to see you. He's been asking around about us."

"Us? There's no us." I was still upset with him. How could he suspect anyone in my family of criminal behavior?

"Well, he seems to think there is. Or I should say that he hopes there isn't. See, he wants to ask you out."

"How do you—"

"Secrets don't stay that way for long around here. You know that."

"But why do you care?" Afraid he might say, *Trust me, I don't,* I quickly changed the question into a statement. "I mean, it's really none of your business."

"He's a jackass! Being employed by the county board, I deal with him on a regular basis. And ever since the robbery at the pharmacy, I've had to spend even more time with him." He stopped for a beat. "He's also a womanizer."

I thought of Grace. "Yet you've done nothing about that."

"I can't if no one files a complaint."

I was worn out and cranky. And arguing with Karl wouldn't convince him of Erin's innocence.

Besides, I appreciated his interest in me—or more accurately, my safety. Even if I'd never admit it to anyone. His concern warmed my insides like hot coffee on a cold day. Speaking of which… "How about a cup of coffee, Karl?" Before overthinking the invitation, which probably would have resulted in me withdrawing it, I opened the front door and motioned him inside.

While appearing wary, he followed me through the foyer and into the dining room after I convinced him that he didn't need to remove his boots.

"What's with the lanterns?" He pointed to them as we passed the patio door.

"We used them before the electricity got hooked up. Will took a couple back to the farm but insisted I keep those. I've been meaning to put them in the garage."

Entering the kitchen, he waved his apple core at me, and I gestured toward the cupboard beneath the sink. He opened the door and tossed the core into the trash. "Hey, did you get a whiff of Betcher's cologne? It smelled like 'eau de lutefisk.'"

"Oh? You're familiar with that scent?"

He sat at the kitchen table and unzipped his jacket. "Still a smartass, huh?" His lips twitched, like he was doing his best to refrain from laughing.

As for me, I set my purse on the counter and poured coffee and water into the coffee maker before draping my coat over the back of the chair opposite him. "It's too early for supper," I said as I sat down, "even for us old fogies. But I have some caramel chocolate chip bars. Grace brought them home from the café. Would you care for one?"

"No, I'm fine."

"You sure?"

"Yep."

I had a lot to say but found I wasn't eager to begin. Discussing Erin would likely end with us yelling at each other, and I wanted to delay that. You see, it felt good to sit there with him, pretending that my life was normal. So that's what I did, while the coffee pot gurgled and the refrigerator hummed.

And Karl? He jingled the contents of his pants pockets. The setting was clearly too intimate for him—the two of us at the kitchen table, like an old couple. I smiled at his unease but hid it behind my fist while pretending to cough. Most of the time, I was the one who felt awkward during our encounters. Being in my house—on my own turf, so to speak—evidently made a difference. I'd have to remember that.

For now, though, it was in my best interest—and my duty as a host—to make him comfortable. As a result, I did what Minnesotans routinely do when in search of a tension-free topic of conversation. I turned to the weather. "I understand it's supposed to get nasty overnight."

At that, Karl visibly relaxed, removing his hands from his pockets. "According to the radar, three to four inches of snow. Wind gusts up to fifty miles an hour."

"That'll make for a real mess in the morning."

He nodded. "I can drop by and give you a hand with the shoveling, if you want."

Anyone with an ounce of common sense would have accepted his offer. But I couldn't. As far as I was concerned, clearing the driveway of someone other than a family member or a neighbor was far more intimate than visiting over coffee. "No, that's okay. I can handle it. I have a new snowblower."

"Oh. That's good. What is it?"

"Huh?" I fiddled with the grocery list lying in the middle of the table.

"The snowblower," he said. "What kind is it?"

"Oh, a Toro."

"Yeah, they're good machines." Obviously, that was all he had to say about that because he went back to jingling his pockets.

And since I, too, had nothing more to add, I retreated to the counter to pour us each some coffee. "Black?"

"Yep."

Giving him one cup, I sat down with the other.

As I sipped, I watched him squirm for some time before deciding to put him out of his misery—by getting down to business. But I couldn't start by discussing Erin. That would have made me emotional. So I began with, "Any sign of Tweety?"

He set his cup down. It was plain to see that he was relieved to discuss something less personal. At least when chatting with me. And I wasn't sure what to make of that. "No," he said. "No sign of her yet."

"Can't you ping her cell phone or something?"

He almost smiled. "We're trying, Doris, but nothing gets done as fast as it does on television."

With his index finger, he began wiping away the crumbs that were caught along the edge of my drop-leaf table. Of course, some women would have been mortified, presuming that he was criticizing their housekeeping. But it didn't bother me in the least. Although that wouldn't have been the case years ago.

While married, I'd taken great pride in my house-cleaning abilities. I was a pathetic cook but a fantastic housekeeper. Grace said it was because I cleaned at night, when the kids were asleep, Bill was out gallivanting, and I was consumed by angst. She claimed that when things grew especially tense between Bill and me, she smelled disinfectant and furniture polish all the way down our gravel drive.

Following Bill's death, however, I seldom cleaned. A spotless house was no longer important to me. Consequently, Karl's "white glove" treatment caused me no consternation.

"As for the $100 bills I got from you," Karl said, disrupting my thoughts, "Gustaf confirmed that the paper band around them is identical to the bands on the other money packs in the bank."

"Do the serial numbers match those on record?"

"The bank doesn't track serial numbers."

"Oh. Umm…" I cleared my mind with a shake of my head, determined to remain focused on our chat and not his finger. "Does Tweety have an account there?"

"Yeah, she does all of her banking with Gustaf, but she pretty much lives paycheck to paycheck, so there isn't any reason for her to have that much money on hand. In other words, the money she has most likely came from Wilma's accounts, via Buck Daniel."

Karl wiped his finger on the front of his shirt, then placed his hand in his lap, which was a good thing because I was just about to stab him with the pen lying next to my grocery list. Okay, his Mr. Clean routine may have made me a bit batty, after all.

Nevertheless, I attempted to act normal. "Are you certain of the money's origin, Karl? Last time you were here, you weren't."

"Well, I hadn't spoken with Gustaf then." He waited a beat. "And I was angry with you. You can drive me crazy."

I went squinty-eyed. "In my defense, it's a short drive."

"You really are a pain in the—"

"Hey!" I snatched the pen and my grocery list. "I'm not such a bad person. I can be nice. For example, I want to thank you for clearing Will."

He flashed a calloused palm in my direction. "No thanks necessary. Facts are facts. The evidence doesn't point to Will as Buck Daniel's killer."

I doodled on my grocery list. "What about Erin?" I drew a poor likeness of a cow next to the word "milk."

"Doris, she lied to—"

"Yeah, yeah, we've been all through that. I'm talking—"

"A second time."

"What?" I dropped my pen.

"She lied about where she was the night of the robbery. The night Buck was killed."

I set aside my grocery list.

"When I left here last night, I drove back to the office to meet with Tweety," he explained. "As you're aware, she didn't show. But while I waited, I reamed out Ed for how he'd handled things at her apartment on Saturday night. He got scared that I was gonna fire him or something and came clean about everything, including the fact that Erin wasn't with him from around 10:45 p.m. to 1:15 a.m. on the night of the robbery."

He sighed, sounding old beyond his years. "I won't even ask if you knew because I'm sure you did."

I couldn't look at him. My eyes would give me away. Staring at my coffee cup probably did, too.

"Doris, I hafta take Erin in for questioning. Do you have any idea where she is? Her car's parked behind the café, but Grace claims she doesn't know anything."

My heart picked up its pace, as if determined to outrun Karl and his words. And while I appreciated its resolve, I knew my heart and the rest of me were stuck right where they were. "Both Erin and I were at the café this morning, Karl. Why didn't you say anything then?"

He arched a brow. "Did you really want me to lead your daughter out of a busy café in handcuffs?"

Hearing that, I couldn't process anything else that he said. His lips seemed out of sync with the words emanating from them. Even so, I understood one thing for certain: Sheriff Ingebretsen suspected my daughter of murder and appeared resolute in arresting her.

Chapter 24

After Karl left, I was at my wits' end. I hunted all over for my cell phone, only to discover it in my purse, where I'd already searched twice. I called Erin and explained what had transpired, and I assured her that I hadn't let on where she was. Next, I called Grace, who said she was still at the café and would remain there most of the evening. After that, I picked up Rose, who wasn't ready to leave the senior center.

As we headed downtown, she grumbled, "I could of gotten a ride home later."

"We have to meet with Grace," I replied before relaying to her that the sheriff had insisted on questioning Erin and that Dr. Betcher was "well known" to Tweety. "So," I concluded, "even though we can't do much about Karl being a first-class jerk, we can—and have to—come up with a plan to zero in on both Betcher and Tweety."

Since the café was closed and the front door was locked, I drove around to the rear of the building and parked in the alley, behind Grace's jeep. Other than the dirty light above the café's back door and the blue light of a street lamp fifty feet away, the alley was dark and the dumpster sat in the shadows, hiding who knew what.

Insisting that Rose stay put until I could assist her, I made my way around the hood of the car, carefully sliding my feet along the icy pavement. *Ting!* I lurched, and if I hadn't grasped the Ford emblem on the grill, I would have landed on my rear end.

I spotted a cat playing with an empty pop can. It eyed me with an expression that indicated it found me lacking. A wuss, if you will. Then again, I may have been projecting. The alley frightened me. And my family's recent troubles and my inability to remedy them had left me feeling woefully inadequate. Even so, I scowled at the cat, letting it know that while I might be a wuss, I'd sleep indoors when the day was done.

"I can walk," Rose groused as I made an effort to help her from the car.

"Fine." I dropped her arm. "You're awfully owly."

"Well, I was on fire. I already had two bingos and knew I'd win the blackout game. I could feel it in my bones."

"Rose, you have osteoporosis. Your bones are full of holes. You're feeling air. Or blood. Not bingo wins."

"Goes to show what you know."

"Well, excuse me. I thought you'd want to be in on this conversation."

"I do. But it could of waited another hour. Nothin' would of changed by then."

The café door squeaked as I ushered in my ill-tempered companion. "What was the blackout prize?"

Rose stomped her boots on the floor mat. "Two free Meals on Wheels tickets."

"Worth around $10, right? So I'll give you $10."

"That's not the point."

"What are you two squabbling about?" Grace stood behind the stainless-steel prep table, carving raw meat into serving-sized slices. Her apron was smeared with blood, as were her hands and the table.

"Doris is being Mrs. Bossy Pants." Rose paid little attention to the meat piled high on one side of the table or the mound of discarded fat and bones on the other. Having lived the vast majority of her life here, among farmers and hunters, she was comfortable with the various stages of butchering and meat preparation.

I, on the other hand, avoided anything to do with raw meat because of my overactive gag reflex.

"She's angry because I picked her up before the blackout game," I said to Grace while hooking a thumb in Rose's direction.

Grace, in turn, peered at Rose. "Don't you play enough bingo at assisted living?"

"You can never play too much bingo. And bingo at the senior center is way better. At assisted living, the prizes are usually candy bars or pieces of fruit, and fresh fruit gives me the trots."

Handing me her coat, Rose climbed onto a stool at the prep table. "So, Grace, what ya preparin' there?"

"Venison steaks for the Wildlife Feed. It's only two days away."

"Yah, well, I haven't been to it in a couple years." Rose's tone was laced with self-pity. "I guess everyone's been too busy to take me."

My eyes crossed. "Rose, you know darn well everyone in the family works this dinner. It's a fundraiser. And you also know that we always come and get you the following morning, so we can spend Thanksgiving Day together."

"You mean, so I can eat leftovers."

Grace waved a serious-looking knife. "After preparing all of this food, I'm not about to cook a traditional Thanksgiving dinner, too."

Rose appeared sheepish. "Sorry. I'm just upset." She blew out a tired breath. "Now I can only pray to Jesus, Mary, and Joseph that Leah Erickson doesn't win the blackout game. Accordin' to practically everyone at the senior center, she gloats for days after a big win."

"Well, if you want to spend Thanksgiving somewhere else, that's fine with me." After hanging both of our coats in the utility closet, I claimed my own stool but did my best to look anywhere except at the raw meat, the clumps of fat, or the heap of bloody bones. "I certainly don't want you with us if you don't want to be here."

"Of course I wanna be here." She swiveled toward Grace. "So what can I do for you now and at the dinner? And more importantly, what ya servin'?"

Grace stabbed the slab of venison on the carving board, freeing her hands to gesture as she spoke. "I've got everything under control for now. The pheasant and walleye are prepped and in the walk-in cooler. And, as you can see, I'm almost done with the venison. But there will be plenty for you to do at the dinner itself. Allie's still sick. And God only knows where Tweety is or what will happen once she's found." She eyed me. "Remind Erin, Will, and Sophie, okay?"

The metallic smell of blood bit my nose, prompting me to swallow hard and scoot my stool back a foot or two. "Erin may be unavailable." I then repeated everything I had shared with Rose.

Once I was finished, Rose repositioned her dentures with a click. "I still refuse to believe that Dr. Betcher and Tweety were in cahoots. Tweety might of killed Buck Daniel on her own. But Dr. Betcher had no part in it."

I recounted Erin's argument: "Buck Daniel was killed shortly after the robbery and long before most people in town even knew about it. But Betcher knew."

"And," Rose countered, "if Tweety was involved in those robbery shenanigans, she would of known, too."

"But why would she be a part of the robbery?" Grace tossed several more pieces of venison into the roasting pan. "She doesn't do drugs. Never has, from what I gather."

"Well," I said, "whether or not she was directly involved in the robbery, she was aware of Buck's plan. I overheard her discussing everything with Berta in the grocery store the day after the robbery took place. She justified all of Buck's actions, including stealing the pills."

Rose actually raised her hand, as if seeking permission to speak. "The way I figure it, followin' the robbery, Tweety met up with Buck. But rather than helpin' him get out of town, she killed him, got rid of the pills and the backpack, but kept the cash for herself."

"Whoa!" Grace was clearly impressed. "That was some quick thinking, Rose."

Rose tapped her temple. "No moss growin' here."

I disagreed. Not about the moss. But about Tweety killing Buck on her own. "Do you truly believe Tweety could have done all of that by herself? Without leaving a trace? I don't. Besides, we can't forget, Erin's convinced that Betcher's the killer or at least involved to some extent."

"And what did Karl have to say about that?" Grace wanted to know.

"We didn't discuss it. After he confirmed that the money in Tweety's apartment came from Wilma's accounts, he started accusing Erin of this and that, and things deteriorated. He stormed out before I had a chance to ask him about Betcher."

Rose pointed a crooked finger in my face. "Maybe Erin only thinks that Dr. Betcher's connected to the murder because you haven't told her about Tweety havin' Wilma's money."

I shook my head dismissively. "Rose, there's more to it than that."

"I don't know," she argued. "Holdin' back information doesn't seem like a good idea. Especially since we're supposedly workin' together on this."

"I have to agree." Grace leveled her knife at me. "You should talk to Erin. Tell her about our visit to Tweety's apartment."

I sighed and stared at the floor. They were right, of course. Erin deserved to know everything, even though I doubted it would alter her take on Betcher's involvement in the murder. And because of that, I continued to drag my feet when it came to confessing what Grace and I had done. Still… "Okay, I'll think about it."

Rose reached over and patted my hand. "It's the right thing to do. Plus, as I said, I don't see Dr. Betcher partnerin' with Tweety Jacobson. Why would he?"

Grace waggled her brows. "Do I have to explain the facts of life to you, Rose?" Glancing my way, she added, "The far better question is, why would she want to be with him?"

"Well," I replied, "he is the chief doctor in the county. And even if we aren't impressed by that, some people are. And then, of course, there's his car."

Grace outright laughed.

Meanwhile, Rose applied a serious expression to her face. "Don't be too quick to dismiss the influence of a car there. A car can make a girl go loopy sometimes. I should know."

She stared at the stainless-steel refrigerator, as if watching something in the shine. "Did I ever tell you about when I went out with Ted Torgason? He drove a 1954 ruby-red Corvette. I'd spend time with him and that car at the drop of a hat. I'd even skip work at the creamery. Yah, deep down, I knew he was no good. But I didn't wanna give up ridin' in that car." She shrugged her bony shoulders, as if to say, *Who could blame me?*

"Anyways, when I discovered he'd been two-timin' me, I actually got livid with both of them—him and the car—like the car was partly responsible for our relationship going kaput. Silly, I know, but that's how I felt. To pay them back, I poured uncooked rice down the Corvette's heatin' vents and—"

"Oh my God!" Grace dropped her knife, and it clattered against the metal table. "That's where you got the idea, Doris?"

"Yeah, well, Rose might have mentioned it."

"You mean to say you did the old rice trick?" Rose beamed with pride. "You never told me."

"It was no big deal," I assured her. "And it's really not worth discussing now, either. So don't, particularly around Sheriff Ingebretsen. In fact, let's move on."

"Not so fast." Rose obviously wasn't ready to go anywhere else just yet. "Have either of you ever tried any of my other revenge tactics?" She allowed her gaze to shift between Grace and me. "My favorite's the skunk payback. I used it on Bob Iverson."

Merely mentioning his name caused her to chuckle. "He really wasn't much of a catch, but I went out with him bein' the war was on and most of the good men were gone. He was 4-F. He didn't pass the physical because he had six toes on his left foot, and the army didn't think he'd be able to handle all the marchin'. I personally thought he'd be better at it, havin' that extra piggy and all. But the army said no. Go figure."

221

She clicked her dentures, struggling to get a decent fit. "Anyways, after he two-timed me, I caught a skunk in a live trap and set it free in his house. When he got home from bein' with Harriot, the harlot, the skunk did what skunks do, and Bob had to move out of his house and back in with his mother. Not at first, mind ya. She made him live in the garage until he quit stinkin."

Neither Grace nor I said a word. We just stared at her, agog.

As for Rose, she acted as if what she'd done was perfectly reasonable. But who was I to judge? I had no regrets about Destiny Delovely's Mustang.

"The point bein'," Rose went on to say, "a two-timin' man can make a woman take drastic measures."

While I knew first-hand that she spoke the truth, I couldn't figure out how her point pertained to our discussion.

"You see," she added, as if reading my mind, "since Buck Daniel two-timed Erin, he probably did the same to Tweety. But when Tweety found out, she more than likely decided to kill him. Tweety can be pretty vicious, don't ya know. Accordin' to Ole, she's so ornery that when she dies, the devil won't even let her into hell."

Rose eyed Grace and me, sparks of life flashing through her murky irises. "Because Tweety no doubt knew about Buck's plan to take Wilma's money, she must of decided to wait until after he did that before she whacked him. But bein' he withdrew the money just a few hours before he robbed the pharmacy, she ended up killin' him and stealin' the money at the same time. Then she started spendin' the money right here in town." She tsked. "Dr. Betcher wouldn't of let any partner of his do that. He's too smart."

Again, Grace and I just stared. I didn't necessarily agree with all aspects of Rose's theory, yet I found it compelling and her, extraordinary. No doubt about it, Rose O'Brian remained one sharp cookie. And I decided right then and there that I wanted to be just like her when I was ninety. Well, maybe not just like her. I wasn't a fan of her gravity-fraught body. Not that mine was great. But at least I didn't worry about pinching my boobs in the waistband of my lavender sweatpants. Not yet, at any rate.

With a clang, Grace secured the cover on her roaster and lugged it to the fridge. "When we finally get this mess settled, we should take a trip. The three of us and Erin. We deserve a getaway."

I agreed, which surprised her.

"Really, Doris?" She slid the roaster onto an empty shelf. "You never go on vacation."

"That's not true. Bill and I wintered in Arizona two years ago and Florida the year before that."

She was quick to refute me. "You rented a trailer in a park full of other Midwestern farmers desperate to escape the cold. You spent your days playing whist and bingo. Not exactly what I call an adventurous getaway."

"We enjoyed ourselves."

Grace returned to the table. "Clobber me if I ever suggest doing anything so boring."

"Keep it up and I'll reserve you a camper, then find a big stick."

Rose edged off her stool. "You two go on arguin' there. I hafta grab my purse. I forgot it in the car, and I wanna take my pill, so I can get some shut-eye later."

I raised my hand. "I'll get it."

Rose pressed her fists to her hips—or the place her hips would have been if, during the last several years, they hadn't slid down her legs and disappeared altogether. "Doris, you're smotherin' me. Now go ahead and fight with your sister. I'll be back in a minute. Then we can discuss what to do about Erin. And where we should go on our vacation. I'm thinkin' Hawaii." With that, she performed a few hula motions before trundling toward the door without her coat.

I knew better than to say anything more.

Chapter 25

After Rose made her way outside, I held my breath, averted my eyes, and filled another roaster with raw venison before shoving it in the fridge, next to the one Grace already had in there. The shelves above and below them were empty, but Grace assured me that they'd be filled with Jell-O salads, hot dishes, and bars by Wednesday morning.

As she finished updating me on the food lineup, which included rhubarb pudding among many of my other favorites, a shriek pierced the air. It came from the alley, and the two of us rushed to the door.

Yanking it open, I peered outside. Rose was on the ground near my car. I expected a leg or an arm to be posed at an odd angle, but all of her appendages seemed to be aligned properly. Still, she was sitting on the ground, her head lolled against the building, and the alley cat at her side.

"Shoo!" I brushed the cat away and crouched beside her. "What happened? Are you okay?" A quick survey indicated no blood. "You shouldn't have come out here. I knew you'd slip."

"Uff-da. I didn't slip. I got pushed."

"What?" I glanced at the cat. While I didn't like it much, I couldn't believe it was the guilty party, unless... "You tripped over the cat?"

As Grace stepped closer, she also shooed the cat. But because her hands were stained with venison blood, her efforts accomplished even less than mine.

"No," Rose groaned. "Someone came around the corner, pushed me down, and ran away."

With only the dim light from the fixture above the door to guide me, I checked the perimeter of the building. Because the snow was hard-packed, I didn't spot any fresh footprints. Proceeding to the middle of the alley and on toward Main Street, I saw no one. Hallock was a ghost town.

I was about to head back to the café, assuming Rose's assailant was long gone, when out of the corner of my eye, I caught a glimpse of someone among the shadows on the alley side of the brewery across the street. I jogged to the curb to get a closer look, and the person took off. No surprise there. Although I did surprise myself when I gave chase.

From my initial vantage point, about forty feet back, I noted that Rose's attacker was good sized and dressed in dark clothing, from skull cap to running shoes. I desperately wanted to close the gap between us, but I was afraid to move any faster because the ice underfoot had me slipping as it was.

Taking a hard right, the person I was after fled down another alley and through the dim glow of another streetlight. Even though I still had them in my sights, my breathing had become ragged, and I was losing ground.

Reaching the post office, the perpetrator turned right again, as I involuntarily bent at the waist and gulped air. Only after breathing in enough oxygen to ward off a heart attack did I push on. But, by then, it was too late. I saw no one.

Limping back to the café, I massaged the stitch in my side. And when a breeze swirled around me, I hugged myself, wishing I had worn my jacket.

What would you have done if you'd actually caught the guy? I wondered while reviewing the chase in my mind. Wrestle them to the ground? I hadn't wrestled anyone in fifty years. Not since I was twelve, when I'd pounded Grace for blabbing to Johnny Larson that I begged Mom for a training bra, only to have her say, "No. They aren't big enough."

Approaching the café's back door, I came across a small mound of blood-stained snow, and my breath stalled in my achy throat.

"Is Rose okay?" I rasped as I rushed inside.

"She's fine." Grace hovered over her, a cloth in hand.

"Then why is there blood outside?" I blinked to adjust my eyes to the light. "There wasn't any before."

Grace wiped smudges from Rose's sweatsuit. "She made me clean the venison blood from my hands before helping her off the ground."

Rose sat cattywampus on her stool. "I didn't want her to ruin my clothes. Blood's hard to remove from polyester."

"Was someone out there?" Grace asked.

"Yeah. One person. But I couldn't catch them."

"Any idea who it was?"

"No. They were bigger and faster than me."

Rose remained silent and pale, leading me to wonder out loud, "Are you sure you're okay?"

"Oh, yah. I got a mite cold and dirty, that's all." She hesitated. "I guess I got kind of scared, too." Her brogue was back and thicker than at any time since the night of the robbery.

"We've been arguing about going to the hospital," Grace informed me.

Rose extended her chin, elongating the waddle beneath it. "I told her I won't go, but she can if she wants."

"At the very least, you should see a doctor." I pressed my hand against her forehead. Why? I had no idea. It wasn't like she'd come down with the flu. Besides, my hand was too cold to determine anything, anyhow. "You look kind of pasty."

"Of course I look pasty. So do you and Grace. It's winter. And we live in Minnesota, for land sakes."

"This isn't up for debate." I employed my stern mother's voice, the one I'd used on my kids when they were belligerent—and far younger.

"Then call Dr. Betcher," she said, "and get him to come over here, because I won't go to the hospital. And now that's he's back in town, he's the only doctor I'll let examine me."

She assumed that my poor opinion of Dr. Betcher would prevent me from placing the call. I could tell by the I-dare-you look in her eyes. But she was wrong.

I opened my purse and retrieved my wallet. "I have his card. And he wrote his personal cell phone number on the back."

"Why on earth do you have—" Grace began.

But I interrupted. "He gave it to me the night of the robbery. When we took Rose home against his advice."

⊗ ⊗ ⊗

I had barely returned my phone to my purse when Dr. Betcher burst through the back door. "I happened to be nearby." He was dressed in dark athletic clothing: a navy ski jacket and skull cap, nylon workout pants, and tennis shoes. He looked haggard.

228

Right away I got suspicious. "Were you out jogging or something?" Rose may have adeptly argued the unlikelihood of him teaming up with Tweety to murder Buck Daniel, but I remained unconvinced of his innocence.

Stuffing his gloves into his jacket pockets, Dr. Betcher turned his back on me and my inquiry and knelt next to Rose. "What happened, dear?"

She repeated the story as he checked her pulse. Opening his medical bag, he retrieved a pen light, and shined a fine beam in her eyes. After that, he placed his stethoscope against her chest and said, "Big breaths."

"Huh?" Rose glanced down at her chest. "You really think so? They used to be way bigger. When I was younger."

Betcher's cheeks flushed the color of Grace's venison.

I raised my voice and spoke through a barely restrained giggle. "Rose, he wants you to take some big breaths."

"Oh." Her cheeks pinked up. "I can do that."

When she was done, Dr. Betcher confirmed to the floor because he was obviously too embarrassed to address her face, "You're fine, Rose."

And Rose lost no time in shooting Grace and me an I-told-you-so glare. "I thought as much, but you know how some folks are."

"Well, you can never be too careful. Doris was right to call me. And because I want to be extra careful, I'd like to admit you to the hospital overnight for observation."

Rose almost fell off her stool. "Wait a gall-darn minute! You just said I was fine."

"I don't want to take any chances. I like you, and I want you around for a long time to come. My medical practice wouldn't be the same without you."

Grace and I circled away from Betcher and Rose long enough to point our index fingers down our throats and pretend to gag.

"Well, if you insist," Rose acquiesced, as we spooled back around. "But just for tonight." Either her fall had left her with a tick, or she'd fluttered her eyelashes at him.

"That's all I'm asking." He assisted her to her feet.

"I'll grab her coat," I informed him, "along with mine."

"What?" Dr. Betcher was clearly surprised. "Doris, it's not necessary for you to come with us."

"Oh, believe me, it is." With a mere glance, I assured both Grace and Rose that Dr. Betcher wasn't about to take Rose anywhere on her own.

Grace tilted her head in agreement, while Rose conveyed by way of the evil eye that she'd thoroughly enjoy slapping me. I didn't care.

I retrieved our coats and we were almost out the door when Deputy Monson and a howl of cold air stumbled in.

The deputy wore the requisite brown bomber jacket and fleece-lined hat, the flaps hanging over his ears and the strap dangling beneath his chin. "Where do you think you're going?" He slammed the door shut.

"Who called you?" I asked.

Grace answered the deputy first. "They're taking Rose to the hospital for monitoring."

She then told me, "I called the sheriff's office as soon as I brought Rose back inside."

"I'm fine," Rose confirmed for the deputy's benefit. "Dr. Betcher just likes to fuss over me." Another flutter of her eyelashes. She definitely needed her head examined.

Deputy Monson's gaze darted between Grace and me, as if unsure where to direct his comments. He ultimately chose a spot somewhere between us. Fine with me. I couldn't look him in the eye, anyhow. "I checked the entire block," he reported to that spot, "but I didn't see anything other than some snow by the door that appears to have blood in it. I'll take a sample and—"

"No need." Grace flapped her hand. "It's venison blood."

"Venison blood?" he echoed.

She didn't elaborate.

"What about the sheriff?" I wiggled my index finger to get the deputy's attention. "Is he stopping by?"

"No." Deputy Monson sniffled against his drippy nose. "I can handle this by myself."

That was debatable. I'd seen him in action. And in my opinion, Rose deserved better.

"It's just that Dr. Betcher and I were with the sheriff earlier today," I said, "so I guess I expected him to show up now, too."

"Well, he can't. He's working another case."

"Another case?" Because Hallock wasn't exactly a hotbed of criminal activity, I was certain "the other case" involved the search for Tweety.

Deputy Monson tightened his lips until they all but disappeared. He had learned his lesson. He wasn't about to say anything more.

Eventually, though, he had to open his mouth to speak to Rose. "I need to get a few things straight with you," he said, while Dr. Betcher appeared as if he might object. But Ed hurried and asked, "Are you sure you didn't just fall out there? The alley's pretty darn slippery. I almost took a tumble myself."

Rose narrowed her eyes. "I got shoved, young man."

"Someone ran down the alley," I added by way of confirmation. "I chased them, but they got away. I didn't get much of a look at them, either."

"Was it a man or a woman?" the deputy asked.

I had to confess, "I have no idea. Just a good-sized individual."

He was visibly disappointed in my observational skills. Then again, I wasn't particularly impressed with his law enforcement prowess.

"How about you?" He again addressed Rose. "Can you remember anything about your attacker?"

"Well, he wore a ski mask."

"Uh-huh!" he shouted, and we all jumped. "So it was a man!"

Rose looked at Ed as if she wanted to slap him. Not long ago, she had liked the guy. She thought he was smart enough to clear Erin. But now? Obviously, not so much. "I don't know, Deputy," she said. "It happened so fast that he—or she—may not of seen me at all. At least not before runnin' me down."

"What?" Ed edged backward until he bumped against the door. "You mean you weren't intentionally attacked?"

"Uff-da, how am I supposed to know their intentions?" The adrenaline surge caused by the assault had begun to ebb, and the reality of what had happened was settling in. Rose's shoulders curved as she started to fold in on herself. "I grabbed my purse from the car, and the next thing I knew, I was on the ground. The person who ran into me—or pushed me or whatever—stopped for a second. That's how I saw that they had a ski mask pulled over their face. Then they took off."

Dr. Betcher slid in front of Rose. "And we're going to do the same, Deputy Monson. Take off, that is. Any other questions will have to wait for another time."

Chapter 26

When I woke up Tuesday morning, I forced myself out of bed and peeked between the blinds. Four to five inches of snow had fallen overnight. Even so, I wouldn't have to get dressed and clear my sidewalk and driveway because Will had done it. I watched him push my snowblower back into the garage and lean my shovel against the outside wall before returning to his pickup.

Chilled, I slid back under the covers, grabbed my phone, and texted, *Come in. I'll make coffee.* It would be good for him to be here when Erin arrived.

He responded, *Cant. 2 much to do.*

Noting that it was later than I had thought, I again rolled out of bed, padded into the bathroom, and used the toilet before cowering in front of the scale. After winning a debate with myself, however, I skipped checking my weight. I already had too much stress in my life. I didn't need any more by watching the numbers on my scale climb like those on a gas pump.

Instead, I splashed water on my face, patted it dry, and stared into the mirror. My mother stared back. When had I grown so old? The years had passed too quickly, even if some of them had been hellacious. I flicked the loose skin along my jawline. Oh well, at least it was my mother in the mirror and not my grandmother. Or worse yet, Grandpa Anderson.

Once downstairs, I started a pot of coffee. While it perked, I paced through the dining room and the living room and back into the kitchen, repeatedly checking the time and the driveway. I was on the lookout for Erin. She had phoned late last night, updating me with the news that she'd spoken with the sheriff and was to meet with him first thing this morning. I, in turn, had filled her in on Rose. And before hanging up, she'd promised to stop by the house as soon as the sheriff was done with her. Unless he threw her in jail. In that case, she'd only call. I assured her she wasn't funny.

When the coffee quit dribbling into the pot, I filled my cup and waited for the aroma to raise my energy level. It didn't. So rather than making another pass through the main floor, I opted for a seat at the round oak table in the dining room. Almost daily, the sun gleamed through the bay window and the patio door, encouraging the plants in the room to stretch and me to thrive. But that wouldn't happen this morning—not my part, anyhow.

I surveyed the stray pieces surrounding the Last Supper puzzle in front of me. My brain was foggy, and I felt weighed down by melancholy. Okay, by a few extra pounds, too. But mostly by melancholy.

As I picked up a piece, thinking it might be the one that would finish Judas's face, I accidently elbowed several other pieces onto the floor. And while I was stooped over to gather them up, a couple stomps in the entry signaled Erin's arrival and startled me into ramming my head against the table's underbelly.

As I checked my head for blood, my daughter plodded stocking-footed through the foyer and into the dining room. She was dressed in a black pantsuit and her hair was pulled back into its customary bun. She even wore a dash of eye makeup.

"I couldn't sleep," she said while continuing into the kitchen, where I heard her pour some coffee. "Then it took me an hour to shovel my driveway. One of these days I'll have to build a garage and buy a snowblower."

Once back in the dining room, she sat down with a sigh. "I went to the hospital to check on Nana. It was like six a.m., and she already was holding court in her room."

"I'll pick her up after Betcher's done with rounds." No blood on my head but definitely an egg. "Will spent the night with her, but he was just out front, moving snow, so I assume Sophie's with her now."

"She is. She said Will wasn't too happy about having to sleep at the hospital. Especially in Rose's room." Erin gave the puzzle a cursory glance. Her eyes were red and puffy and as tired-looking as her voice sounded. "I guess her snoring is a lot like rolling thunder."

That explained why Will had refused my coffee invitation. He was angry. I figured as much since no farmer was too busy for morning coffee post-harvest. "Yeah," I said, "Will thought I was ridiculous for insisting that she not be left alone there. But he wouldn't let me stay. Said that after sitting in a chair all night, I'd hobble for a week."

After a nod to indicate that she agreed with her brother, Erin drank her coffee, while I made to mental note to patch things up with Will. Later. Right now, I had to find out about Erin's meeting with the sheriff.

As I waited for her to speak, I reminded myself to let her raise the subject. After all, reasonable mothers didn't nag. Two seconds later, though, when I couldn't bear her silence any longer, I blurted, "What happened with the sheriff?"

She chewed her bottom lip. "Odds are, the county board will insist that he fire me."

I think I heard my heart break. "I'm sorry, Erin."

"I explained why I lied, and he said he understood, but..." She teared up.

"When will you find out for sure?"

"The county board meets next week. Gustaf's already received 'renewed calls for my dismissal.'" Her tenor implied a direct quote. "However, getting fired is the least of my worries."

She fidgeted with the handle of her mug. "Karl questioned me some more about Buck's death. He said that since I lied and don't have anyone to corroborate my whereabouts for several hours on the night Buck was murdered, I'll remain a suspect. And suspended."

While it wasn't what either of us had wanted to hear, I wasn't surprised.

"But he also said that he recovered some of the money Buck withdrew from Wilma's bank accounts." She gave me a second to ponder that, though under the circumstances, I didn't need that long. "The events surrounding the recovery point to someone other than me being involved. But he doesn't want me to mention that to anyone, so mum's the word."

I put my cup to my lips, only to set it down again. "Did he say anything else about the money or how it was discovered?"

"No. And I haven't heard a thing, which means he must have pursued the lead himself."

"Ed isn't aware of anything?"

"I called him on my way over here. He's in the dark, too."

Hmm. Maybe my antics in Tweety's apartment could remain hidden from the general public—and my children—after all. True, I didn't like secrets. Although I didn't care to be humiliated in the eyes of my children, either.

But who was I kidding? I had to tell Erin what had happened, if for no other reason than I couldn't depend on Karl to keep quiet. "So," I began, "you've got to be pleased that Karl's looking at other people." It's just that making my confession wasn't easy, which was saying a lot given that I was Catholic.

"Yeah, unless that's just what he wants me to believe."

"Huh?"

"Karl's a master at lulling people into complacency, Mom. He leads them to believe that they're in the clear. Then, when they let down their guard, he swoops in and gets them. Of course, we've never had a murder around here before, but that's what he's done in robbery and drug cases."

"Really?" I had never viewed Karl as sneaky, the drive-in incident with his old girlfriend notwithstanding. Then again, I didn't really know him anymore. Forty-five years had passed since we'd spent much time together. He may have changed. Most likely he had. Heck, for all I knew, he'd become an ax murderer. An ax murderer who couldn't keep a secret.

"Well, I suppose," Erin said, slapping her thighs, "I better go."

"No! Not yet. I've got something to say." Anxiety pooled in my stomach as I started with, "On Saturday night, Grace and I snuck into Tweety's apartment..." And it nearly overflowed, which would have been incredibly embarrassing, by the time I ended with, "Anyhow, I didn't tell you earlier because I didn't want you to think we were loony."

My daughter stared at me stone-faced as she processed everything. I practically saw the wheels rotating in her head. And when she got done, she scooted back her chair, folded her arms across her chest, and pursed her lips. Then, after a few moments, she doubled over with laughter. "I can't believe it! I just can't believe it."

Because I was relieved that she wasn't furious with me, I laughed, too. But it wasn't long before our laughter gave way to tears. Erin likely cried because she was scared of what lay ahead for her, while I cried because I loved her more than life itself.

"I really can't believe you two did that for me." She wiped her face with her napkin and, in the process, smeared mascara across her temples.

"I can't believe it, either."

Catching her breath, she hiccupped. "I suppose you don't want me to say anything to Ed."

I flashed her the side eye. "Not unless you have a death wish."

"Okay. I'll merely tell him that you learned Tweety has some of Buck's money. He'll assume you got the information from Karl."

Erin stood, dropping her napkin on the table, next to her cup. "Speaking of Ed, I'm off to meet him. We have a couple of leads to follow."

"Care to share?"

"Only if they pan out."

I cleaned the mascara from her face with my napkin. "I'm sorry I didn't get a chance to speak with Gerti yesterday. I got flustered when Betcher showed up here, and I guess I forgot about it. But I'll do it today, before I check Rose out of the hospital."

"Don't worry. It's probably not important, anyway. At dinner last night, Les—I mean, Dr. Osgood—said Gerti's been head nurse way too long. He said most staff members, including Dr. Betcher, agree that she should retire, but Betcher won't push her out because she's been there since Moses was a baby."

"Hey!" I punched her in the shoulder. "She's only my age. She's not even eligible for social security yet."

Erin scrunched her face and rubbed her arm, but she didn't apologize. She simply spoke around the foot in her mouth. "I guess she's become so rigid that she cares more about regulations than patients. And that's what the argument between her and Dr. Betcher was all about."

"Really? I thought it was about medication."

"Yeah, the regulations covering the distribution of medication to hospital patients and the people who reside in assisted living and the nursing home."

"Hmm. Interesting." And somewhat perplexing. I'd always been under the impression that Gerti was a compassionate nurse, who put her patients first.

"Anyway, don't go out of your way to visit with her on my account." Erin moved toward the entry.

And I followed. "While we're on the subject of Dr. Osgood, how was your date?"

She slipped her boots on. "He's nice, Mom. Really nice. He didn't only go on about himself. He was interested in my life, too. Particularly everything I'm going through now. My only complaint was that right after you phoned, he got called back to the hospital, cutting our evening short."

"I didn't mean to interrupt you guys, but I thought you'd want to know that Karl was searching for you."

"No worries. I stopped in to see Les in his office at the medical center this morning, before I visited Rose."

She shrugged into her coat. "I still can't believe you and Grace actually caught Ed without his shirt and almost without his—"

"Not another word!"

"But—"

"I mean it, Erin! Zip it!"

"That's what you should have told Ed."

Chapter 27

After Erin left, I rushed upstairs and got dressed. I pulled on a pair of black jeans and added a black turtleneck and a long black-and-white color-blocked sweater. To my way of thinking, wearing black, a slimming color, was necessary due to the trouble I'd had curbing my appetite as of late. To further distract from my waistline, I also went with thick eyeliner, gunked-up lashes, and poofy hair.

As soon as I arrived at the medical center, I made a beeline for Gerti's office. After what Erin had said, my curiosity was piqued. I couldn't pass up speaking with her.

Gerti's office was only a couple doors down from Dr. Osgood's office. And like his door, hers was open. But unlike him, she was at her desk, hunched over a stack of papers.

I knocked on the metal doorframe, and she raised her eyes over the rims of reading glasses tethered to a gold chain and perched on the end of her pug nose.

"Why, Doris, it's great to see you!" She dropped the glasses, leaving them to dangle against her chest, and scurried toward me. Her hips were far wider than when we were together last and her shirt hugged her upper arms and chest, the buttons straining. I'm ashamed to say her appearance lifted my spirits. I appreciated that I wasn't the only one struggling with middle-age weight gain.

"It's been way too long." Her pixie cut was henna red, a bottle shade of her natural color. And while the freckles on her cheeks had faded, her face remained youthful looking.

Because she, too, was Scandinavian, our hug was clumsy.

"I haven't seen you since Bill's funeral," she said while removing her arms from around me. "I still can't believe he's gone. We're too young to be widows."

"It's been three years since Ivan's death, right?"

She nodded. "I hope you're not here for medical reasons. From what I understand, you've had a tough go of it since Bill's passing. I'm sorry I haven't visited. I've buried myself in my work. It's how I've coped."

"First of all, no apology necessary. If there's one thing I've learned, it's that we do what we have to do to get through the rough times. And if our friends don't understand or can't accept that, they're not really our friends."

"Amen!" She led me to a pair of narrow office chairs in front of her streamlined desk. "Have a seat." She motioned to one of the uncomfortable-looking modern chairs while sitting in the other. "I hope you can visit for a few minutes."

"I'm here to pick up Rose. She's living with me temporarily, and she was hospitalized overnight for observation. I'm early, though."

"I heard what happened. Has the sheriff determined if she was actually attacked?"

"Not yet. But we should learn something soon."

Gerti shook her head. "You certainly have been through more than your share of turmoil lately, haven't you?"

"Well, I wouldn't complain if my life settled down some."
She winked. "I have one word for you, Doris: Zoloft."

"What?"

"After Ivan died, I fell into a funk. And the last several months around here haven't been any picnic, either. So I started taking Zoloft for depression and anxiety. It's caused me to gain some weight." She swept her hand along her torso. "But I feel much better."

"I'm glad. Although what do you mean, 'the last several months around here haven't been a picnic'? You've always loved working here."

"Before Dr. Osgood arrived, I did." She drew her lips together, like she'd sucked a lemon. "Do you remember *Leave It to Beaver*?"

"Of course." Although I couldn't imagine what that had to do with anything.

"Well, Dr. Osgood is the Eddie Haskell of this medical center." She inflated her voice to a sickening pitch. "'Good morning, Mrs. Bengston. Don't you look lovely, Mrs. Bengston.' Yet behind my back, he usurps my power and alienates my nurses every chance he gets."

"What does Dr. Betcher say about that? He oversees the doctors, right?"

"Yeah, he manages the doctors, while I'm in charge of the nurses. And I always believed we were like-minded as to medical care. But about six months ago, when I got fed up with Dr. Osgood, I went to Andrew to complain. And he got furious—with me! He said I was too hard on Osgood and the nurses. He said I had to 'lighten up.' Otherwise, we'd lose employees, and it was next to impossible to get folks to come all the way up here to work. According to him, he had a bugger of a time bringing Dr. Osgood on board, even with the medical school loan-forgiveness program."

"Could there be any truth to that?"

Gerti slouched in her chair, her tone mimicking her posture. "Possibly. But he went ballistic. Totally out of control. I had to walk away."

"You said the argument occurred six months ago?"

She nodded and, in doing so, confirmed that, contrary to my earlier impression, the argument had no bearing on either the robbery or the murder. It had taken place well beforehand. In other words, the corner-booth ladies had gotten their stories wrong.

"He avoided me for a long time after that," she went on to explain. "And when he finally came in, ostensibly to apologize, he made excuses. Said he was under a lot of strain."

"Strain?"

"Because of the robbery. It had happened a day or two earlier. And he was upset that the security camera in the pharmacy hadn't been working at the time. You see, he'd forgotten to get it fixed. He said it was an innocent mistake, but the board members were fit to be tied because there was no footage to provide to law enforcement. Gustaf, in particular, was giving him a hard time."

"I didn't realize that Gustaf was on the medical center board."

"Oh, yeah. Nothing in this town operates effectively without him. You know that." She snorted her derision. "He enjoys reminding Andrew that he's his boss. We have a CEO, of course, but the board oversees the chief of staff."

She smoothed her skirt. "To make a long story short, I told him that since our falling-out had taken place well before the robbery, blaming his bad behavior on 'strain' caused by that crime didn't even make sense. He got pissy. So I then said I intended to file a formal complaint against him." She raised her chin, clearly proud of herself. "Of course, hearing that, he practically fell all over himself, demonstrating how sorry he was. But I said it was too late. That is, unless he agreed to do something about his temper—like counseling."

"And he agreed?" I asked the question, already aware of the answer thanks to Will.

"He had no choice. I stood my ground." Another tilt of her chin, her nose pointing to the ceiling. "With everything he'd gone through in the Twin Cities, he couldn't stand the thought of another complaint being lodged against him."

"Were you afraid, Gerti?"

"No. I reminded him that I was his friend. And he's aware he doesn't have many of those. I also said he needed professional help before his temper got him into real trouble. He's now in an anger management group that meets in Crookston a couple times a month. I pray it will do him some good."

Since her argument with Betcher had nothing to do with the crimes that concerned me, there really wasn't any point in asking her more questions. But because any insights she had regarding Dr. Betcher might come in handy when I confronted him, I continued to probe.

"Gerti, are you aware that the women who hang out in the corner booth at the café have been discussing that argument again recently?"

"Oh?" She pursed her lips in concentration. "I guess I shouldn't be surprised." She propped an elbow on the arm of her chair and rested her chin in the palm of her hand. "Are you acquainted with Erma Landers? She's one of the old crows in that café group."

"Yeah. She used to be a Peterson from out by Halma. Her older sister was friends with my mom and Rose O'Brian. And she was married to a Wheeler years ago, if I'm not mistaken."

"That's right. And her son, Myles, was married to Jenny Inggrim until she caught him with Ivy Baker a few years back."

I racked my brain. "I don't remember that. Then again, I was always so busy out on the farm that I barely made it to town to buy groceries. I never had time to hang around and catch up on what was going on with everyone."

"In that case, let me tell you, because it was quite the scandal." Gerti scooted forward in her chair, bracing her forearms against her thighs, a mischievous expression on her face. "One day, Jenny stopped by Ivy's house to drop off a book for book club. She laid it on the kitchen counter and was about to leave when she heard voices. She followed the sound and ended up peeking into the sunroom that Ivy's husband had converted into exercise space. And lo and behold, there were Ivy and Myles going at it on Ivy's husband's weight bench."

"Oh, yeah. I do recall Grace mentioning something about that." Although I didn't see how it pertained to our discussion.

"Well," Gerti continued, "when Myles spotted his wife in the doorway, he heaved Ivy off his chest, and she fell on the floor, landing on a barbell and bursting one of her breast implants."

"Ouch!" My arms involuntarily crossed my bust.

"And Myles?" Gerti was practically giddy. "He was trussed up like a Thanksgiving turkey. I guess Ivy had used those stretchy resistance bands on him. And because he couldn't move very fast all tied up, he made an easy target for Jenny, who whipped a table lamp at him, smacking him in the middle of his forehead. He ended up with a concussion, ten stitches, and hefty child-support payments."

"What happened to Ivy?"

"She moved to St. Paul, where she's now a 'personal trainer.'" Gerti waggled her eyebrows. "Myles lives in a broken-down double-wide near Lancaster. And he and Jenny's daughter,

Lola, is one of the newer nurses up here. I'd love to say that she takes after her mother, but I can't. She chases around like her dad and runs at the mouth like her paternal grandmother, Erma Landers."

"So she's the source of the gossip about your argument with Betcher?"

"Odds are."

"But why is it of interest to anyone now? It's old news."

Gerti gave that some thought. "Probably because the sheriff's been digging around here again lately, just like after the robbery."

"But you said the argument had nothing to do with the robbery."

"True. Although..." She seemed to grow pensive, as if we were veering too closely to a subject she wasn't comfortable discussing. "Why does any of this matter to you, Doris?"

"Well..." I inhaled a fortifying breath. "I'm sure you've heard the rumor about Erin's supposed involvement in Buck Daniel's murder." I could barely get the words out. "Of course, it's preposterous. Even so, we've got to address it, or she could lose her job or worse."

"Still, I don't see how—"

"Erin believes that the pharmacy robbery and Buck Daniel's murder were connected in some way because they occurred one right after the other. Then, when she heard that your argument with Dr. Betcher had something to do with the dissemination of pharmacy medication to patients, she got to wondering if it was connected, too. You see, Buck Daniel had a lot of drugs in his system when he was murdered, which was only a few hours after he robbed the pharmacy."

Gerti looked appalled. "You aren't suggesting that Dr. Betcher or I had anything to do with any of that, are you?"

"No! Of course not." At least, not you. "And based on what you've said, the timing's all wrong. Nonetheless, I'd like to know more about how the distribution of medication is done."

"Why?"

I shrugged. "I'm curious. It was the basis of your argument, with Dr. Betcher, wasn't it?"

"Yes, though..." Gerti appeared suspicious, and rightly so. But like most professionals, she couldn't refrain from discussing her work, particularly when asked directly about it. "Well," she said, sitting straighter in her chair, "we have a protocol that's supposed to be followed whenever a patient needs medication. It requires the nurse or doctor to check out the drugs from the pharmacy and sign for them in a log. That same nurse or doctor is then responsible for personally administering the medication to the patient."

"So someone wasn't following those procedures?"

A knock at the door disrupted Gerti's response.

I glanced over my shoulder to find Dr. Osgood leaning against the doorjamb. "Do you have a minute, Mrs. Bengston?" he asked. "We have a situation."

Gerti stiffened.

"It's okay," I told her while wondering how much he had heard. "I have to go, although I'd really like to finish our talk."

She hugged herself, undeniably uncomfortable with the situation. "I don't know, Doris. I'm pretty busy."

Snatching a business card and a pen from the front of her desk, I scribbled down my cell phone number. "Please call me," I pleaded in a whisper. "The sooner the better."

Chapter 28

As I wandered down the medical center's nearly deserted corridor, I came across Vern Olinski. He had been the pharmacist for as long as I could remember. He'd also been one of my mother's friends. And while I hadn't seen him in ages, he looked the same.

Day in and day out, Vern dressed in black, yet I doubted he worried about appearing overweight. He was tall, stooped, and so skinny that his torso was concave. As for his face, it gave the impression that it was slipping right off of his skull. And while white tufts of hair sprouted from his oversized ears, none grew on top of his head. But it was his hooked nose that everyone noticed first. It made him look like a vulture—a Disney cartoon vulture.

I hadn't planned on speaking with the man, though once I saw him, I decided to ask him to confirm what Gerti couldn't because of Dr. Osgood's inconvenient arrival at her office: Had Dr. Betcher skirted the medication distribution protocol? It wouldn't definitively prove that he'd played a role in Buck Daniel's death, but it would point to further unethical behavior.

"Hello, Mr. Olinski."

The old man studied me through goggle-like glasses. "Doris Connor? Is that you?"

"Yep. How are you?"

"Been better." He dipped his head, his body wobbled, and for a moment, I was concerned that he might tip right over. "Goodness gracious, girl, I haven't seen you in forever and a day."

"Yeah, well, life never seems to slow down, even though I've retired from farming." I offered him a smile. "I thought you'd be retired by now, too. But here you are."

"Oh, the young whippersnappers around here would love to get rid of me. But I don't know what I'd do with myself."

"Mr. Olinski, I can't imagine anyone wanting to get rid of you. You're an institution."

"Oh, they wanna do things their way." He stepped closer, like he was readying himself to share something confidential. "They don't care about rules and regulations," he whispered. "Fact is, I just came from getting interrogated again by that Dr. Osgood." He pronounced his name as if he didn't care for the taste of it. "He and that nurse—"

"Gerti Bengston?"

"Oh, for sure, she came along at the end there. But I'm referring to that other one. The young one. The one who'll need a ladder just to get over herself." He smacked his lips. "Lola Landers."

"I know the name." Thanks to Gerti. "But I can't place her."

"Well, if you were a guy, and she were on her back, you would. That's how I understand it, anyways."

Having no wish to pursue that particular topic, I said, "You sure seem upset. What exactly happened?"

The old man glanced to his right, then his left, before once more lowering his voice. "They've been nitpicking, trying to come up with something that'll justify giving me the boot. And since the robbery, it's only gotten worse. But they'll never find anything 'cause I'm good at my job."

His whisper had given way to a much louder grumble as well as some arm waving. "The night of the robbery, I locked everything up tight before I went home, just like I always do. Sheriff Ingebretsen interviewed me the following day. And he was here again this morning. And both times, he said I did fine."

"Then I'm sure you did."

"But they're out to get me," he shouted. "Mark my words, they're out to get me!"

It was my turn to check the hallway. I fully expected to see heads bopping out of offices left and right. But the hall remained empty. "Mr. Olinski, calm down. It can't be good for you to get so upset."

He covered his face with shaky, age-ravaged hands. "I'm okay. They just rile me something fierce."

"You don't seem okay. How about taking a break and having a cup of tea with me? That is, if I can find one."

"Yeah, that might not be a bad idea." He drew in a deep breath, and as his chest filled, his posture straightened. Yet upon exhaling, he deflated again like a forgotten party balloon. "I keep both tea and coffee in my office, right over there." As with Ole, he pointed a finger that was so bent I couldn't determine if his office was in front of us or all the way on the opposite side of the hall. "My tech can handle the counter a little while longer."

After hobbling across the corridor, he unlocked a door, and I followed him into a room the size of a storage closet.

Six-by-eight, drab green, with no windows. A small desk with a large, antiquated computer filled most of the space, while a file cabinet and a visitor's chair fought over what was left. The desk was strewn with files and printouts. And on top of the file cabinet, a Mr. Coffee, and a teapot on a hot plate crowded several mugs, a carton of tea bags, a container of coffee, and a jar of non-dairy creamer.

"Have a seat." Olinski chose a mug. "Coffee or tea?"

"Coffee. Black. Thank you." As I sat down, my knees scraped the front of his desk.

He handed me my coffee before pouring himself a cup of hot water, selecting a tea bag, and sliding behind his metal desk into his padded chair. Sweeping a printout out of his way with a broad stroke of his arm, he made room for his cup.

"Have I ever told you how much you look like your mother?" He grinned, showing off stained picket-fence teeth. "Though she was years ahead of me in school, I always had a crush on her. She was pretty. And nice. Even to us younger kids. We rode the same bus, don't ya know." He shared that story every time I ran into him.

"She cared for you, too. And Grace and I will never forget how attentive you were when she was dying."

He dipped his tea bag into his cup, as if he were toying with a fishing line, and I thought about leaving him alone, now that he had relaxed some. But I couldn't do that. I'd be going up against Dr. Betcher shortly, and I wanted a few more answers if I could get them.

Glancing at the schoolhouse clock on his wall, I saw that time was getting away from me, so I went ahead and asked the most important question straight away: "Mr. Olinski, does Dr. Betcher disregard the protocol for receiving and administering medication to patients?"

"What?" Mr. Olinski let go of his tea bag, and it plopped into his cup of water. "Where in the Sam Hill did you hear that?"

"Around." I leaned forward, our faces no more than a couple of feet apart. "I don't expect you to disclose any confidential information. Just say yes or no."

"But why?"

Because of my time constraints, I offered him the Reader's Digest condensed version of the story of Buck and Erin's relationship as well as one about Will's fight with Buck. I also summarized Erin's suspicions about Dr. Betcher.

When I finished, Mr. Olinski shook his head. "Well, I'll be. I certainly had nothing to do with any of that business."

"Of course you didn't. You're a highly regarded pharmacist, and the medical center and this town are lucky to have you. But there's someone on staff who's not as reputable as you."

He chuckled. "Trust me, Doris, there's more than one."

"Well, I'm referring to Dr. Betcher. I want to know if he balks at the medication distribution rules."

"I'm not sure what to say."

"You mean you don't know?"

"I mean it wouldn't be right for me to discuss hospital business." He glanced at me, then past me, and his jaw went slack.

I, in turn, swiveled my head like it was on a stick. There was Dr. Betcher in the doorway, Dr. Osgood at his side.

"What's going on?" Betcher glared at me as if he'd actually enjoy seeing my head on a stick.

"Umm… nothing. I just stopped by to visit with Mr. Olinski." I had no idea how much the doctors had heard, but I pretended "nothing at all." It was the only way to keep from wetting my pants.

Betcher glanced at the pharmacist before again homing in on me. "Someone alerted me. They said you were badgering Mr. Olinski in the hallway."

"Me? Badgering Mr. Olinski?"

Both Betcher and Osgood eyed the pharmacist, clearly waiting for him to corroborate the allegation.

"On the contrary," I rushed to volunteer before the old man had a chance to open his mouth. "I just got done assuring him that the medical center is lucky to still have him on the job."

"Well… umm… of course we are." Dr. Betcher was at an apparent loss of words.

I, on the other hand, had an abundance of them. Sometimes, the tendency to ramble when nervous came in handy. "Dr. Betcher, were you aware that Mr. Olinski was acquainted with my mother? They rode the same bus to school. Well, I suppose they rode it home again, too. But that's beside the point."

Betcher glanced at Olinski, "Everything's really okay here?"

"Yeah. We were only visiting." Mr. Olinski stood, visibly twitchy with nerves. "But I hafta get back out front." He then squeezed past the three of us and out the door, hobbling faster than I'd thought possible for a person with horseshoe posture.

As for the doctors, they traded looks, plainly unsure what to do next. "Well, I suppose," Betcher finally uttered as he turned away.

"Wait!" I shouted

Dr. Betcher jumped, then tripped, barely catching himself on the door handle.

"I want to speak with you, Doctor. That is, if you have a minute."

He smoothed his shirt and hoisted his belt to its usual location just below his collarbone. "I'm sorry, Doris, but we're on our way to a meeting."

Believe it or not, I was actually disappointed. I was ready to do battle. True, I didn't have a definitive answer about his probable abuse of protocol, but I was pretty sure. "Will you be long?"

"I'm not sure, I suppose I can call you when we're done."

"Okay. Please do."

"In the meantime, you may take Rose home. She's been discharged, and she's ready to go. Has been for a while. Just remember, she has to rest the remainder of the day. And you should stay close by, in case she needs anything."

Chapter 29

Under a gray-painted sky, Rose and I approached my porch, where the sheriff appeared to be holding up the front door with his shoulder.

"I didn't see your car," I yelled through a gust of wind.

He canted his head to indicate where he had parked along a bank of snow, almost a block away. "I thought you might keep driving if you saw it."

"I may have, but Rose is pooped."

Leaning into the stair rail, Rose climbed the three steps to the porch. "With all the visitin' I did at the hospital, I'm all tuckered out."

Karl hooked her arm through his. "I hope I didn't pelt you with too many questions. I only wanted to follow up. See if you remembered anything else about last night."

"Nah, you weren't any bother. I'd been up for hours by the time you came by my room."

I weaved around them, opened the door to the welcoming warm air, and led them through the entry and into the foyer.

"Rose, let's get you settled in your room. I'll put your boots and coat away afterward."

"I'll wait here," Karl assured—or warned—me. "We have to talk."

"In that case, have a seat in the living room."

A few minutes later, that's where I found him, seated in what had been Bill's leather club chair. Because no one had sat there since Bill's death, I was taken aback by the sight.

My reaction wasn't lost on Karl, who halfway stood. "Should I move?"

I switched on the wall sconces and handed him a bottle of water while keeping one for myself. "It's fine. Sit down."

After flipping on the fireplace, I curled into the corner of the couch and folded my stocking feet under me. "Now, what's up?"

He swallowed water, his Adam's apple bobbing. "I got a call from Dr. Betcher," he said once he was done drinking. "He claimed that you were snooping around the medical center, causing a stir."

I yanked my own bottle from my lips, and water dribbled down my chin. "A stir?" I wiped it with my sleeve. "I visited with Gerti Bengston, who happens to be a friend. And I said hello to Mr. Olinski."

He narrowed his eyes, no doubt wary of my version of events. Go figure.

"So what does he want?" I asked. "Are you supposed to arrest me?"

"No. He just thought I might have some influence over you." He snorted at the likelihood of that.

"Ha-ha." Undoubtedly, I'd fashion a better comeback later. Probably while in the shower. I was dynamite at creating snappy retorts while shampooing. But that did little for me now. "Anyhow, Karl, don't you find it odd that Betcher wasted no time in calling you?"

Notwithstanding the drive-in ordeal or what Erin had suggested, I had difficulty believing that Karl Ingebretsen had morphed into someone who could use people. Set them up. Or trick them. Sure, he could be a big galoot, and he was one hundred percent wrong about my kids. But he'd always possessed a strong moral compass, and I couldn't imagine that he had thrown it away.

Then again, maybe that was mere wishful thinking on my part because I needed his assistance. While I knew Dr. Betcher and Tweety were mixed up in the robbery and murder, Erin and I couldn't seem to puzzle out the particulars. We were closing in. That much was obvious. But with people demanding a speedy arrest, we probably didn't have the time necessary to solve the case on our own. Nor did we have the time to hire a professional investigator and bring him—or her—up to speed. In other words, I had no choice but to take a chance on Karl.

"Karl," I said, clearing my throat, "I have a couple theories about the murder that I'd like to discuss with you."

He sighed. "Why doesn't that surprise me?"

He certainly could push my buttons. "Fine, then. Forget it. I just assumed you'd be interested since you haven't managed to solve the case on your own—or even with the assistance of state law enforcement."

He scowled, and I felt a rush of satisfaction knowing that I could push his, too.

"Okay, Doris, go ahead. Tell me what you've got." He didn't strike me as all that eager to hear me out.

I didn't let that stop me. "Dr. Betcher killed Buck Daniel," I stated as fact. "It may have been an accident. And someone else may have been in on it. But Dr. Betcher was definitely behind it."

259

"Really? And what makes you say that?"

I rattled off a litany of evidence. I explained how Betcher had disappeared from the hospital soon after the robbery and shortly before Buck's death. "That establishes opportunity." And I surmised how his career would have been destroyed if Buck had been apprehended and provided an opportunity to confess everything he knew. "That's also why Betcher had to get rid of him. Buck would have divulged their scheme."

"What scheme?"

"Oh, come on. It's obvious. Betcher was providing Buck and who knows how many others with pills on the sly. But Buck became addicted and out of control, so Betcher had to cut him off. Buck, though, needed the pills and robbed the pharmacy. Then Betcher killed him. Sure, it's possible that Betcher didn't mean to do it. But he had to get Buck out of the picture. And that establishes motive. It also explains why Betcher didn't want me poking around the medical center today."

"You said you were only visiting."

I ignored both his comment and his tone and went on to outline Betcher's anger issues as well as the procedures normally followed by the doctors and nurses to obtain medication for their patients. "While neither Gerti nor Mr. Olinski got the chance to name names, I'm certain Dr. Betcher was the primary violator of the rules. Why else would he and Gerti have argued over them? Even if their argument was well before the robbery and murder."

I was on a roll, becoming more and more animated as I continued. My head moved to the beat of my voice, and my hands weaved through the air like I was doing the Macarena. "It's my guess that Betcher signed out the pills on behalf of his patients, but rather than administering them, he sold them to folks like Buck Daniels. Betcher has a lot of older patients, and they'd never question him. They think he's a god." Done with what I considered a pretty good hypothesis, I downed the remainder of my water and waited for him to respond.

"Not bad, Doris, although you left a few holes."

"Which you can help me fill, right?"

He set his water bottle on a dusty coaster on the dusty end table and braced his hands against his knees, his forearms taut. "Why would I do that?"

"Because I'm Erin and Will's mother, and they're implicated in this... kerfuffle."

"Kerfuffle?"

"I couldn't think of another word for it. Not unless I swore."

He shook his head. "I already assured you that Will is in the clear."

"But can I believe you?" I mumbled.

"Huh?"

I drummed my empty water bottle against my calf. I had to be careful. I didn't want to tick him off with my accusations. "Well, Karl, from what I understand, you... umm... sometimes let suspects think they're off the hook, only to reel them in later, when they slip up. And while that's probably an acceptable practice to use with hardened criminals, it doesn't strike me as appropriate with–"

"Doris," he interrupted as he glared at me. "Shut up."

"What did you say?"

"You're suggesting that I tricked Will, and I won't stand for that."

"Well–"

"Your son is in the clear. I don't know any other way to put it." He somehow managed to sound both sincere and angry, and that left me feeling relieved and full of shame.

"As for your theory about Buck Daniel's murder," he went on to say, "you failed to account for the fact that Tweety is in possession of the money that Buck withdrew from his grandmother's bank accounts."

I stopped him right there. "As I said, he probably had someone working with him, and that someone was most likely Tweety. You know, he admitted that they dated."

He threw his hands up. "Well, then, case closed. If they dated, they clearly partnered to kill Buck, too. After all, I'm sure they couldn't pass up stealing $10,000 or a backpack full of pills, even if Betcher probably has a hundred times that amount of money in the bank and oversees an entire pharmacy."

"You don't need to get sarcastic. I agree that some parts of my theory don't make sense. That's why I need your help."

He dropped his head back against the top of the leather chair and muttered something to the ceiling.

"What was that?" I asked.

He shifted his eyes in my direction but refrained from raising his head, as if conversing with me left him utterly exhausted. "Betcher's not a suspect."

"What do you mean he's not a suspect? I just went through—"

"Doris, he can't be."

"Well, of course he—"

"He's left-handed. Like your son. Haven't you noticed?"

"Huh?" He had to be wrong. But he nodded to confirm what he had said. I, in turn, gave my head a couple of stiff shakes to clear my mind of everything else in an effort to concentrate on my encounters with the doctor.

Until recently, I hadn't had many dealings with the man, so I zeroed in on a few from the past several weeks. In my mind's eye, I first saw Dr. Betcher write his phone number on the back of the business card he gave me. Next, I saw him repeatedly adjust his glasses—and himself. And, yes, he had done them all with his left hand.

"And you call yourself a detective." Karl teased, prompting me to give him the evil eye until he added, "Oh, come on, Doris. Don't feel bad. We all make mistakes."

But I wasn't ready to admit to this one. Not yet, at any rate. "Are you positive that the killer had to be right-handed?"

He drank the rest of his water before answering. "Buck and his killer were face-to-face. A left-handed person would have been forced to reach across his—or her—body to hit Buck on the left side of his head. Not very likely. In fact, not likely at all."

"Still, I can't believe—"

"Even so, I'm impressed. You demonstrated solid deductive skills. Although I'm surprised you didn't suggest that Betcher hired Buck to rob the pharmacy because he, too, was addicted to opioids, but he wanted Buck to assume all of the criminal risk." He twisted the cap on his empty water bottle. "That would have explained why Betcher's been so irritable lately. Even more irritable than usual."

My mouth fell open, and I had to close it by pushing up on my chin with my thumb. "That possibility never even occurred to me. Is it true? Is Betcher an addict?"

Karl chuckled. "No, but it was one of my theories early on. And it goes to show that everyone can get things wrong. You just need to keep trying. You have to be tenacious, which you are." He peered at me, the reflection of the flames in the fireplace playing off the side of his face. "It's something I always admired about you, Doris. Yet when I first came back to town, I didn't see it and wondered what had happened to tamp it down. But it's still there."

My face grew warm and I wanted to switch off the fireplace before I started to melt, though I worried that such a move might give me away.

"Anyway, I better go." Karl rose from Bill's chair. "I'm following a few new leads regarding Tweety."

I fanned myself with my hand. "No sign of her yet?"

"None. But I'll find her."

Scrambling off the couch, I stood directly in front of him. "Karl, do you still suspect Erin, too? I need to know. I'm going a little bit crazy here."

As soon as those last words left my mouth, I realized that I had set him up, and I braced myself for a snide reply—a line about me being crazy for as long as he could remember.

Instead, he gazed at me with real tenderness in his eyes, then reached for my shoulders, like he was going to hug me. But just as quickly he wrenched his hands back, as if to avoid getting burned. "Tweety has Buck's money," he said. "Although until I get a chance to interrogate her, I won't know much of anything."

"W-what about Erin?"

He stuffed his hands in his pants pockets and shuffled his feet, the floor creaking beneath the movement. "Buck cheated on her. She lied about him hitting her as well as about where she was the night he died. That's problematic." He cocked his head. "Still, let's take this one step at a time, okay? First, I gotta find Tweety. And I will. I promise."

The moment was heavy with emotion, and I sensed that he was about to reach for me again. But he merely pivoted toward the door. So much for me being clairvoyant—or irresistible.

"As far as what happened to Rose last night," he said over his shoulder as he strode through the foyer, "while we haven't come to any official conclusion, I think it may have been a case of her being in the wrong place at the wrong time."

I tracked him into the entry. "You mean someone ran around the corner of the café and knocked her down accidentally but kept right on going?"

"What can I say? The world's full of jerks." At the door, he zipped his jacket and retrieved his gloves from his pocket.

"What were they running from, Karl? Any idea?"

"None. No break-ins or assaults reported."

At that moment, I realized how overwhelmed and exhausted I was. I felt like crying. I longed for the way things were before the robbery and murder. When Erin was happy at her job. When Rose was safely ensconced in her assisted-living apartment. And when I was dreaming about a new, simpler life.

Karl cleared his throat. "I understand from Ed that Erin told you about my meeting with her this morning."

"Uh-huh. She stopped by here afterward."

He stared at his feet for a moment before raising his head. "Doris, I'm sorry… about all of this. Really, I am."

Chapter 30

It was late afternoon when Karl left my house.

After he crossed the porch and trekked down the sidewalk, I closed my eyes and thumped my head against the door. I had failed Erin for the second time in her life. First, I was unable to create the happy homelife she craved. And now I couldn't seem to protect her from being blamed for a crime she didn't commit.

A knock at the door led my heart to leap into my throat before I swallowed it back down to where it belonged. I switched on the porch light, fully expecting to see Karl in the window, shouting about forgetting something. But it wasn't him. Rather, Dr. Betcher stood there, his white hair and pink complexion illuminated by the overhead light. No doubt about it, he resembled a giant lab rat, yet it was I who eeked.

I reminded myself that he wasn't a murderer. Karl had more or less guaranteed it. Sure, he was a cad. And a pompous ass. But not a murderer. No, I repeated silently, like a mantra, *he is not a murderer.*

I opened the door—just an inch or two. "Yes?"

267

Betcher spoke into the crack. "I was on my way home and saw the sheriff pull out of your driveway. I imagine he was here because of me. That's why I stopped. To apologize. I shouldn't have called him. I was upset, and I reacted without thinking. I normally don't do that. But I've been under a great deal of strain."

"So I've heard. Okay, then. Goodbye." I went to shut the door, but he stopped it from fully closing with the toe of his wingtip.

"Wait! Can we talk?" Evidently seeing the panic on my face, he added, "We can stand out here. I just want to clear the air."

A long moment passed before I was able to cobble together the wherewithal to say, "I don't know, Andrew. I just don't know." *He is not a murderer.*

"Five minutes. That's all I'm asking. I'll leave after that. I promise. Bring your phone with you, if it'll make you more comfortable."

Despite the cold air sneaking into the entry, perspiration collected around my neck and along my cleavage. I was scared of him, even though Karl had assured me that I had no reason to be. And that made me angry—with myself.

In the past, I'd had trouble finding my voice, my backbone, or the exit, particularly when it came to my husband. But he was gone. I was growing stronger. And I wasn't about to backtrack by allowing Andrew Betcher to get the better of me. "Okay. Five minutes. But that's all. I'll be right out."

He pulled his foot back, and I shut and locked the door. I could do this. I simply had to pull up my big-girl panties—the ones with good elastic—and do it.

I collected my jacket from the entry closet and hunted for my phone. Keeping it near seemed like a good idea. Toting a gun seemed a far better one. But I didn't own a gun, so I had to settle for my phone.

I searched for it on the cabinet in the foyer and on the side tables in the living room. I also checked the dining room table as well as the countertop and the table in the kitchen. But nothing. Next, I slipped into Rose's room and spied it on her nightstand, beside her false teeth. I stuffed it in my jacket and tiptoed out, though I could have marched while playing the tuba and she wouldn't have heard a thing. Her snoring was that loud.

Once on the porch, I leaned against the railing alongside the stairs, in case I had to run for my life. You see, something about Dr. Betcher still bothered me. No, that wasn't true. Lots of things about Dr. Betcher still bothered me. Rather than concentrating on them, however, I merely peered over my shoulder, into the sky, where the first stars flickered like errant sparks. "So, what did you want to say?"

Andrew Betcher propped himself against the wall opposite me, his hands in his coat pockets, doing God only knew what. "You think I murdered Buck Daniel, don't you?" He fixed his eyes on me, his gaze assessing. "You also think I was involved in the pharmacy robbery."

"Where on earth did you get such an idea?" I stared at the porch deck and huddled deeper into my jacket. If I could have done so discreetly, I would have pulled it over my head. Not that I was embarrassed.

"I have my sources, Doris. But I can hardly believe it. I regarded us as friends. I'd even hoped for more."

"Well… umm… I'm not sure what to say."

"I didn't kill him."

A breeze swept a tangle of hair across my face, and I tucked it behind my ear. At the same time, I recalled that while the sheriff had convinced me that Dr. Betcher wasn't Buck Daniel's killer, he had failed to address the possibility of Betcher and

Tweety being partners in the crime. And while I had difficulty believing she'd been the one to strike the fatal blow, I could have been wrong. It was known to happen on occasion. "What about Tweety? What's going on between you two?"

Betcher pushed off the wall and stepped toward me, prompting me to clutch the phone in my pocket. I had no idea why. If he wanted to attack me, I doubt he'd let me make a phone call first.

"Why are you so obsessed with Tweety? I meant what I said, Doris. It's not becoming. Sure, you're way older than her, but older women have some good qualities, and accomplished men like myself are sometimes willing to look beyond youth and vitality. We can appreciate an older woman's desire to nurture."

My jaw dropped and while scraping it off the frosty porch deck, I guaranteed him, "I have absolutely no desire to 'nurture' you. And I'm not obsessed with Tweety. I have a very good reason for posing my question."

He sighed, clearly weary of me, which seemed to be a common theme among the men who happened to cross my path. When I had more time, I'd have to ponder why.

"As I told you previously," he replied, "I went out with her a couple of times. That's all."

"When did you last see her?"

"I don't know. A few days ago?"

"What?" The icicles along the overhang cracked at the shrillness of my voice, and I hopped away from the railing when they speared the crusty snow behind me.

"Doris, calm down," he said, steadying me by gripping my upper arms. "I can't help but see her. She works at the café. The only one in town."

Hearing that, I wiggled out of his grasp and fisted my hands. I wanted to punch him. In part, because he wasn't the killer, and I longed to wake up from this nightmare. But mostly, because he irritated the heck out of me. "I meant personally, Andrew. When was the last time you spent time with her away from the café? Just the two of you?"

"Oh." He tapped his toe. "A year ago, more or less."

"And you haven't had anything to do with her personally since?"

He slapped his forehead. "I've told you that a million times! But you just won't believe me. Or you won't listen. Or..."

He went on ranting, but I quit listening. I had a lot to think about, although it all boiled down to one question: Was he lying, or was Tweety alone responsible for Buck Daniel's death?

Sure, I'd agreed to hunt for evidence against her to prove my own kids' innocence. But I would have done anything for them. And after discovering Wilma's money in her apartment, I'd even gone so far as to allege that she probably had participated in one or both of the crimes in some capacity. But the actual murderer?

Yes, I'd suggested as much to Karl, but I never truly believed it. While she was mean enough, she wasn't smart enough. Then again, criminals weren't necessarily smart. Besides, as Erin had pointed out, all of us possessed the capability to murder if pushed too far. And Buck Daniel may have done just that: pushed Tweety 'too far.'

"Doris," Betcher said, putting a stop to my ruminations, "I'll tell you the same thing I told the sheriff. Instead of badgering me, you should investigate Gustaf Gustafson."

"Huh? Gustaf? Where did that come from?"

As a train whistled its way through town, Betcher went back to leaning against the house. The cold air carried the train sounds as if the tracks ran right past my place rather than a mile away.

271

"We had a county board meeting last night," he said once the night was quiet again. "That's why I was close by when you called about Rose's accident. As usual, Gustaf was late. So while we waited for him, the other board members and I discussed the status of the robbery and murder investigations. Some of the men expressed concern that, for personal reasons, the sheriff may have failed to pursue all of the leads as aggressively as warranted."

"Are you suggesting that my kids—"

"Will and Erin were mentioned. But, for the most part, I'm referring to Gustaf. See, as chair of the county board, he's the sheriff's primary boss. And as the town crier, he has the ear of everyone."

"What exactly are you implying, Andrew?"

He paced back and forth, the porch light casting his shadow along the wall. "The wife of one of the board members has a friend who works as a cashier at the bank. She said she happened by Gustaf's office when Buck was in there on the day of the pharmacy robbery. She heard them arguing about the balances in Wilma's accounts. Buck maintained that they were lower than they should have been, while Gustaf insisted they weren't."

A coyote howled, the sound coming from near the river, behind the house. After another one answered, they both fell silent, and Andrew proceeded. "Gustaf ultimately instructed a cashier to close Wilma's accounts and give all of her money to Buck in $100 bills, as he requested. Once she had, Buck stuffed the money into a backpack and left. But not before threatening Gustaf."

"Threatening him how?"

"He evidently said, 'This isn't the end. You will pay me what I'm owed, Gustaf. Or else.'"

"And?"

"The bank employee contacted the sheriff the next day, shortly after you and Rose discovered Buck's body in the dumpster behind the café. The sheriff stopped in the bank a couple of times, asked a few questions, and reviewed some records. That was it."

He resurrected a memory for me. "I guess I do recall something about Karl checking out the bank. But I'd assumed he merely wanted to verify that Buck was authorized to withdraw Wilma's funds."

"That's what Gustaf wanted people to think. Even before the sheriff made any inquiries at the bank, Gustaf shared his version of events with anyone who'd listen."

The doctor was right about that. In the café on the morning after the pharmacy robbery, Gustaf had reported to the sheriff—at high volume—that Buck Daniel was a money-grubbing scoundrel who couldn't be trusted.

"So you think Gustaf murdered Buck over some impropriety at the bank?" I asked.

"It's not just me. Lots of people think so. And they believe that the sheriff failed to pursue the allegation as diligently as it deserved."

"Because he was afraid of losing his job?"

Betcher wrinkled his nose in an effort to adjust his glasses without the use of his hands, which remained otherwise occupied in his coat pockets. "Doris, Gustaf oversees the county board like a dictator, although he has no more power than the rest of us board members. He also acts as if he has the final say regarding county employees, including the sheriff, notwithstanding the fact that he was voted in by the people."

For someone who was appalled at being the subject of rumors, Andrew Betcher certainly didn't mind spreading them. And that led me to distrust what he was saying.

273

Even so, I continued to let him speak. "Per the men on the county board, Gustaf's been skimming money from accounts for years. Never a lot. And usually from seniors who reside in the nursing home or assisted living. You know, people whose bank statements aren't scrutinized very closely by anyone."

"And nothing has ever been done about it?"

"It's difficult to prove. Whenever Gustaf's confronted, he claims the missing funds are fees. Or he blames one of his girls for making an accounting error. Then he simply credits the account."

The wind had found its way inside my jacket, and I shivered. "But that's not what you're suggesting happened in this case."

"No. In this case, Gustaf embezzled quite a lot. Why? I'm not sure. Maybe he's in dire straits. In addition to being a heavy drinker, he gambles. And from what I gather, his wife does, too."

"But why Wilma's accounts?"

He squinted, as if giving the question considerable thought, though his expression came across as rehearsed. "Quite possibly because Buck Daniel was her guardian, and during the last couple months of his life, he was too strung out on pills to pay any attention to her finances."

Hmm. Maybe there was something to his accusations. Still, for some reason, they felt off.

Slipping past him, I moved toward the door, more than ready to go inside. "Andrew, this sounds like a lot of speculation."

"Well, it makes far more sense than suspecting me of murdering Buck Daniel."

"Perhaps." And with that, I left him alone on the porch.

Chapter 31

As soon as I was in the house, I locked the door, nestled under an afghan on the couch, and stared into the fire. I had a lot to contemplate. And when I was finished contemplating, I called Erin to report that Karl had more or less sworn that Dr. Betcher was innocent of murder. She wasn't surprised, because Ed had also spoken with the sheriff.

I then floated the idea that Betcher was involved in one or both of the crimes in some other way. But, in the end, Erin claimed that Rose was probably right. If Dr. Betcher had been complicit in any respect, he wouldn't have allowed Tweety to be so reckless with the money.

So, with that in mind, I went on to summarize Betcher's allegations against Gustaf.

In response, Erin said, "On the one hand, Mom, I still have trouble getting past the fact that Betcher isn't the killer. But on the other hand, he may be on to something. Remember, Gustaf's father had a reputation for being a shrewd and somewhat dishonest banker, and people say Gustaf's just like him. Though I don't recall his father ever being accused of murder."

I watched the flames lick the fireplace glass as I rewrapped my afghan around me. "Erin, what do you remember about Karl's investigation of Gustaf and the bank? What was the scuttlebutt?"

Erin waited a couple of beats before she answered, and I imagined her silently piecing together her recollections. "I believe the sheriff handled it on his own."

"Did you ever hear anything about Buck threatening Gustaf?"

Erin scoffed. "Gladys Knutson was the only teller who supposedly heard that. And since she's a busybody, no one took what she said seriously. Behind her back, they call her Gladys Kravitz."

"Who?"

"You know. The nosy next-door neighbor on the *Bewitched* reruns."

"Hmm. I suppose that's what you call me, too."

Rather than deny it, she merely said, "Right after I started at the sheriff's office, Nellie Nordling reported the same kind of deal. It seems that shortly after her grandma moved into the nursing home, her bank account came up short. Nellie complained to Gustaf about the discrepancy, and he credited the account."

Putting aside the idea that my daughter considered me a busybody, I reflected on my bank accounts as well as those I oversaw for Rose. "I've never had any issues with the bank. But I don't pay particularly close attention. I will from now on."

"And I'll run all of this past Ed, Mom." Erin's words were clipped, signaling that she was ready to hang up. "He might be aware of something more. And as soon as I hang up, I'll call a couple friends who work at the bank."

I nodded, as if she were in the room with me. "Because I don't know what else I can do, I'll pay Gustaf a visit tonight. And I'll ask Grace to come with me since he's more likely to open up to her." The cuckoo struck seven o'clock. "I suppose it's possible that he killed Buck, although I can't see him palling around with Tweety. And because she has Buck's money, she had to be involved."

"Well, Karl said she banked with Gustaf, so maybe there's a link there."

"I suppose anything's possible, Erin. And we certainly don't want to leave any stone unturned."

"You know where to find him, don't you?"

"Yep."

"And if he's not there, you'll have to drive to the casino in Thief River Falls."

After assuring her that I'd phone her later with what I learned, I went to disconnect but stopped short. "Hey, Erin, don't forget to be at the café at nine o'clock tomorrow morning to finish prepping. The fundraiser begins at four."

"Just a heads up, Ed will be with me. As of this afternoon, he can't leave my side." She made a noise that was part giggle, part growl.

◎ ◎ ◎

After serving Rose a bowl of chicken noodle soup in her room because she was too worn out to get out of bed, I ate alone at the kitchen table, my supper consisting of a rhubarb muffin and a cup of coffee. Coffee usually was a no-no for me in the evening, but I wouldn't sleep much tonight, anyhow. Not with all that was on my mind.

I rinsed my cup and set it in the sink, then called Will, who agreed to stop in and check on Rose while I was gone. When he asked where I was headed, I said I had to assist Grace with "last-minute things" for the fundraiser dinner. Yeah, I'd become a hopeless liar.

When I got to the Eagles, Gustaf's white Navigator was parked outside. I recognized it because of the vanity license plate that read, "MONEY."

As I climbed over the snowbank that barricaded the sidewalk, my snow boots filled with snow, and I dumped them out while leaning against the tired brick building and standing on one foot, then the other. After that, I hustled through the door, barely noticing the sign that advertised the upcoming fish-fry season.

Gustaf was seated at the bend in the bar, playing pull-tabs. The place was otherwise unoccupied except for the bartender, who was washing glasses, and the two guys hunched over the pool table.

I slid onto a stool kitty-corner from Gustaf and breathed a sigh of relief when Grace shuffled in and claimed the stool between us.

Milt, the bartender, made his way over. He was in his late sixties and as bald as a newborn. While fingering the red suspenders that traversed his sizeable belly, he said, "Hi, ladies," after which he gave me the once-over before adding, "Haven't seen you in here for ages."

"I've been busy with the move and helping Rose. She's staying with me temporarily."

"Well, what can I get you?"

I went with a bottle of Miller Lite, while Grace opted for a glass of the house wine.

As Milt wandered off, I canvassed the room. "It never changes, does it?"

Dark paneling lined the walls, assorted neon beer signs scoring them. A single Naugahyde booth hugged one end of the space, while wooden pub tables and high stools populated the rest. The bar opened into a cafeteria-style dining room packed with metal tables and folding chairs and smelling of beer and French fries and a bit of tedium. A paper banner on the beige wall announced that the bingo jackpot was $1,000. If Rose found out, she'd never again be satisfied with the prizes offered at the senior center or assisted living.

When Milt brought our drinks, I edged a twenty-dollar bill his way before ignoring the glass in favor of the bottle. I drew a long swallow, the burn actually feeling good as the beer made its way down my gullet.

Setting the bottle on the bar, I wiped my hands, wet with condensation, and nudged Grace with my knee. She glanced at me, and I bobbed my head toward Gustaf. His head was bobbing, too. If we were to learn anything from him, we'd have to get on it. And by "we," I meant Grace.

"Hi, Gustaf," she said.

He peered at her through eyes that suggested he hadn't seen her come in. And perhaps he hadn't. He may have been occupied in his own boozy world. "Hi, yourself," he slurred.

"Have you heard anything new about the robbery or murder investigations?" she asked.

A moment passed before he shook his head, like he had to think about how to do it.

"Well," she continued, "I've come up with a couple more questions that I'm sure only you can answer."

"Only me?" He peeked out from beneath his heavy eyelids. "Why only me?"

"Because you're in the know."

Hearing that, he attempted to sit a little prouder but couldn't manage the pose for more than a second or two before again slumping over his glass and a pile of discarded pull-tabs. "Ya betcha. Nothing gets past me."

Grace was the right person to take the lead on this particular mission. She knew how to play Gustaf Gustafson, as evidenced by the job she had done on him in the café. But because I sensed that we were running out of time, my anxiety level was climbing, and her nonchalant approach was grating on me. Consequently, I budded in. "I'm not so sure about that, Gustaf. I think a lot of things get past you."

He flinched and nearly tumbled right off his stool. "What exactly are you insinuating?"

Grace scowled at me, but I pretended not to notice. "The way I understand it, there've been a lot of irregularities in the accounts at your bank. So it's obvious that you have trouble staying on top of things."

Gustaf steadied himself by gripping the edge of the bar. "I don't have to sit here and listen to this." He attempted to stand, but his whole body swayed.

"Whoa!" Grace hopped off her stool and snagged his left arm while I rushed to grab his right. As I did, a question came to mind.

"Gustaf, are you right-handed?"

"Huh?"

"Just tell me. Are you right-handed?"

He scrutinized both of his hands before pretending to write in the air. "Yeah. I guess I am." He seemed genuinely surprised.

My sister peered at me over his beer-keg chest and stomach. "We better take him home."

To Milt, she hollered, "Gustaf's had more than his share. And we're headed out. So we'll drop him off."

Milt nodded, and I hissed under my breath, "Why are we leaving? We haven't asked him hardly anything yet."

"My dear sister," Grace replied while Gustaf rocked between us, demonstrating that he was too drunk to register our exchange, "if we want to find out anything, we need to get him alone. We may also have to ply him with coffee or more liquor than Milt will allow. Now, help me drag his sorry butt to your car."

◎ ◎ ◎

Because Gustaf adamantly refused coffee, we stopped at the local off-sale and purchased a pint of Jack Daniel's, his liquor of choice. From there, we drove into the country south of town. The road was gravel, snow-packed, and hardly wide enough for two cars to pass. But that didn't present a problem, since we never met another vehicle.

The sky was now chock-full of stars. The lights in the town of Kennedy, almost ten miles down the road, shimmered like candles. And the green hue in the sky in my rearview mirror hinted at the aurora borealis.

I was behind the wheel and Grace was in the passenger seat, playing hostess. Gustaf was in the back seat, sipping his whiskey from a Styrofoam coffee cup Grace had found on the floor in front of her. And Johnny Cash was on the radio, singing, Kris Kristofferson's "Sunday Morning Coming Down."

I wasn't crazy about Gustaf being in my car. He stunk. On top of that, I didn't like playing games with him. I just wanted him to answer a few questions, after which, I planned to return home and go to bed. As a result, even though Grace had lectured me on the importance of allowing her to handle Gustaf, as well as the whiskey, I lowered the volume on Johnny and said, "Now, Gustaf, what happened between you and Buck Daniel at your bank?"

Gustaf bent his head toward my sister and opened his mouth, the smell of booze permeating the car and causing my eyes to water. "I won't talk to her," he confided to Grace while pointing a thumb in my direction. "She's not very nice. Fact is, she's a bi–Oh, sorry, Gracie. I won't say that word in front of you. You're a lady. But it rhymes with 'witch.'" He sipped from his cup. "Back in high school, she and some other bit–I mean witches–stole my underwear."

Grace reached around the bucket seat and patted his knee. "Yeah, she's kind of a loser. But what can I do? She's my sister."

Another drink from his cup. "I can sorta relate. Not that I have siblings, mind you. But I never liked my old man. Nope, never liked him at all. He made me become a banker, don't you know. I didn't want to. But he made me."

Johnny sang, "And somewhere far away, a lonely bell was ringing, and it echoed through the canyons, like the disappearing dreams of yesterday." Gustaf pointed to the radio. "This song makes me really sad."

I wanted to assure him that being trapped in a car with him made me really sad, but I didn't. I merely switched off the radio.

"Yah," he muttered almost to himself, "my dream was to buy the bowling alley. I was a darn good bowler back in the day."

He stuck his cup out, and Grace added another splash of whiskey. By way of a nod that I spotted in the rearview mirror, he asked for more. She gave it to him before he said, "Gracie, because I've always liked you, I'll share something else with you."

In the mirror, I watched his features contort. He must have been thinking. It appeared painful.

"I never wanted to marry Louise," he announced, like that was news.

"Really?" Grace feigned shock. She, like everyone else in town, knew full well that Gustaf hated his wife. He disparaged her every chance he got.

"My father said I had to drop Janice and marry Louise because her father was a big farmer. Said it would be a great match for everyone concerned." He burped.

"Wasn't Janice pregnant?" Grace asked.

"He didn't care. He paid her to leave town. But you know what's worse than that?" Whiskey sloshed over the side of his cup as he juddered his hands for emphasis. "I had to spend the rest of my life with Louise. Although two good things happened." He held up four fingers. "One, she never got pregnant. And B, if I ever need a heart transplant, I can take hers. It's barely been used."

"Gustaf," Grace scolded, "that's not very nice."

"Neither is she."

He burped again. "I guess I shouldn't complain, though. I've got a lot going for me. I'm one of the most influ… influen… most important men in the county." His tongue was thick and growing thicker by the minute. "I even have a chance for a decent family life. That is, if she doesn't ruin it."

"What do you mean?" Grace asked.

"Nothing." He put a fat finger to his lips. "I can't say."

"Oh, come on. Tell us," Grace gently prodded. "You must be referring to your wife. But how could she ruin your life any more at this point?"

I couldn't take it. Grace was way too nice. "Gustaf," I shouted over my shoulder, "is she gambling away all your money? Is that what you mean?"

He sniggered. "You've been listening to Andrew Betcher and those other jealous fools on the county board, haven't you, Doris?" He sprayed spittle with every consonant. "That doesn't surprise me. You're the type."

283

I wiped the right side of my face on my coat sleeve. "Well, the rumor is, you're experiencing financial hardship."

I again glanced in the rearview mirror. He was doing that "come here" finger wiggle—but only to Grace. "I have more money than God." He attempted to whisper, but he couldn't do it. "And Louise doesn't know about most of it."

Grace eyed me, the two of us plainly thinking along the same lines. "Where did it come from, Gustaf?" she asked. "You aren't stealing from your bank customers, are you?"

"What?" He went for indignant but was far too drunk to be anything other than repulsive. "I'd never do that."

I butted in again. "Then why'd Buck Daniel accuse you of shorting his grandmother's accounts?"

Another burp. And I got concerned. That much burping wasn't good.

"I'm just not a real good banker. That's all. My heart's not in it. So I don't train my girls very well, and they make mistakes. Sometimes I make mistakes, too, because I'm daydreaming… about being a pro bowler."

Turning off the gravel road, onto Highway 75, I headed back to Hallock. If we didn't get anything worthwhile out of him by the time we pulled into his driveway, we would need another plan. One that didn't include being confined to a vehicle with him. The fumes were getting to me, and it was too cold to open a window.

"Okay, Gustaf," I said, taking one last stab at him, so to speak, "your incompetence and your staff's poor training might explain small account discrepancies. But the word is that Buck Daniel accused you of skimming a lot of money."

As I glanced in the mirror, he scooted forward and waved his cup back and forth between Grace and me. Predictably, he lost control of it, the cup remaining suspended in mid-air for a long moment before it fell and landed in my lap. Whiskey soaked my crotch and I jerked the wheel. The car fishtailed. The tires rumbled along the gravel shoulder. Grace yelped. I overcorrected. And the car slid on a patch of ice. I clamped down on the steering wheel as well as my back molars.

When we finally bumped to a stop, Grace swore while digging through the glove box. After locating two napkins, she wiped her face with one and handed me the other. I swiped at my pants a few times before giving up.

For his part, Gustaf went on as if nothing had happened. "Oh, yeah, Buck Daniel withdrew wads of cash. But toward the end there, when his drug problem got real bad, I don't think he even remembered stopping in at the bank. Though I have records that prove otherwise."

I tossed Gustaf's Styrofoam cup on the floor and contemplated tossing him from the car. But, of course, I couldn't. He was way too big. Besides, even though he was drunker than anyone had a right to be, the description of his pathetic banking practices and Buck Daniel's drug-addled mind rang true. And they, most likely, were reason enough for the sheriff to limit his investigation of Gustaf and his bank.

Realizing I still had a few more blocks before reaching Gustaf's house, I posed what seemed like the next logical question: "Gustaf, if you didn't siphon funds from your bank customers' accounts, where did you get all of the money you claim to have?"

He gazed at me through bloodshot eyes and opened his mouth. But rather than speaking, he threw up.

Chapter 32

Grace arrived home shortly after me. Joining me in the kitchen, she plopped on the empty chair at the little table. "Stick a fork in me. I'm done."

I checked the clock above the sink. Almost eleven. "Yeah, it's late."

"I need to grab a shower and go to bed. Tomorrow will be a long day."

"I have to shower, too." I sniffed myself. "I smell like a distillery."

"You won't get any argument from me."

Dropping my head back, I closed my eyes. "Rose and I will come to the café around seven or so."

"If she's up by then." Grace pitched a thumb toward Rose's bedroom. "She's not just sawing logs. She's clearing a whole damn forest." Which was true. All the common nighttime noises in our old house were drowned out by the chainsaw-like buzz emanating from behind her door.

"So," I began as I lifted my head and my voice, "should we discuss what happened?"

"You mean with Gustaf? What's there to say other than I may have dislocated my shoulder dragging him to his porch?" She extended her left arm and repeatedly bent it.

"I hope he doesn't freeze out there."

"I hope no one recognized us. Me with his hands. You with his feet. And his butt plowing through the snow. Thank God his wife wasn't home."

I dismissed the entire matter with a shudder. "I can hardly believe that Gustaf is rich because he's a successful gambler. But he said Karl knows all about it, so it must be true."

Grace nodded. "There's been gossip about him on that front in the café for years, but nothing concrete. Goes to show that he can keep his mouth shut when he wants to."

I slid down in my chair until my butt teetered on the edge of my seat. I was fading fast. "You know, even though it would have been great if Gustaf had confessed to killing Buck Daniel, I wasn't surprised that he didn't. Or that he has nothing but contempt for Tweety."

"Yeah, I didn't realize how mean she was to him."

"Well, we haven't exactly been his bosom buddies, either, Grace. Much to his disappointment. At least as far as you're concerned."

"Ha-ha." Grace propped her elbow on the table and rested her head on her fist. "I have to admit that by the time our little joyride was over, I felt kind of sorry for the guy."

What?" I slapped her forearm, and her head slipped off her fist and almost bounced on the table. "He puked all over my back seat!"

"Oh, it wasn't that bad. It mostly hit the floor. And it came out pretty easily."

"You didn't have to ride home with me. My car stinks, even after the car wash. I'll have to have it professionally detailed."

Yawning, she pushed her chair away from the table and slapped her thighs. "Well, I suppose."

"No! You can't go. Not yet." I sat up straight and opened my eyes wide, using my fingers like toothpicks. "We have to decide what to do about Erin. Even if Tweety alone was responsible for Buck's death, Karl's having a tough time locating her. And since he's getting pressured to arrest somebody, I'm scared—"

"He won't arrest Erin—or anyone else—unless he has direct evidence. The state law enforcement guys wouldn't allow it. And the county attorney wouldn't agree to file charges."

"How do you know?"

She smiled coyly. "I phoned him. The county attorney, that is. You may recall that we dated briefly when he and his wife were separated. They've reconciled, but we've remained friends."

"Well, what if Tweety's never found? You think the folks around here will be fine with no one taking responsibility for Buck's death?" Another thought popped into my head. "And if the real killer remains at large, will Ed stay attached to Erin's hip forever?"

Grace kicked me under the table. "Having Ed with her is a good thing. He's protecting her against any crazies who may want to take matters into their own hands."

"What? Why would... how do you know..."

"Karl didn't tell you because he didn't want to alarm you. He also hoped to avoid having you go all Rambo—Rambette—whatever."

"Wait a second, Grace. You spoke to Karl?"

"Yeah. He called me on my way home. I guess I'm the more level-headed sister. Who would have guessed?"

Okay. That hurt. But I shook it off. I had to keep focused on the matter at hand. "Are you suggesting that there are people out there who truly want to harm my daughter?"

"Well, Buck must have had a few friends. And, of course, there's Tweety and Berta."

I rose from my chair and paced around the room. Because it was a small space, I pretty much just circled the table. "I can't imagine Berta or Tweety actually going after her."

"Probably not. They'd most likely get a crazy friend or relative to do it in exchange for roadkill and a six-pack."

That stopped me in my tracks. "Which means we've got to do something. We have to help Karl find Tweety before someone gets to Erin." I marched out of the room, having no idea where I was headed. "We can't go to bed. Not now."

"Doris, come on back here," Grace hollered. "Karl has things under control. In fact, he hopes to have Tweety apprehended by morning. And who knows? I may have been wrong about that whole roadkill and six-pack thing."

Returning to the kitchen, I leaned against the doorway. "But we have to—"

"Listen, Karl doesn't want you to interfere. So don't. Let him do his job." She stood. "But just in case you get any harebrained ideas, I hid your keys."

"You what?"

"I hid your keys."

"Grace, you're a twit."

"Sticks and stones."

My insides simmered with rage. "Did Karl ask you to do that?"

Grace didn't answer, choosing, instead, to make her way past me and through the dining room and the foyer and up the stairs, the creaks underfoot logging her every step. The door to the attic squeaked open and closed, and she was out of earshot.

◎   ◎   ◎

290

I rummaged around the house for my car keys. I had no idea where I'd go after I found them, but that wasn't the point. I was furious with Grace and Karl. But mostly with Tweety. After all, she was Buck Daniel's murderer. She had to be. And as such, she had caused this entire shitstorm—I mean mess.

In the entry closet, I examined every coat pocket and checked all the boots and shoes. I scoured the junk drawer in the credenza in the foyer and under the sofa cushions in the living room. I found nothing but a five-dollar bill, a partial pack of cherry Life Savers, and enough popcorn under the couch cushions to last through *Gone with the Wind*.

Grace must have taken the keys upstairs. She probably had them tucked under her pillow. Of course, I had a spare—which I had given to her to keep for me. I'd have to rethink that sometime.

I headed upstairs, unconsciously stomping to the rhythm of Rose's snoring. I envisioned storming into Grace's attic suite and body slamming her like I'd done when we were young. But who was I kidding? I barely had enough energy to make it to the second floor. If I showered and called Erin before I collapsed, I'd be doing well. Lambasting Grace—and locating Tweety—would have to wait until morning.

At the top of the stairs, I gazed out the window. The sky was milky with starlight. Closing my eyes, I made a wish. I wished for a quiet, stress-free life. After the events of the last several weeks, I wasn't even sure I wanted my family nearby. Though I didn't want any of them residing in the state pen, either.

To that end, I made another plea. This one to God. Granted, when it came to my prayers getting answered, my record was sketchy. Even so, I promised God that I'd try to be a better person if Erin was exonerated.

After a quick sign of the cross, I opened my eyes to movement out by the garage. I cupped my hands to the window for a better look. It wasn't a deer. It only had two legs. And it wasn't a bear. Too agile. No question about it, it was human.

My initial impulse was to yell for Grace, but I was still miffed at her. Besides, I didn't want my voice to travel through the drafty window and scare off the prowler. Nor did I want to alarm Rose. Instead, I pulled my phone from the back pocket of my jeans and called Erin. I'd dismissed the notion of phoning Karl. He was in pursuit of Tweety. And I was miffed at him, too.

"Erin," I whispered when she picked up, "someone's lurking around outside the house. By the garage."

"Are you okay?"

"Yeah, but you and Ed better get over here right away. Park down the road. I don't want them to see you and run off."

"We're on our way. Stay inside. And lock the doors."

I disconnected and tiptoed downstairs, fully intending to check the front door, then wait. But once I was in the entry, I found myself slipping into my jacket and boots and furtively stepping outside, off the porch, and along the sidewalk. I figured I had no choice. Who knew how long it would take Erin and Ed to arrive? And what if the trespasser got antsy?

Positive he—or she—had moved to the far side of the garage, I scurried to the side closest to the house. There, I picked up the snow shovel Will had failed to put away and, holding it hand over hand, like a bat, crept past the first bay door and on to the next.

The sound of boots crunching hard-topped snow led me to hold my breath. I pressed my back against the garage and rotated the shovel until the flat side of the metal scoop was at head height.

More clomping from around the corner, just outside of view. My lips trembled, and my shoulder and thigh muscles stiffened. I gripped the shovel tighter. And that's when the prowler traipsed into the open, only an arm's length away. I attempted to make recognition, but because of the dark—and the ski mask over his face—I was at a loss.

Spotting me, the prowler shrieked like the unwitting victim in a horror film, and I did the same. And when both of us were done shrieking, I whacked him with my shovel, and he fell to the ground. True, his fall may have had more to do with slipping on the ice than getting slapped on the shoulder with a shovel. Even so, there he was, face down on the cement apron of my driveway.

Having no idea what to do next, I let my instincts take over. And my instincts thought it would be a good idea to jump on his back and scream for Grace. So that's what I did.

"Get off of me," my captive growled.

"Not a chance. And if you try anything, I'll hit you again. This time on the head." I had no intention of hitting anyone on the head. I may have, if my life had been in danger, but that didn't appear to be the case. I had the prowler pinned. He wasn't going anywhere. I am woman! Hear me roar!

"What the hell's going on?" Grace shouted.

I twisted in her direction and did a double take as she shuffled toward me.

She had a towel wrapped around her hair. Her snow boots stopped midway up her bare legs. And her quilted car coat only covered a portion of her chest and even less of her nether region. "What?" she snarled, when she noticed me staring. "I just got out of the shower, okay?"

I tossed my shovel aside. "I caught a prowler."

"Who is it?"

"I don't know. I'm afraid to flip him over by myself. Come help me."

"Not dressed like this!"

"Mom!" Over my other shoulder, I saw Erin and Ed jogging up the driveway. "Didn't I tell you to wait for us?"

Because it wasn't really a question, I didn't bother to answer. Instead, I merely yielded control of my prisoner to the two of them and shuffled over to Grace, who appeared mesmerized by the scene.

"You realize you're still all but naked, don't you?" I nodded at Ed, who couldn't seem to decide whether to ogle Grace or aid my daughter in subduing our intruder.

Grace dropped her eyes and caught sight of herself. "Oh my God!" Then with those words hanging in the cold night air, she began a backward march toward the house, yanking on the hem of her coat as she went.

"Well, well, well, who do we have here?" I recognized that voice and spun around to watch the sheriff amble up the drive.

He followed his question with a tip of the head toward Ed. "Thanks for the call."

In response, Ed twirled the intruder around while Erin snatched the ski mask from his head.

And that's when we all got a good look at—Tweety!

"Well, I'll be," Karl muttered. "No wonder I couldn't find you at the motel."

"Huh?" I grunted. "You were looking for her at a motel?"

"What exactly's going on here?" he asked me.

Of course, I noted that he had ignored my question about Tweety and the motel in favor of posing one of his own. Yet I answered, "What does it look like? I just caught her sneaking around my property."

Karl sniffed. "I mean you smell like a brewery, and Grace is walking backward half naked. What's going on?"

I waved him off. "It's a long story. And it has nothing to do with Tweety. So why were you looking for her in a motel?"

His crow's feet crinkled. "You jealous?"

I rolled my eyes, although in the dark, it was pointless. "How come everyone thinks I'm jealous of Tweety? I just find it strange that all of the men around—"

He talked over me. "She's been holed up in a motel in Thief River."

Next, he raised his voice even more to address Erin and Ed. "Take her inside. I have a slew of questions for her."

To me, he added, "You're okay with that, aren't you?"

I checked behind me, certain he was speaking to someone else. After all, there was no reason for him to interrogate Tweety Jacobson in my house.

"I figured you'd want to be in on this, that's all," he said, as if psychic.

"Well, sure. Go ahead." I acted like it was no big deal. Like I hosted police interrogations all of the time. But on the inside, I was as excited as a dog with two tails.

Chapter 33

Entering the dining room from the kitchen, I asked, "Who wants coffee?"

Lines ploughed across Karl's forehead as he claimed a chair from around my oak table. "This isn't a social gathering, Doris. We're here to question Tweety."

"But I already started the coffee." And it was a social gathering as far as I was concerned. Specifically, a celebration. Tweety was in custody, so Erin was off the hook. "Now, who wants a cup?"

"I'll have one." That was Erin as she retrieved a linen tablecloth from the top drawer of the hutch. "Ed, help me cover Mom and Rose's puzzle?"

"Sure. The Last Supper, huh?" Yep, Ed Monson was a trained investigator. Nothing escaped him. "I'll take some coffee," he added while carefully covering Jesus, the disciples, and about one hundred random puzzle pieces. "That is, if it's no bother, Mrs. Connor."

Because I still had trouble looking him in the eye, I answered his shirt. "No bother at all."

Erin took a seat and Ed claimed the one next to her, while Tweety grabbed the chair between him and Karl, scudding as close to Ed as she could without climbing on his lap. "I'll have some, too," she said. "With cream and sugar, if you got it."

"I thought you'd carry your own," I mumbled, recalling the stolen stash of condiments in her apartment.

"What was that?" She cocked her head. "I didn't hear you."

"Never mind." I turned away. "How about you, Karl?"

He sighed. "I suppose."

As I retreated to the kitchen, I heard Grace creak down the stairs and into the foyer. "Well, well, the gang's all here," she joked in a sing-song voice while passing through the dining room.

Joining me in the kitchen, she actually laughed out loud at the shocked expression on my face. You see, she was dressed in plaid pajama pants, a waffle-knit top, and a ratty-looking terry-cloth bathrobe. Her hair was damp and straight, a pink plait hanging down the left side. She was also makeup free. Grace normally didn't let people see her like that–less than totally put together. Then again, she normally didn't go outside half naked. Yeah, it had been an unusual night.

"I need coffee," she said. "Otherwise, I'll fall asleep. And I don't want to miss a minute of this." After I handed her a cup, she shuffled toward the fridge. "I'll grab some bars for everyone."

"We don't have any."

"Yes, we do. I hid them under the frozen vegetables, where you would never look."

I climbed onto my high horse. "For your information, I'm eating better these days."

"Yet you didn't find the bars, did you?"

As she rummaged through the freezer, Rose padded in from her bedroom in her fuzzy bathrobe and matching slippers. "What's going on? What did I miss?" Her hair was matted. Her glasses were askew. And she had forgotten her teeth.

Leaving Grace to fill her in, I made my way into the dining room and around the table, serving my guests brimming cups of coffee. When I got to Tweety, I also provided her with a few sugar packs, a couple cream tubs, as well as a verbal jab: "Just like at home, huh?" Without responding to the confused look on her face, I set my tray in the middle of the table and took a seat to Karl's right.

"Can we begin now?" He was noticeably irritated.

"No! Not yet!" Grace hurried in with chocolate-chip cookie bars. She handed the plate to Karl, collected a chair from the corner of the room, and wedged it in next to Erin. "Okay, go ahead."

"No! Wait!" Rose scuffed into the room, a stack of paper napkins in her hands. She tossed them on the table and eased herself onto the chair I had saved for her. Eyeing each person around the table, one at a time, she then said—or, more accurately, gummed, "Well, now, isn't this a fine howdy-a-do?"

Karl frowned.

And Rose nudged my leg, and whispered, "I'd take one of those bars."

I shook my head. The expression on Karl's face suggested that it would be best if we all sat still for a while. Besides, I reminded her on a whisper of my own, "You forgot your teeth."

"So, Tweety..." Karl raised his voice, no doubt to signal that I should pipe down. "What were you doing prowling around outside?" He fidgeted with the plate of bars, obviously unsure what to do with it. For a moment, it appeared as if he might pass it around, but the moment passed, and he set it down.

Meanwhile, Tweety lifted her square chin and replied, "I did what I was told to do. That's what."

Karl, still in his bomber jacket, propped his leather-padded elbows on the table and steepled his fingers. "What's that supposed to mean?" His register had dropped to a level that surely made hardened criminals quake.

And Tweety did some quaking of her own. "Well… umm… I was ordered to leave some money behind the garage."

"What money?" he barked more than asked.

Tweety glanced at Ed, clearly imploring him to come to her aid. But he only had eyes for his coffee cup. "The money Buck gave me," she responded once she evidently realized that she was on her own. "The money from his granny's bank accounts."

Karl bent a little closer to her. "It's out there now?"

Under the lights of the overhead chandelier and with coffee and bars at the ready, Tweety's interrogation may have appeared laid-back. Still, she'd gotten the message that Karl wasn't fooling around. It was apparent by the continued quiver in her voice. "Yeah. It's in a Walmart bag."

Karl nodded at Ed, who remained fixated on his cup until Karl cleared his throat. At that, Ed flinched, pushed away from the table, grabbed his jacket from the back of his chair, and hightailed it outside.

After the front door closed, Karl said, "Now, Tweety, why were you supposed to leave the money here, at Doris's house?"

Tweety leveled her gaze at Erin. "She said she'd make sure that I ended up in jail if I didn't."

Everyone swiveled their heads in Erin's direction.

"You're crazy," Erin snarled. "I did no such thing."

Karl raised his hand, and Erin immediately stopped talking. It was almost like he was a magician, and I envied him that particular trick.

He next asked Tweety, "When did all of this allegedly occur?"

Even though I only saw his profile, I was certain Karl had his cop face on. I could tell by the distress in Tweety's eyes. "First, she left a note under the door to my apartment. I found it Sunday afternoon. It said, 'Tweety, I know you have the money, and I want it. Put it in a bag and drop the bag behind the dumpster at the café no later than nine o'clock tonight. If you don't, you'll be sorry.'"

"You're sure that's how it read?"

"Well, Sheriff, I don't have a pornographic memory or nothing, so I can't be one hundred percent positive. But I'm pretty sure."

Grace snickered until Karl shot her a withering look. Yep, he was quite a magician. He even possessed the ability to silence my sister.

"How do you know Erin wrote the note, Tweety?" he went on to ask. "Was it signed?"

Tweety began an eye roll but must have thought better of it. "Of course it wasn't signed. But her name was attached to the text messages she sent me yesterday and today."

"She sent you text messages?" Karl was clearly surprised.

"Well, yeah." Tweety halfway stood to pull her phone from the back pocket of her jeans. Not an easy task. Those jeans were tight. "You see, after I got the note on Sunday, I got scared and drove to Thief River to hide out. I only planned to spend Sunday night in the motel there, but I watched movies so late that I slept past checkout. That meant I had to pay for Monday, too."

Karl's coffee cup was halfway to his mouth when he set it back down. "What does that have to do with the texts?"

"Well, I hung around Thief River on Monday and ate an early supper. They have a Chinese place there that I really like. And that's when I got the first text." She scrolled through her messages. "I knew it was from Erin because her name's in my contact list being I get her to fill in for me at the café sometimes. So it's automatically on her texts."

"And?"

"And she said I blew it by not leaving the money behind the dumpster on Sunday night, but she'd give me another chance. But if I didn't leave the money behind the café by nine o'clock Monday night—you know, last night—I'd end up in big trouble." She glared at Erin.

Erin glared right back. "I didn't text you." She retrieved her own cell phone from her jacket pocket and began sifting through her messages.

"Tweety?" Karl raised a finger to get her attention. "Why didn't you call my office and report that you'd been threatened?"

Tweety started to speak, only to stop when the cuckoo clock in the foyer struck 1:00 a.m. It was followed by a tinny chorus of "Edelweiss." And when the song was over, Tweety wondered aloud, "That's from that one movie, right?" She gazed at each person around the table, as if she expected someone to answer. No one did.

Karl, however, grunted. And Tweety must have understood what that meant because she immediately responded, "I didn't call you because you'd never believe that Buck gave me the money. You'd think that I killed him for it. That's why I didn't call Ed, either."

I bent around Karl and said, "You raise a good point, Tweety. Why on earth would Buck Daniel give you his money?"

She braced herself, her visible fear of Karl replaced with unfiltered resentment of me. "Well, if you must know, Mrs. Budinski, we were gonna run off together. He put the money in a duffle bag in the trunk of my car while I was at that retirement party at the distillery. He said he had one last errand and left with his backpack."

"He didn't take your car?" That was Karl.

"No. Although I didn't really see him leave. It was cold, and I went back inside. I figured he took his motorcycle or met someone or something. But he never came back. And he didn't call the next day. Then he was found in the dumpster, deader than Grandma's old cat after that bad freeze a few years back."

Erin poked an accusatory finger at Tweety. "When Ed and I interviewed you at the distillery that night, you claimed you never saw Buck after the robbery."

Tweety shrugged in defiance. "I guess I forgot. So sue me."

Karl glowered at Erin and me. Apparently, he preferred to handle his interrogations on his own. "So, Tweety," he eventually said, his countenance indicating that he dared us to interrupt him, "do you still have the note that was left under your door?"

Tweety fidgeted. "I threw it in the dumpster before I drove to Thief River. I didn't want anything to do with it."

Erin slapped her hand on the table. "A likely story!"

A mere look from Karl, and she sank in her chair.

"Tweety," he then said, "Let's go back to what you did after you got the text message last night."

Tweety grinned. "That's easy. First off, I finished my Chinese dinner. I wasn't gonna waste it. Chinese food's expensive. And I really like it."

Karl may have growled.

So Tweety hurried on. "Then I drove back here to Hallock. I could have kept the money, you know. Buck called it 'our' money. But it wasn't worth the hassle. And I'd already used some of it." She hesitated, as if unsure about confessing to that. "Anyways, I parked my car behind the post office because I didn't want nobody to see it, and I walked toward the café. But when I headed down the alley, I got a funny feeling, like someone was watching me. What is that called? A sick sense?"

Without so much as a glimpse her way, I was certain that Grace had tied herself in knots to keep from laughing.

"I peeked over my shoulder." Tweety continued, having no clue how dumb she sounded. "And sure enough, someone was coming for me. They were dressed in black and had a ski mask pulled over their face. And because that really freaked me out, I took off."

"Where'd you go?" Karl asked.

"I ran behind the café, past Doris and Grace's cars, and all the way down to the grain elevator without stopping. That's where I stayed until I went back to the café later on. I still wanted to get rid of the money. It was causing me way too much trouble. But a squad car was there, so I didn't take the chance. Plus, I was hungry. You know how it is with Chinese food. You're hungry again two hours later."

"Tweety, you're lying!" I pushed to my feet, my chair screeching and almost tipping over.

"No, I'm not, Doris. Chinese food always leaves me—"

"I don't care about that!" I leaned past Karl. "You were the one with the ski mask last night because you had it on tonight, too. And that means, among other things, you shoved Rose to the ground!"

Rose muttered, "For land sake."

Meanwhile Tweety shouted, "I don't know what the heck you're talking about. I only wore a ski mask tonight because the guy chasing me last night had one on, and it seemed like a good disguise."

"You actually expect me to believe that?" I pressed my palms against the table, puzzle pieces poking my skin through the tablecloth.

"Mom's right." Erin waved her phone in the air.

Karl stood and, in doing so, shouldered me back down onto my chair. "That's enough! All of you, quiet down."

"But Tweety's lying," Erin persisted. To prove her point, she reached across the table and handed her phone to Karl. "Her name doesn't appear on any of my outgoing texts."

"Well, you must have deleted them because they're right here." Tweety tapped her phone, her fingernails clicking against the screen.

Karl silently studied Erin's phone before laying it on the table and doing the same with Tweety's. "She's right, Erin," he said only after reviewing both of them a second time. "The texts are on Tweety's phone. One from yesterday evening and another from early this morning. And your name's attached to each one."

"See?" Tweety taunted. "I told you. And how dumb are you, anyways? Why'd you change your mind and have me leave the money right here at your mom's house?" She shook her head. "Like that wouldn't be a dead giveaway."

Ed swaggered in, a Walmart bag in his hand. "Got it, sheriff. There's $5,000 in here. Five packs with ten one hundred dollar bills in each pack. And all of the packs are wrapped in those paper bands."

"Only $5,000?" Karl eyed Tweety.

She shrugged. "What can I say? A girl's gotta live."

"I didn't see anything else around the garage," Ed went on to report after a sniffle. "Nothing inside, either."

"Wait a minute. You went in the garage?" Karl closed his eyes and pinched the bridge of his nose. "We don't have a warrant, and you didn't get permission from the owner to do that."

"Well, I didn't find anything, so no biggie."

Karl mumbled something under his breath before voicing out loud, "Erin and Tweety, you better come down to the station with Ed and me." He checked his watch. "And given the late hour, plan to spend the rest of the night there. This is going to take some time to sort out."

"Well, now," Rose muttered, "isn't this a—"

I scowled, and she pressed her lips together, pretending to lock them with her thumb and forefinger.

Chapter 34

Wednesday morning, Rose accompanied Grace to the café right after dawn. I didn't go. I had to hire a lawyer for Erin and make sense out of everything that had happened. I accomplished the former right after eight o'clock. The latter would take a lot longer.

Sitting at the dining room table in my bathrobe, I sipped my coffee. It was bitter. Yet I kept drinking. I also gnawed on what was left of the chocolate chip bars. Because they'd been left uncovered on the kitchen counter all night, they tasted like dust. But that didn't stop me from eating them, one right after the other.

Before going to bed, Grace and I had cleared the table, tossing the tablecloth into the wash. Now as the sun shined through the bay window, the rays reflected off the lanterns on the floor by the patio door and created a halo over the puzzle Jesus.

When the cuckoo clock struck nine, I dragged myself upstairs, phoned Will, and brought him up to date. He insisted on meeting me at the sheriff's office at eleven, when I was scheduled to confer with Erin, her new lawyer, Karl, and the county attorney. Some of the law enforcement folks from the state's Bureau of Criminal Apprehension would be there, too.

After disconnecting, I showered and dug through my drawers until I found my newest underwear set. I also picked out my best black jeans and a long, small-print sweater. I used the blow-dryer on my hair, smudged eyeliner around my eyes, and added a few swipes of mascara. I had to feel well-composed. Otherwise, I'd blubber at the mere sight of my daughter.

Grace had left my keys on the credenza. I used them to lock the house and, after that, spent five minutes searching for the courage to press the garage-door remote. I had no idea why I was so tense. Ed had checked the garage the previous evening, and Grace had backed her car out earlier this morning, and neither had been attacked. Besides, Tweety was Buck Daniel's killer, regardless of what her phone might suggest, and she was in custody.

With that in mind, I ordered myself to buzz the overhead door. And once it was up, I ran as fast as I could to my car, jumped inside, and hit the automatic locks.

At the courthouse, I found a parking spot, then patted the top of my head for my reading glasses. They weren't there. I dug through my purse. Not there, either. Normally, I would have tried to get by without them, but because I presumed there'd be material to review, I had no choice but to go home and get them. At the same time, I'd grab a can of Glade. Until sliding behind the wheel, I'd forgotten how bad my car smelled. And it was too cold—and I was too jittery—to drive with the windows down.

As I turned down my driveway, I saw an older black Camry but no one in or around it. "That's strange." I pulled in beside the unfamiliar car, eased myself from behind the wheel, and started down the sidewalk.

When the side door to the garage came into view, I noticed that it was open. Since Grace and I had remotes, we seldom used that door, and seeing it ajar caused me pause.

Moving closer, I swore I heard something scraping along the concrete floor inside. I envisioned someone dragging a dead body, but just as quickly, I mentally slapped myself and pledged to forgo television mysteries for a while.

Despite being panicky, I was determined to inspect the garage like a mature adult and eased into the snow between the sidewalk and the garage, pressed my back against the exterior wall, next to the open door, and listened—to nothing. Perhaps the noise had been just the rustling of rabbits in the bushes. But lead-footed rabbits? And what about the open door? Perhaps Deputy Monson had failed to close it tightly, and the wind had pushed it open. Then Grace and Rose, running late earlier this morning, hadn't noticed it. *Hmm.*

Peeking through the doorway, I caught the faint light of the bare bulb hanging from the ceiling, and my heart crawled into my throat. There was no reason for that light to be on. Still, I spotted nothing else out of the ordinary. And with both my car and Grace's Jeep gone, I had no difficulty scanning the entire space.

Because the garage was new, we hadn't had time to clutter it. The lawn mower and snowblower were parked against the north wall, where they belonged. All of the lawn and garden tools, including the shovel I'd used on Tweety, hung from hooks on two-by-four supports along the east wall. And to my right, against the west wall, lawn chairs were folded and neatly stacked.

Stepping all the way in, I studied the space more closely. That's when I saw something heaped next to a fifty-pound bag of sidewalk salt—a bag I was certain that Will had propped against the opposite wall.

I squinted for a better look but still couldn't identify the mound and edged even closer. I smelled cinnamon. And the mound raised its head.

It was young Dr. Osgood. And he had a pistol in his hand. "You weren't supposed to be here," he said in a matter-of-fact manner. "You were supposed to be at the sheriff's office."

"How did you—"

"I called your son. Claimed to be worried about Erin. He was more than happy to explain everything. So why aren't you there?"

"I forgot my reading glasses."

"Too bad."

The hamster in my head jumped on its wheel and raced for comprehension of the scene: A disheveled Dr. Osgood, his hair sticking up all over the place like he'd just gotten out of bed. His eyes were crazed, as if he'd been living a nightmare. And his peacoat was buttoned wrong. Did I mention that he also had a gun in his hand? And a backpack at his feet?

"What are you doing?" As the hamster picked up speed, more thoughts fell into place. "That's Buck Daniel's backpack, isn't it?"

Dr. Osgood smiled. But there was nothing charming about the expression. Rather, it chilled me to my core.

"Did you kill Buck Daniel?" I wasn't sure why I asked the question. I didn't really want to know the answer. At least not at that moment, while I was alone with him.

"It was an accident." He rubbed his whisker-stubbled chin. "But I knew no one would believe me."

The room began to spin. "I think I'm going to be sick. I have to sit down."

He motioned toward the ground with his gun. "On the cement."

"I can't. It's too cold. I won't be able to get up again." I swayed, and he grabbed the back of my neck. Shoving my head to my knees, he ordered me to breathe. And I did until he yanked me up again, his grip still firm.

He poked the barrel of his gun between my shoulder blades and demanded that I walk slowly toward the house. "Any funny business and I'll shoot you."

Like most avid crime-show viewers, I, on occasion, had imagined what I'd do in this type of situation. I had wanted to believe that I'd fight back at the first opportunity or feign a seizure of some kind to put my assailant off guard. In reality, though, I only did as I was instructed. I slogged toward the house, the sour taste of terror in my mouth. I heard nothing except the wind howling warnings through the trees. And, of course, I didn't see a darn thing. No people. Not even any cars. Because I had to live off by myself.

◎ ◎ ◎

After I unlocked the door, Dr. Osgood prodded me into the dining room. I sat at the table, and he dropped onto the seat next to me. I scudded my chair forward so I could lean on the table for support, while he pushed his chair back so he could watch the driveway through the bay windows and, at the same time, keep his gun trained on me.

"Why did you kill him?" I asked, recalling that the cops on television stressed how important it was to keep the guy with the gun talking. He was less apt to shoot if his mouth was moving. I only hoped that Osgood had watched those same shows and remembered his part.

"Buck told me that he and Tweety were leaving town," he said. "He had enough pills for a while and close to ten grand from his grandmother's bank accounts. I agreed it was the right thing to do. Leave town, I mean. I couldn't risk selling to him anymore. In fact, I'd cut him off a week before the robbery."

"Why didn't he go?"

"He said he would contact me when he needed more pills. If I refused to send them to him, he'd alert the authorities, informing them that I'd been hawking my patients' medication." Dr. Osgood shifted the pistol to his left hand and, with his right, retrieved a cinnamon candy from the pocket of his khaki pants. After using his teeth to unwrap it, he popped the candy into his mouth, dropped the wrapper on the floor, and returned the gun to his other hand. "I said I didn't believe him. If he was willing to blackmail me, he wouldn't have robbed the pharmacy. He would have simply blackmailed me. But he laughed at that. Said he couldn't give me up without implicating himself. That's why he couldn't do it—or even threaten to do it—while he was in town. Although he definitely could from some other place, where they'd never find him."

"So you killed him?"

He crushed the candy with his molars. I flinched at the sound. He snorted a laugh.

"I did my best to reason with him," he explained. "But he was a jerk. And higher than a kite. So it wasn't my fault that he died. I had a good thing going. I'd prescribe and check out pain medication for people in the nursing home and assisted living and pocket it to sell later."

"But what about your patients?"

He swallowed what remained of the candy and skimmed his teeth with his tongue. "They always have pain of one kind or another. I gave them Tylenol and Ibuprofen."

"That's awful." I didn't mean to say that. It just slipped out. I certainly didn't want to antagonize him. After all, he had the gun.

"Don't get all self-righteous!" he yelled, and I cowered. "You're just like your friend Gerti Bengston. I'd sometimes sweet-talk the nurses into handing over pain pills that they had signed out, assuring them that I'd administer the medication when I made my rounds. But every once in a while, Gerti would find out and blow a gasket." He mimicked her in the voice of a cackling witch: "Whoever signs out the meds must administer the meds. No exceptions."

Because I was too scared to think straight, my mind tripped from thoughts of the medical center and pills to Buck Daniel and the café, leaving no rhyme or reason to the order of my questions. "Why'd you stuff the body in the dumpster behind the café?"

"That was a no-brainer." He slouched in his chair. "Since this town only has one café, I've eaten there every morning since I moved here. And because I'm low man at the medical center, I have to be at work early, which means I'm usually the first customer in the café. That's how I knew the dumpster got emptied every Wednesday morning, shortly after six. And that's why, when Buck died—in the wee hours of a Wednesday morning—I deposited him in the dumpster, assuming he'd soon be on his way to the landfill."

"But the garbage truck broke down."

"Yeah, I didn't expect that."

My thoughts remained jumbled. "I still don't understand why you did it."

"I just said. I figured he'd get buried in the landfill."

"No! I meant, why'd you sell pills?"

He uncrossed his legs, leaned toward me, the gun only an inch from my heart, and spoke slowly, as if I were so stupid that I needed to see his lips move to comprehend his words. "For—the—money." His breath smelled of cinnamon. My stomach roiled. And I pledged never to eat anything with cinnamon again. "I may be a doctor," he added, "but I don't make a lot. Mostly, I work in return for student-loan forgiveness."

"I can't believe you're all that poor."

"Well, it's not the life I expected, that's for sure." He shook his head, as if truly disgusted. "I realized how unfair things were as soon as I moved up here. I saw all of these rich farm kids driving around in their fancy pickups, most of them doing nothing for work, while I'd been working my ass off since I was thirteen. So when those brats started coming in with their sports injuries and such, I recognized an opportunity to make some extra money. You see, a few were damn willing to pay big bucks to remain pain-free." As was Buck Daniel.

"You actually jeopardized their health and your future for a little extra cash?"

"Who are you to judge me?" His eyes blazed with fury, and I mentally cuffed myself for saying anything. "It wasn't supposed to be a risk," he continued. "Not even after Buck died. He was an addict, and his only living relative didn't know what day it was. So no one was supposed to care. But the sheriff had to poke around. Erin, too. Then you got nosy."

"I am not nosy."

"Whatever."

I was wearing down. Holding death at bay was grueling. Nevertheless, I did my best to keep him talking, while I prayed for a plan of escape to come to me. Given my recent prayer results, however, I didn't hold out a lot of hope. "Why'd you involve me in all of this? Why'd you come here?"

Osgood stood and studied the puzzle. "Blame your daughter." He picked up a piece and fit it in to finish Judas's hand. I'd been searching for that piece for days.

"At first, I only wanted to keep tabs on the investigation," he said. "And I thought Erin–suspended or not–would be a good source of information, which she was. But the more she told me, the more concerned I got." He kept his eyes on the puzzle but his gun on me. "That's why I invited her to dinner with me in Grand Forks. I wanted to discuss everything at length, and I couldn't do that very well in the café while she waited tables."

He noticed a couple puzzle pieces on the floor and bent over to pick them up. I thought about kicking him. After all, he was only a few feet away. But just as quickly he was upright again, a smirk on his face, as if he grasped what I'd been contemplating.

"I didn't have a plan initially," he then went on to say. "But when we were in Grand Forks, and Erin went to the bathroom and left her phone on the table, it all came together. I'd use her phone to build evidence against her, in case things fell apart and I needed someone to blame. And I'd simultaneously keep pushing Tweety to hand over Buck's money." He backed against the patio door, almost tripping over the lanterns on the floor. "I'd already left a written note under Tweety's door, but she didn't follow my instructions. She's not particularly bright."

"I don't get it. Buck's been dead for some time now. Why'd you wait so long to go after his money?"

Osgood slid over to the bay window and checked outside. In my imagination, I saw Karl out there. I watched as he raced up the sidewalk, broke down the door, and knocked Osgood out cold with a single punch. But when Osgood ambled away, I realized that Karl wasn't really there. I was on my own.

Osgood spun his chair around and straddled it like a horse, his gun resting on his crossed arms. "After Buck died, I opened his backpack, expecting to find pills and close to ten thousand dollars in cash. But only the pills were there. He'd stolen dozens of bottles and wanted to sell me the ones he'd never use. He said I'd make a good profit off of them. And he was right. I told those kids the pills were this or that, and they were only too happy to buy them, regardless of what they really were. Still, I was disappointed about the money."

"Yet you waited."

"I didn't want to draw attention to myself. But when I began to feel the heat, I decided I better prepare to leave town, in case it came to that. Of course, taking off would mean giving up my career as a doctor, which, in turn, would require way more cash than I had socked away. So that's when I made up my mind to take Buck's money. From what he had said when we met the night of the robbery, I was pretty sure that Tweety had it or knew where to find it."

"But it wasn't ten grand. Tweety had spent a lot of it."

Anger darkened his features. "I didn't know that until your son filled me in this morning." He paused. His mind was obviously elsewhere, no doubt thinking black thoughts.

As for me, my mind was busy reviewing escape scenarios:

In the first one, I knocked Osgood down, kicked his gun away, and beat him through the patio door and into the woods, along the river. But, from there, I wasn't sure where to go.

In the second, I simply ran out the front door, jumped into my car, and speeded away. Osgood was thirty years younger than me and in great shape, though, so I'd never outrun him. And if he was any good with that gun of his, he'd shoot me, as promised.

As for the third plan—

"Okay," Osgood shouted, making me jump, "I've got everything figured out." He stood and gestured with his gun. "Let's go."

My phone rang. "Umm... I should probably get that first."

"Very funny. Where is it? Your phone?"

"I'm not sure. I misplace it a lot. But it sounds like it might be upstairs. I'll go check." I slowly rose from my chair.

And he shoved me back down, his lips receding to reveal his perfect teeth as well as a sneer. "I don't think so."

The ringing stopped.

"It may have been the sheriff's office," I warned him. "They may be wondering where I am."

"Which is precisely why we're leaving."

"Where are we going?"

"The medical center. You see, Mrs. Connor, you're about to have a heart attack. The stress of the past month has proven too much for you." He tsked. "I happened to discover you on the floor when I stopped over to see if Erin had been released from police custody. Naturally, I rushed you to the hospital, but it was too late. Despite my best efforts, you died."

"But I'm fine."

"You won't be for long. I have syringes and medication in my medical bag. And my bag is in the car. I always carry it with me. Most doctors do. Just in case we run into a problem. And guess what? You're a problem. Now move!"

Chapter 35

Once more I rose from my chair, only to drop back onto it again. "Ouch!"

"Quit stalling," Dr. Osgood advised.

"I'm not." I was. But only because I didn't want to get injected with some drug, suffer a heart attack, and die. "I have trouble with my sciatic nerve. Sometimes it causes me a lot of pain. Sometimes it hurts so bad I can't walk." I rubbed my thigh for effect.

"Well, you better deal with it, or I'll shoot you right here. I'd rather not. I really like my new plan. I'll be a hero. But shooting you will work, too. That's what I was going to do, you know. After you found me in the garage, I decided I'd bring you in here, where you'd become the 'victim of a home invasion.' So I guess it's up to you."

I didn't care for either option, although going with him allowed me more time. Consequently, I took to my feet and slowly moved around the back of my chair, hoping that a viable plan for escape would occur to me—soon.

He poked the barrel of the gun into my back. "Keep moving. We'll leave the same way we came in."

Blood pounded in my head. My breathing became more erratic. And my vision blurred. The puzzle Jesus got fuzzy, and there were way more than twelve apostles around the Last Supper table. I figured that Osgood wouldn't have to induce a heart attack because I was having one on my own.

One more step. Then another. And a notion of sorts finally fought its way through the muddle that was my brain. It wasn't much. In fact, it was merely a version of one of my earlier pathetic ideas, which meant that it probably wouldn't work. But it was the only chance I had.

With a moan, I slumped to the floor, as if my "sore" leg had given out. "Oh, my leg. My leg."

I wasn't much of an actor, but during my fall, I managed to knock over his chair, making sure it landed between the two of us. Osgood tripped over it, and at the same time, I lunged for one of the lanterns.

In my peripheral vision, I saw him regain his balance. I got so scared that my heart forgot to beat while I waited for a gunshot and the accompanying pain. But neither came.

My phone rang again. The clock in the foyer cuckooed. And I twisted onto my back and blindly swung the lantern.

I struck his hand. His gun slammed against the patio door and went off, the bullet shattering the cuckoo clock. Osgood bent to retrieve his weapon, and I whipped the lantern at him again. This time I connected with the side of his head. He fell on top of me, oozing blood. And I screamed.

The front door burst open and Karl rushed in, his gun drawn. He was followed by Erin and Ed, both brandishing their weapons. Will brought up the rear, empty-handed.

"Are you okay?" Karl yelled.

"I think so."

"Did you shoot him?"

"No. I knocked him out with the lantern. But he shot the cuckoo."

He visibly relaxed. "I never liked that clock, anyhow."

My teeth chattered. "V-very funny. N-now get him off m-me."

Karl cuffed Osgood's hands behind his back and rolled him over as Ed made a phone call, presumably to the hospital, requesting an ambulance.

"It's okay, Doris," Karl assured me. "You're safe. Now give me the lantern." I didn't realize that I had it poised over my head, ready to strike again. I had a death grip on the handle, and he had to pry my fingers away.

"Mom, are you okay?" Will knelt down next to me.

"Yeah. This is his blood. Not mine."

My son's face showed relief, but he couldn't articulate it. Instead, he merely said, "I knew those lanterns would come in handy."

Erin joined him on the floor, wrapping me in a big hug. A genuine hug, undeniably the result of the Irish blood that coursed through half of her veins.

"Honey," I said into her neck, "I know you don't want me to interfere in your life. But I have to say, I really hope you never go out with Dr. Osgood again."

"Oh, shut up," she replied between sniffles.

◎ ◎ ◎

The next day was Thanksgiving, and a group of us met to eat leftovers in the café. We had pushed two tables together, both crowded with platters of meat, salads, and bars.

Will and Sophie were in Fargo with her parents, but the other members of my family, including Rose, were with Grace and me. As were Karl and Ed. And it was no shock that our conversation centered on what had transpired at my house the day before.

"Well, it was a good thing that Ed searched Mom's garage." Erin fluttered her eyelashes and teased, "He's my hero."

Karl countered, "He didn't have the right to go in there. The state guys weren't too happy with him."

"Still, he confirmed that Buck's backpack wasn't there on Tuesday night. And I couldn't have put it in there after that because you had me in jail."

"Well, he's lucky Osgood plans to plead guilty." Karl rested his fork on his plate. "Otherwise, we'd have a potential problem at trial."

"You two realize that I'm sitting right here, don't you?" Ed waved a steak knife in the air, a piece of venison stuck on the tip of it.

"I still don't understand why he planted Buck's backpack in my garage," I said. "If he wanted to frame Erin, why didn't he go to her house?"

"He did," Ed said on a swallow. "But when he got there, he discovered that she didn't have a garage. He couldn't believe it. When he confessed, he kept saying, 'Who doesn't have a garage in Minnesota?'"

"Someone who lives on a law enforcement salary," Erin muttered.

Which prompted another question from me, this one directed to my daughter. "Didn't he notice your lack of a garage when he picked you up for your dinner date in Grand Forks?"

She wiped her mouth with a napkin and slumped back in her chair, the sunlight brightening her features as it beamed through the plate-glass windows. "He picked me up and dropped me off here at the café. That's where my car was. And because I had a change of clothes in my car, I didn't need to go home to get ready."

"Anyways," Ed said as he loaded up his plate with more meat, "after Osgood discovered that Erin was garageless, he decided to dump the backpack in one of her closets. But he couldn't do that, either, because, as he said, 'She locks her damn doors. She's the only person in town who locks her damn doors.'"

Erin shrugged. "What can I say? I'm a cop. I'm serious about security."

"That's why," Ed concluded, "he had to stick the backpack in your garage, Mrs. Connor. He planned to tip off our office, then influence public opinion by hinting to a few of the gossipers at the medical center that Erin hid it there, hoping she'd soon get the chance to get rid of it permanently."

Grace set her coffee cup on the table and tugged on her t shirt. It read, *Don't Flatter Yourself. I Only Look Up To You Because I'm Short.* "I still don't quite understand what happened on Monday night. After Osgood and Erin drove back from Grand Forks, and he dropped her off at the café."

Karl responded, "He went home and changed his clothes. And when he returned to collect the money, he found Doris's SUV in back, next to your Jeep. That rattled him. Only your car had been there originally, and he figured he could handle you if need be. But when he saw Doris's car, too, he decided he better grab the money from Tweety before she even got to the dumpster." He paused to clear his throat. "Yet as we know, Tweety outran him, passing both cars without incident, while he got held up when he bumped into Rose. And after that, he retreated into the shadows, only to have Doris chase after him."

"That no-good pipsqueak," Rose grumbled. "Here I went on and on to folks about how he wasn't such a bad doctor."

Erin reached for the last cinnamon muffin, the ones that had been my favorite. "Mom, do you want it?"

I shuddered. "No! I'll never eat anything with cinnamon again."

She appeared perplexed by what probably seemed to be an overreaction to a simple seasoning. But she merely shrugged and bit into the muffin before proceeding to talk with her mouth full. It was one of the habits she shared with her brother, and it drove me nuts. And once again, I wondered if that was their intent. "Well," she said as she chewed, "I can't believe he thought he'd get away with it. Didn't he realize we'd finger him as soon as we determined that the text messages to Tweety were sent when he had access to my phone? First, in the restaurant in Grand Forks? Then on Tuesday morning at the medical center, when he practically begged me to leave my purse in his office while I visited with Rose?"

"He didn't see that as a problem." Ed had almost cleared another plate of food. "He said it would have been your word against his. And since he'd be seen as the wonderful young man who had attempted to save your mother's life, while you're a known liar, people would have believed him." Right away Ed cringed. "Sorry, Erin. I didn't mean–"

"Don't apologize. It's true. I lied. And everyone found out."

It wasn't fair. Because of the events of the last several weeks, I'd become a liar, too. Like mother, like daughter. Yet I wouldn't pay a price for my fabrications–at least not in this world. But it would be a while before the folks around Hallock forgave Erin her transgressions.

"Okay," Ed said, "We all lie. But why on earth did you share the password to your phone with the guy?"

Embarrassment bloomed on Erin's cheeks. "We both were using our phones, and he asked, and it seemed innocent."

"Karl," Grace said, "did Osgood happen to confess as to why he changed the location of the money drop for Tuesday night?"

Karl tossed his napkin on his plate, covering a pile of fish bones. "He said he found the alley behind the café too hard to control. He figured an out-of-the-way place would be better. And he was familiar with Doris's house because of the commotion caused when it was moved to town. According to him, using Doris's property also had the added bonus of further linking Erin to everything."

"I have one more question," my sister said. "Why did Osgood defend Dr. Betcher so adamantly? Why didn't he let him take the fall for all of this?"

Erin twiddled her finger to signal she had the answer. "Les didn't want law enforcement anywhere near the medical center for fear that they might discover what he was up to. So he did his best to make everyone there look innocent, unless they posed a perceived threat to him, in which case, he worked to get them fired."

Karl propped his elbows on the table, his chin on his knuckles. "Even though he was preparing to leave town if necessary, he didn't want to go. He was a doctor, after all. And another four years and two months and he'd have most of his school debt forgiven."

I mulled over everything. All but one of my questions had been answered. "Karl, did Osgood say where Buck's murder took place?"

The sheriff nodded. "Buck texted him, offering to sell him some of the pills from the robbery. They agreed to meet along County Road 13, out by the distillery. Buck left his bike in a ditch and went with Osgood in his car. They conducted their business on a field road, behind a stand of trees. And that's where Osgood killed him."

"So I take it that Osgood is right-handed?" That was me.

Karl offered a confirming nod before he went on to say, "Osgood left the body out there but threw the murder weapon, a rock, into a culvert, along with Buck's keys, phone, and wallet. He then drove back to town, stole a body bag from the medical center, and returned to stuff Buck into it. After that, he dumped the body in the dumpster and burned the body bag in his fireplace." Karl stopped, only to start again after obviously recalling something more. "As for Buck's motorcycle, Osgood said he never got a chance to get rid of it. That's why we found it exactly where Buck had left it."

As he spoke, I came up with one more loose end that, in my mind, needed to be tied up. "Was Tweety involved in the robbery or the murder in any way?"

Karl rubbed the back of his neck, as if massaging his response. "She claims she wasn't. She said Buck may have mentioned something to her about his plans to rob the pharmacy, but she didn't recall for sure. She said he was a big talker, so she didn't believe much of what he told her. Still, because she had no trouble believing him when he asked her to run off with him, I think she knew more than she's letting on. But the county attorney won't charge her. There's not enough evidence."

"Well," Grace said, "I'm glad this whole ordeal is over. Although I still don't understand how you guys determined that Doris was in trouble."

Karl eyed me again before he replied, "When she didn't show up for our meeting at the courthouse, I phoned her. She didn't answer. Erin had already outlined her theory about Les Osgood and the text messages. It made sense, so I contacted the medical center in an effort to follow up, but no one knew where Osgood was. I tried to get a hold of Gerti, but she was out for the day. That's when I spoke with Old Man Olinski and pressured him into sharing with me that it was Osgood, not Betcher, who routinely failed to adhere to the protocol for distributing medication." He paused, as if to let us think about that. "Anyway, armed with that information, we then headed to Doris's house, while the state guys checked out Osgood's house. We called her again along the way but still no answer. And when we got there, Erin recognized Osgood's sedan in her driveway."

Grace slapped the table. "Okay, that's enough. Let's clean up and go home. The café's not open again until Monday, and I plan to sleep until then."

I rose from my chair. "Grace is right. Let's take a break from all of this." I picked up a plate and scraped the food scraps into an empty serving bowl. After that, I picked up another and did the same. As I worked, I tried to keep from thinking about Les Osgood and what he had done, but the images from the previous day stubbornly lingered in my mind.

"Want some help?"

I jumped, fumbling the plate in my hand.

Karl steadied my arm. "Sorry. I didn't mean to startle you."

"I guess I'm still jittery. I've never had someone try to kill me before."

"You can always see someone about that, you know. Or, there are pills."

I snorted. "I'm doing my best to avoid more therapy. And after everything that's happened, I probably won't even take an aspirin for a long time."

"Well, you can talk to me if you want. I've been there a couple of times myself."

"Thanks for the offer, but I'll be fine."

Grace passed by and handed Karl a stack of Tupperware containers. He set all but one on the table.

"The county board meets on Monday," he proceeded to inform me while spooning leftover Jell-O into the plastic dish. "I plan to tell them that it was Erin who figured out that Osgood was our guy. The head of the Bureau of Criminal Apprehension is also faxing a letter to that effect. I don't know if it will help, but we'll make the case for keeping her on."

"I really appreciate it. I'm sure Erin does, too."

He glanced around the table, his gaze settling on Rose. She was seated on one chair, her legs propped up on another. "Now what about Rose?" He pointed to her with his spoon. "Is she soon headed back to assisted living?"

I scraped gristle from yet another plate. "We haven't had a chance to discuss it. But I'm going to invite her to stay on with me for a while."

"Really?"

"Yeah, I think she needs me."

He cocked his head. I wasn't fooling him.

"Okay, okay. I need her, too."

He chuckled at that. "And what's next for you, Doris?"

I feigned great interest in the bowl of food scraps in front of me. I couldn't look at him because what I was about to say felt too personal. Still, I wanted to explain what was going on with me. "I'm not sure, Karl. These last several weeks were far more eventful than I liked. Although I did learn a few things."

"Such as?"

"Oh, I don't know." Then again, maybe I couldn't tell him how just a few months ago, I'd felt like a horse that had been put out to pasture. I was old, undesirable, and not much use to anyone, or so it seemed. And worst of all, on some level, I actually longed for the isolation because I was tired of being abused, ignored, and invisible.

Yet in spite of all the turmoil as of late—and yesterday, in particular—I had come to realize that I was still pretty darn tough. And I had a lot to offer. Sure, my therapist had made that point often enough, but it had never sunk in. I had to learn it for myself.

"So, anyways," Karl said into the awkward silence, "I was wondering if sometime you'd like to go to a fish fry at the Eagles with me now that they've started up again?"

"What?" Another plate almost slipped from my hands.

"A fish fry," he repeated, rescuing the dish before I broke it. "At the Eagles."

Maybe I wasn't so tough, after all. All of a sudden, my knees could barely hold me up. "I'm just not sure, Karl." I leaned against the table. "I haven't been on a date in years. Not that it was an option when I was married. Although Bill didn't seem to think that should stand in the way. He dated anytime and anywhere. In the tractor. The combine. Wherever." I had to stop talking. And I really wanted to. But I was physically unable to do it. "I guess it just wasn't my thing. I'm not saying dating, per se. Dating's fine. In fact, we used to date. Remember? But dating while married is another matter."

Certain I was making a complete fool of myself, I scoped out the room until I spotted Grace. I willed her to come to my rescue, but she turned away. As did practically everyone else. It was like they were intentionally ignoring me.

"You're rambling again, Doris." Karl's crows' feet crinkled.

"No, I'm not. I'm just explaining how things are."

"But it's only a fish fry."

"I understand. Still—"

"A fish fry," he repeated. "It's not like I asked you to marry me."

THE END

329

State Fair M&M Cookies

3 sticks butter, creamed
½ c. butter-flavored Crisco
1-½ c. white sugar
1-½ c. dark brown sugar
4 large eggs
4 tsp. vanilla

4-½ c. all-purpose flour, sifted
2 tsp. baking soda
1-¾ tsp. salt
5-¼ c. old-fashioned oatmeal
2 c. semi-sweet chocolate chips
2 c. plain M&Ms

Using an electric beater, mix together the ingredients in the left-hand column—in order. Then slowly stir in the flour, baking soda, and salt. (Baking Tip: Use a glass mixing bowl and a wooden spoon.) Next, stir in the oatmeal. (Do not use quick-cooking oatmeal.) Finally, stir in the chocolate chips and M&Ms. Drop by spoon or ice cream scoop onto a nonstick baking sheet. (Baking Tip: For uniform cookies, only place dough around the outside of the baking sheet.) Bake in a 350-degree oven (preheated) for 12 to 15 minutes. Do not overbake. Makes about 4 dozen big cookies.

Wild Rice Hot Dish

1 small onion, chopped
2 c. fresh mushrooms, sliced
½ c. butter
1 tsp. salt
1 c. wild rice, rinsed but *not* cooked
2 c. liquid (water or chicken broth)
½ c. raw potatoes (sliced into small pieces)
½ c. raw carrots (sliced into small pieces)

In a large skillet, fry onion and mushrooms in the butter for about 2 minutes, stirring occasionally. Then add salt, wild rice, vegetables, and liquid. Stir. Next, cover and simmer until rice is cooked and liquid is absorbed (about 35-40 mins.). Makes 8 ½-cup servings.

Cinnamon Muffins

Batter:

1-½ c. sifted, all-purpose flour	¼ c. butter-flavored Crisco
½ c. white sugar	1 large egg
2 tsp. baking powder	½ c. milk
½ tsp. salt	

In a large bowl, mix the ingredients in the left-hand column. Then cut the Crisco into the mixture until it resembles coarse crumbs. Mix the large egg with the milk. Next, stir in the egg-milk mixture. Do not over-stir. Finally, place ½ of the batter in lined muffin cups, filling each cup only ¼ full.

Nut Mixture: 1 T. flour
¼ c. light brown sugar   1 tsp. ground cinnamon
¼ c. chopped walnuts   1 T. melted butter

Combine the above ingredients. Then sprinkle that mixture over the partially filled muffin cups. Next, pour the remaining batter on top, filling each cup about ¾ full. Bake in a 350-degree oven (preheated) for about 20 minutes. Makes about 12 muffins.

Creamy Tater-Tot Hot Dish

1.5 lbs. ground beef
2 cans cream of mushroom soup
1 can of sweet corn
1 bag of tater tots
Salt and pepper to taste

Brown the ground beef, then drain, rinse, and return to the pan. Add soup. Drain corn and add it to the soup/meat mixture. Spread evenly in a greased 9"x13" glass baking dish. Top the mixture with tater tots in a single layer. Bake in a 425-degree oven (preheated) for 35-45 minutes, or until the tater tots are crispy and the meat mixture bubbles. Cool slightly before serving.

White Chicken Chili

4 skinless chicken breasts
4 c. chicken broth
1 can Great Northern white beans
1 can white chili beans
1 can green chilies
1 can Ro-Tel

1 can sweet corn
½ c. cream cheese
½ c. cheddar cheese
1 pkg. McCormick white
   chili seasoning
Diced jalapeños to taste

Place chicken breasts (thawed) in a large crockpot. Add chicken broth and turn Crock-Pot to medium heat. Allow chicken to cook until it easily falls apart. Then shred the chicken with a fork. Add Great Northern white beans (not drained), white chili beans (not drained), green chilies (not drained), Ro-Tel (not drained), and corn (drained). Keep Crock-Pot at medium heat and add the seasoning mix. Stir. Next, add both cheeses and allow them to melt. Finally, stir the entire mixture until creamy and add jalapeños to taste. Turn Crock-Pot to low and serve.

Chocolate-Cherry Cake

Cake:
1 pkg. Pillsbury-Plus devil's food cake mix
2 large eggs, beaten
1 tsp. almond extract
1 can (21 oz.) cherry pie filling

Using an electric beater, beat cake mix, eggs, and almond extract. Then using a wooden spoon, fold in cherry pie filling. Pour into a greased and floured 9"x13" cake pan. Bake in a

350-degree oven (preheated) for 20-30 minutes. The cake is done when you stick a toothpick in it and it comes out clean.

Frosting:

1 c. white sugar

⅓ c. milk

5 T. margarine

1 pkg. (6 oz. or 1 c.) semi-sweet chocolate chips

In a small saucepan, mix the ingredients in the above left-hand column, bringing the mixture to a boil, then boiling it for one minute, stirring constantly. Next, remove the pan from heat and stir in the chocolate chips, stirring until smooth. Immediately pour over the cake and smooth. Let cool before serving.

Baked Cornbread Hot Dish

2 lbs. ground beef

1 small onion, diced

2 cloves garlic, minced

1 16-oz. jar salsa

2 6.5-oz. pkg. Martha White
   yellow cornbread mix

1 14.75-oz. can creamed corn

2 c. shredded Mexican-style cheese

16 slices pickled jalapeños

Optional toppings:

sour cream

pico de gallo

salsa

In a large skillet, brown ground beef with onions and garlic. Drain excess grease. Stir in salsa. Set aside. In a bowl, prepare 1 pkg. of Martha White yellow cornbread mix with ⅔ c. water. Stir well. Then add ½ can of creamed corn. Stir well.

Pour evenly into a sprayed 9"x13" glass baking dish. Spread ground-beef mixture on top of cornbread mixture.

In a separate bowl, prepare the second pkg. of cornbread mix with ⅔ c. of water. Stir well. Then add the remainder of the creamed corn. Stir well. Pour over ground-beef mixture. Top with the cheese. Next, evenly place pickled jalapeño slices on top. Cover with aluminum foil and bake in a 425-degree oven (preheated) for 15 minutes. Remove foil and bake for an additional 10 minutes. Slice and serve with optional toppings, as desired.

Chicken Tetrazzini Baked Hot Dish

6 T. margarine	½ c. grated cheese
6 T. flour	3 c. cooked chicken, cubed
¾ tsp. salt	1 8-oz. can of mushrooms, drained
¼ tsp. pepper	12-oz. spaghetti, cooked and drained
2 c. half-and-half	
1 c. chicken broth	

Melt margarine in a 3-qt. sauce pan. Blend in flour, salt, and pepper. Add half-and-half and broth. Whisk until mixture boils. Remove from heat. Stir in chicken and mushrooms. Toss with spaghetti. Place in a greased 9"x13" glass baking dish. Top with cheese. Bake in a 350-degree oven (preheated) for 30-40 minutes.

Blueberry Streusel Bars with Lemon-Cream Filling

Crust:

1 c. butter, softened	1-⅓ c. light brown sugar, packed
3 c. all-purpose flour	1 tsp. salt
1-½ c. old-fashioned oatmeal	1 tsp. baking powder

In a bowl, blend above ingredients until crumbly. Withhold 2 c. of the mixture and pat the rest into a 9"x13" pan that has been lined with foil, with a 1" overhang on the ends of the pan. Then spray the foil with Pam. Next, bake in a 350-degree oven (preheated) for 12 minutes.

Filling:

2-½ c. fresh blueberries, washed	½ c. lemon juice
1 14-oz. can sweetened condensed milk	2 tsp. lemon zest
1 egg yolk	

Spread the blueberries on the crust right after removing it from the oven. Then in a bowl, mix the other filling ingredients and spread the filling over the blueberries. Bake in a 350-degree oven (preheated) 7-8 minutes, or until it forms a sheen. Remove from oven and spread the remaining crumbs on top. Bake 25-30 more minutes, or until lightly brown.

Let cool 2 hours. Then lift the foil from the pan and slide the bars off the foil and onto a cutting board. Cut and refrigerate until ready to serve.

Quick and Easy Ravioli

1 24-oz. jar spaghetti sauce
1 pkg. frozen ravioli, cheese or meat filled
2 c. shredded mozzarella cheese
1 c. grated Parmesan cheese
Italian spices (basil, oregano, garlic powder)

Pour a thin layer of sauce in the bottom of a Pam-sprayed 9"x9" baking pan. Add a layer of frozen ravioli. Cover the ravioli with a layer of mozzarella cheese, then sprinkle with Parmesan cheese. Next, very lightly sprinkle on the Italian spices. After that, pour a thin layer of sauce on top and repeat everything until all of the ingredients are gone. Bake in a 350-degree oven (preheated) for 60 minutes.

Buttermilk Pancakes

In a bowl, stir the following ingredients:
2 c. all-purpose flour
2 tsp. baking powder
1 tsp. baking soda
½ tsp. salt
3 T. sugar

In a separate bowl, whisk the following ingredients:
2 large eggs, slightly beaten
3 c. buttermilk
4 T. unsalted butter, melted

Add the wet ingredients to the dry ingredients, folding them together. Do not overmix. (Batter will have small lumps.) Heat griddle, testing for readiness by sprinkling a few drops of water on it. If the water bounces and spatters, the griddle is hot enough. (Do not overheat.) Then brush a pat of butter across the griddle. Next, pour about ½ c. of batter onto the griddle for each pancake. When pancakes form bubbles on top and are slightly crusty around the edges (about 2.5 minutes), flip them. Then cook until golden brown (about another minute).

Chicken-and-Stuffing Hot Dish

1 6-oz. box of stuffing mix
1-¼ c. hot water
2 c. cooked chicken, diced
¹/₃ c. sour cream
1 can cream of celery soup
3 c. frozen mixed vegetables

Combine stuffing mix and hot water in a bowl and set aside. In a separate bowl, stir together the other ingredients and spread them into a greased 9"x13" glass baking dish. Top with stuffing. Bake in a 400-degree oven (preheated) for 25-30 minutes, or until lightly brown and bubbly.

Caramel Chocolate Chip Bars

Bars:
1 c. (2 sticks) butter, softened
1-½ c. light brown sugar
1 tsp. vanilla
2 large eggs
2-¼ c. all-purpose flour
1 tsp. baking soda
1 tsp. salt
2 c. milk chocolate chips

Caramel Sauce:
5 oz. evaporated milk
1 11-oz. pkg. caramel bits

Using an electric mixer, beat butter, sugar, and vanilla until fluffy. Then add eggs and mix. Next, add flour, baking soda, and salt, stirring with a wooden spoon. Add chocolate chips and stir. Spread ½ of the batter into a greased 9"x13" pan, setting aside the rest. Bake in a 350-degree oven (preheated) for 10 minutes.

While bars are baking, cook evaporated milk and caramel bits in a saucepan over medium heat until the bits are melted, stirring frequently (about 8 minutes). When bars are done baking, pour caramel sauce over the hot bars. Then with remaining dough, make flattened dollops and place them on top of the caramel. Bake for an additional 15-18 minutes, or until the caramel is bubbling and the dough is golden brown. Cool and serve.

Rhubarb Pudding

8 slices of bread, lightly toasted
1-½ c. milk
¼ c. butter, cubed
5 eggs, lightly beaten
3 c. chopped rhubarb
1-½ c. sugar
½ tsp. ground cinnamon
¼ tsp. salt
½ c. brown sugar (packed)

Remove crust from toast and cut into ½" pieces. Place in a greased 9"x13" baking dish. Set aside. In a large saucepan, heat milk over medium heat until it lightly bubbles. Stir in butter until melted. Pour over toast. Let stand for 15 minutes. In a large bowl, combine the eggs, rhubarb, sugar, cinnamon, and salt and stir into bread mixture. Sprinkle with the brown sugar. Bake in a 350-degree oven (preheated) for 45-50 minutes. Serve warm.

Chicken Ramen Hot Dish

3 pkg. (3 oz. each) ramen noodles, discard seasoning pkg.
2 T. vegetable oil
1 clove garlic
½ tsp. ground ginger
½ large red bell pepper
¾ c. chopped broccoli
¾ c. chopped mushrooms
2 T. soy sauce

2 T. Worcestershire sauce
1 T. ketchup
2-3 tsp. sriracha
1 T. dark brown sugar
½ lb. chicken, chopped into bite-size pieces
Salt and pepper
Toasted sesame seeds
1-2 T. chopped cilantro

Follow package directions to cook the ramen noodles, discarding seasoning packets. Drain noodles and toss with 1 T. vegetable oil. Set aside.

In a large skillet, add remaining vegetable oil and heat over medium heat. Add garlic and ginger. Heat until garlic is soft (about 2 minutes). Add pepper, broccoli, and mushrooms. Heat until vegetables are tender.

In a small bowl, whisk soy sauce, Worcestershire sauce, ketchup, sriracha, and brown sugar. Set aside.

Season chicken with salt and pepper, then cook in skillet, alongside the vegetables, for 2-3 minutes, or until the chicken is no longer pink. Next, combine everything, top with ramen noodles, and toss until noodles are coated in sauce. Add sesame seeds and cilantro. Toss again. Serve.

Rhubarb Muffins

Batter:

¾ c. light brown sugar

½ c. vegetable or canola oil

1 large egg

½ c. buttermilk

1 tsp. vanilla

1-½ c. all-purpose flour

½ tsp. salt

½ tsp. baking soda

½ c. chopped walnuts

1-½ c. chopped rhubarb

Topping:

¼ c. light brown sugar

½ c. ground cinnamon

In a large bowl, combine sugar, oil, egg, buttermilk, and vanilla and mix well. Sift flour, salt, and baking soda into the mixture. Fold in the walnuts and rhubarb. Fill lined muffin cups. Make topping in a small bowl. Then sprinkle it on muffins. Bake in a 325-degree oven (preheated) for 30 minutes. They're done If inserted toothpick comes out clean. Makes 12 muffins.

Chocolate-Chip Cookie Bars

½ c. butter, softened

½ c. white sugar

½ c. light brown sugar

1 large egg

1 tsp. vanilla

1-½ c. all-purpose flour

½ tsp. baking soda

¼ tsp. baking powder

¼ tsp. salt

1 c. semi-sweet chocolate chips

In a mixing bowl, beat together the ingredients in the left-hand column. Then sift in the flour, soda, baking powder, and salt, stirring with a wooden spoon. Fold in the chocolate chips. Spread into a greased 9"x 9" baking pan. Bake in a 350-degree oven (preheated) for 20 minutes.

About the Author

Jeanne Cooney is the author of the popular Hot Dish Heaven mystery series: Hot Dish Heaven (2013), A Second Helping of Murder and Recipes (2014), and A Potluck of Murder and Recipes (2016), all published by North Star Press. Jeanne is a highly sought speaker for conferences, libraries, community gatherings, and organization fundraisers, where she offers her humorous take on life in the Midwest. She and her off-beat mystery books have been featured on television and radio as well as in newspapers and magazines throughout the region. Minnesota Public Radio named Cooney one of a handful of Minnesota-based mystery authors to read. Connect with Jeanne at www. JeanneCooney.com.